D0557681

My Name Is Tom

Jon Reeves

authorHOUSE®

AuthorHouse™ UK
1663 Liberty Drive
Bloomington, IN 47403 USA
www.authorhouse.co.uk
Phone: 0800.197.4150

Published by AuthorHouse 12/15/2015

ISBN: 978-1-5049-9335-7 (sc)
ISBN: 978-1-5049-9334-0 (hc)
ISBN: 978-1-5049-9333-3 (e)

Contents

Conception

It was a warm August night during the first year of a new decade, the 1970s. Two young lovebirds, the girl sixteen, the boy sixteen and one-half, were engaged in an uncomfortable, post-youth-club quickie down the alleyway next to the dry cleaners, somewhere in small-town England.

Almost two minutes later, the two of them relaxed against a cold breeze-block wall to share a paper bag full of Cola Cubes.

"This is so romantic," she said quite genuinely.

"Yeah," he replied, not so convinced. "D'yer wanna do it again?"

"Me knees hurt. Dunno if I can manage it. Suppose we could stand up."

And so with one almighty effort, they rose to their feet to once again begin the act of intercourse. Only this time they had used their last condom.

"We haven't got any johnnies left," he told her.

But it was too late for caution. Their lusts had gotten the better of them.

"This feels much better," he said.

"It really does."

Little did their tiny minds realise exactly how much of an effect that their act of uncontrollable lust might potentially have on the rest of their lives.

He was a man led by his phallus. She was a woman led by her heart. And both his phallus and her heart seemed to be indicating that it was OK to continue.

"I feel weird," she said. "I think I might be falling in love with you."

"Eh?" he replied, voice doused in alarm, "We've only just met."

"Yeah, but it feels right, don't you think?"

And then once again his phallus overruled his head, and he agreed.

"Do you want to do it again?" he said.

"No, thanks."

1. Families

Paul had a lot of spots on his face and neck. One in particular that sat just below his left nostril actually gave the impression of misshaping his top lip. Some others that were once spots in their own rights had joined forces and formed hugely sensitive, bright red areas.

The cause of the problem was mostly adolescence but with an equally hefty helping of bad living and lack of cleaning. He was not a lucky lad. He was well known for it. But now, as he approached his seventeenth birthday, covered in zits, he had a far more pressing issue to deal with.

His girlfriend, Theresa, was pregnant. There was no doubt, although he had tried his hardest to create some, that the child was his. Neither of them were happy about it. But their lack of happiness paled into distant insignificance when compared to the by-now highly developed unhappiness of Theresa's parents.

Christians they might have been, but their attitude towards the impending delivery of their first grandson had been distinctly un-Christian. The poor child didn't stand a chance. Not only was he going to have parents who were still adolescents themselves but also grandparents who thought he was the Antichrist.

Time was getting on, and the big day approached fast. Theresa was almost visibly growing, retaining liquid like a sanitary towel in a previously full tea cup.

"Her body isn't ready for it," her parents would say. Of course, they were right. Sixteen was no age for a woman's body to be treated like this.

Paul's parents had a much more lenient view of the whole situation. Paul himself emerged from a sixteen-year-old uterus. This made his parents twice his age, which in turn made Theresa's parents old enough to be their parents and, thus, Paul's grandparents.

But none of that really mattered. Age didn't really come into it. Well, it did. It was the most important thing. But what really was driving the whole situation out of control were Theresa's parents' religious beliefs.

Neither Paul nor his parents shared those beliefs. And after a lifetime of living with them, Theresa had serious doubts too. Not that she would dare say anything.

She was brought up in a house adorned with crude religious imagery 'round every corner, the most frightening of which was a highly detailed crucifix above the fireplace. It was far too detailed really. You could actually see the indentations on the head of Jesus made by the crown of thorns. And the maker had painstakingly painted hideously accurate scars with drops of blood coming from them. It was like a horror film above the mantelpiece.

Paul's favourite, though, and a secret source of amusement to him, was an embroidered throw depicting Jesus's head draped over the back of the sofa. It was extremely badly made and, due to the size of Jesus's eyes, appeared to be looking at whoever was in the room at the time. When Paul sat on the sofa, he could feel it peering at him over his shoulder. He would often shuffle along in an attempt hide it. But all that did was reveal the Three Wise Men on camels approaching from the East.

Paul regularly had nightmares about it. Why were the Three Wise Men, even when mounted on camels, only the size of Jesus's eyeballs? And why was Jesus a fully grown adult in the same scene as the Wise Men? Surely when they all had been knocking around, Jesus had been just a baby. And by the time Jesus had become a fully grown adult, surely the Wise Men would either have been dead or, at the least, unable to mount a camel. These questions would often lead Paul to wonder whether it was completely accurate or not.

None of it made any sense. But they all knew better than to point any of it out – even Theresa, who was still slightly caught up in the whole thing. She still attended church on a Sunday morning, more now because she was made to by her parents than out of choice, but it would still have been a huge risk to mention her doubts, especially now that she had committed such a terrible sin with Paul.

Eventually the inevitable had to happen. Theresa became suddenly huge, ready to give birth at any minute. And so, as much as neither party wanted to, they knew they would have to arrange for the families to meet up and discuss the future of this poor child.

A date was set. The meeting would take place at Theresa's parents' house on a Sunday afternoon after church and lunch, just two weeks before the due date. Paul informed his parents of this and briefed them on what they could expect from the visit.

"Why are the Three Wise Men only half the size of Jesus's head?" Paul's dad, Tony, said as he sat down on the Shanklins' sofa.

Then he looked up and saw Jesus above the fireplace. Suddenly his original question seemed somewhat pointless.

"Dad, leave it," Paul said under his breath while tending to a weeping spot beginning to gather moisture on his chin.

Luckily for Paul, Tony was no longer saying anything. He was transfixed by the crucifix in front of him. Then, like a scene from a very poor European horror film, his eyes fixed on each religious icon on display in the Shanklins' front room, one after the other at high speed. The soundtrack was hideous. Tony had to put all his effort into not screaming.

Paul's mum, Claire, was just as scared as Tony but, fortunately, able to control her fear and, at the same time, rein Tony's in a bit. She pinched his side in a vain attempt to make him understand that she shared his fears. But it didn't work, and she just hurt him a bit.

"Ow! Jesus bloody Christ, Claire! That really hurt," he said.

"Dad, will you knock it on the head, please?"

Paul knew there was no way back from that comment. Jesus Christ on its own would have been bad enough, but to give him "bloody" as a middle name was crossing a line that could not be backed over.

All eyes were now on Tony. Paul and Theresa tried their hardest to suppress their laughter while Claire resisted the temptation to punch him.

As for Mr and Mrs Shanklin, well, they were as close as you could be to dousing him with holy water.

Despite the tension in the room, so intense that you could have just about seen it, they all knew that they were there to discuss Paul and Theresa's baby. Mr Shanklin decided to take the lead.

"So, we're here to talk about the baby. What are your thoughts?" he said, attempting to sound impartial while still maintaining the same level of judgement he had throughout their visit so far.

No response came. It was only Theresa's parents who thought there was anything to discuss. The rest of the room, with their liberal non-religious way of thinking, just imagined that they would all love the child and watch him grow up to be a good person.

After nearly thirty seconds that felt like several minutes, Tony decided that he had to try and break the silence.

"So," he said. "Are you, er … are you, er … related to Bill Shanklin?"

The Shanklins looked at each other confused. Paul and Theresa put their heads down to mask their laughter, and Claire shook her head.

"I don't know what you mean," Mrs Shanklin said.

"Oh, you know, Bill Shanklin, he's the er, you know, er … the Liverpool manager."

"That's Bill Shankly, Dad."

"Oh right, yeah, Shankly, not Shanklin, isn't it? So what's Shanklin then?"

"It's a town on the Isle of Wight, ain't it?" Paul answered.

"Is it … oh yeah. We've been there, ain't we, Claire?"

"Can you just shut up about that now please, Tony?" Claire said, getting extremely agitated with Tony, but not as agitated as she was about the question posed by Theresa's dad.

"What exactly do you mean by what are our thoughts?" she asked.

"Well, she's not keeping it," Mr Shanklin replied.

And so the silence returned. All eyes were on Mr Shanklin, apart from his wife, that was, who not only knew what he was going to say but agreed with it wholeheartedly.

"Are you serious? Exactly what do you expect she's going to do with it? I could maybe understand you saying this if it was nine bloody months ago," Claire said, only just managing to keep a slight grip on her temper.

"You do not swear in this house," Mrs Shanklin interrupted.

"Bit fucking late for that, ain't it?" Tony added.

"Dad!"

For the next twenty minutes or so, the conversation went nowhere. They were completely at odds with each other. Theresa's parents had their thoughts, and then the rest of the room had theirs. The difference was that her parents' thoughts were based on two things – one, their religious beliefs and, two, what everyone at the church would think of them for allowing their daughter to become pregnant at this age and out of wedlock, which in their eyes, not that they would admit it, was worse than anything.

"So what do you suggest happens then, Mrs Shanklin?" Claire asked.

"I think the only realistic option is adoption. The church will organise everything."

"Oh well, that's just fantastic, isn't it? As long as we've got the church on the case, nothing can go wrong, can it?" Claire replied, trying hard to sound as sarcastic as she could.

"The Lord will guide us," Mr Shanklin added, naturally not picking up on the sarcasm. "Our faith will carry us through."

"Your faith, Mr Shanklin, not ours," Tony added.

The room reached an impasse. There was no way that the Shanklins were going to let the child be brought up by what they described as kids themselves. And there was no way that Paul's parents were about to let the Shanklins force this decision on them.

The discussion had come full circle. The one thing that no one in the room wanted, including them, was for Paul and Theresa to be left to make the decision.

2. Birth, Now Take Him Away

"Here it comes! The head is almost out," said a comically large midwife as she struggled to get low enough to get a good grip on him.

"Is it a boy?" Tony asked.

"We know it's a boy, you idiot. We've known for six months. Just get it out of me." Theresa screamed as she longed to be an expectant mother no more.

Several shouts of "push" and several more deafening screams from the mother later out popped the baby boy.

Theresa cried and took the boy in her arms. The room fell silent, apart from the baby's cry and a slow, pathetic whimper from the newly appointed mother, punctuated with gasps of shock from the respective parents, who now stood on opposite sides of the bed with their war faces on.

"Look at his little face," Theresa said.

"Lovely little face," the midwives said in unison.

Then suddenly the door to the room burst open and in came a heavily sweating Paul. The sheen on his face made his many spots appear even worse than they actually were.

"Did I miss it?" he asked.

The parents of the new mother turned their judgement on him, not dissimilar to the look they had been giving their daughter since she'd sat astride the birthing table just a couple of hours earlier and also since she'd first uttered the words "I am pregnant" almost nine months ago.

"Yes, you missed it," Theresa's mother said, emphasising the "it" to the point where she'd almost spat at him. "Shame you didn't miss nine months ago."

"That's disgusting," Theresa said under her breath.

"What was that?" came the reply from her father, almost spitting himself. She chose not to answer.

The aggressive edge to the proceedings seemed very bizarre to everyone but the family members in the room. Paul made a move towards the child for a closer look but was immediately blocked off by Theresa's parents.

"I think you had better go, Paul. You've done enough damage," Theresa's mother said dismissively.

"Blimey, looks like it," Paul said and pointed towards the now-bleeding mother of his newborn child, and chuckled nervously, as if expecting a similar response from the rest of the room. Theresa shook her head and gestured to Paul to leave. "I'm just saying. Looks like that smarted a bit, eh?"

With Paul now out of the room and making his way down the hall as if nothing had happened, an eerie silence befell the room. Even the newborn baby looked confused. Theresa held him tightly for one last time and then handed him to the priest.

"OK, take him away."

The priest took the boy wrapped in a towel into his arms and turned to leave the room. Now the sounds of the baby's cries were joined by the cries of his mother, as she realised that she would probably never see her son again.

She hoped that maybe in twenty years he might try and find her. Maybe he would try to find Paul and not her. Her face screwed up at the thought, and so she tried to put it out of her mind.

She knew that the likelihood was that she wouldn't be with Paul by then. He was hardly a long term prospect. She imagined that if the boy did search for his dad in the future, Paul would fill his head with stories of how her family had insisted that he be adopted and how he'd had nothing to do with it, which, of course, was largely true, but he was not completely blameless.

Maybe he would be adopted by an awful family and hold it against her. This wasn't going to be easy for her; she knew that. But she also knew that she had to stay positive and get on with her life.

One thing was for sure: she wouldn't forget that funny-looking face in a hurry, and she certainly wouldn't forgive her parents for making her give it up.

"Do you want to give him a name?" the priest said as he stood in the dimly lit doorway.

"No, she doesn't," said her father. "His new family can make that choice."

And with that they were gone.

The next day the newborn, already having an adoptive family waiting for him to be delivered, was placed in a room surrounded by other babies of a similar disposition. A nameless tag was tied around the big toe of his right foot.

On the opposite side of the window to the room stood a couple in their early forties; they were to be the boy's new parents. She was wearing a cross 'round her neck, and he looked slightly bemused by the whole thing. The priest then brought them into the room, reached down to pick up the boy, and handed him to his new mother.

"No, David," she said sternly as his new father went to take him from the priest. "You'll probably drop him, and then where will we be?"

The father looked down as if very used to being admonished in this way.

"Thomas," she said. And so that was his name.

They arrived back at their house at number 1 Shakespeare Road, Druids Heath, Birmingham, to be greeted by all the members of Thomas's new family, including one set of new grandparents on his mother's side, who were a far cry from Paul's parents but not that dissimilar to Theresa's; his new older sister Tracey; and the neighbours, Ann and Barry, from number 3 Shakespeare Road.

His new parents were called Cynthia and David Joyce. And so he was called Thomas Luke Joyce, the newly adopted son of Cynthia and David.

3. You're a Joyce Now, My Boy

Thomas's new family were staunchly religious on Cynthia's side only. David's family were indifferent to the whole concept of religion. But as was always the way in these situations, religion won and would, therefore, play a part in Thomas's upbringing and, if Cynthia and her family had their way, the rest of his life.

David knew that one day Thomas would make his own choice with regards to this, but as far as his new mother and her parents were concerned, there was no option.

Cynthia wasn't a nasty person but had been heavily indoctrinated into this way of thinking by her parents, to the point that, no matter how the world might have changed over the course of Thomas's upbringing, as far as she was concerned, Christianity, or her own personal version of it, would always lead the way.

Both Cynthia and David were brought up during the Second World War and, more often than not, had lived their lives as if it had still been going on. David had joined the air force in his late teens while Cynthia had worked for her uncle Brian three full days a week and one Thursday afternoon per month in his furniture shop until their first child, Tracey, had come along.

They'd met in the late fifties and had moved into their house on Shakespeare Road in the early sixties. Tracey had been born in 1967. They'd always planned to adopt their next child due to complications with Tracey's birth that had rendered Cynthia unable to have any more children. And now they had their family. Not exactly as they had planned, but none the less, their family was complete.

"I christen this child Thomas, in the name of the Father, the Son, and the Holy Spirit," said the same priest who'd delivered the Joyces their new child just a few weeks earlier.

He crossed the boy on the head with a dollop of holy water procured from the font in front of him, and so the christening was complete.

Back at Shakespeare Road, the somewhat-muted celebrations continued, baby Thomas in his crib, balling his eyes out.

"Noisy little bugger, ain't he?" said David's father, also called David. "Who's a noisy little bugger?" He bent down to take a closer look.

You could cut the atmosphere with a blunt knife as he came back up to the full attention of the room.

"I don't think the *B* word is appropriate, Mr Joyce," said Cynthia's mother, whose name was, confusingly, Joyce.

Her stern tone of voice and sour-looking face caused Thomas to fall back into tears. A far cry from the smile that had been raised by the smiling granddad David's attentions. The room had fallen silent once more as Joyce waited for her apology from David.

"Oh for Christ sake, I don't think he'll understand the word *bugger* for a while yet, bloody hell."

David's rant, although it raised a smile from his son and granddaughter Tracey alike, had no such effect on the rest of the room.

"I said no more *B* words, thank you very much, Mr Joyce."

"Which one? Bloody or bugger, or both?" he replied. "When are you going to stop calling me Mr Joyce, Joyce? The kids have been married for nearly ten years now. I've known your smiling bloody face all that time, and you still can't use my first name. Bloody ridiculous, that."

"Will you *stop* saying that, Mr Joyce? Please."

Joyce was now so mad with David, senior, that even the previously smiling young David gave his dad a look that indicated it was time for him to step back from the brink.

"Oh, for f—" David nearly dropped the F-bomb. Even he knew that was a place that he could not come back from and so managed to stop himself from completing the word. "I'm going for a fag. Is that OK with you, your majesty?"

Outside, David was joined by his son.

"Dad, you've got to think of a better way of dealing with Joyce. You know she's wound up as tight as a spring."

"I know she is, son, but I can't help myself. You know what it's like. You can't help it either. The only reason you're keeping schtum now is because you know full well Cynthia will join in if you back me up."

"Right, so if I can make that change surely you can."

"Not sure I want to, son; it's all quite amusing really."

"Just try, would you, Dad?"

With that, the two Davids put their arms around each other and chuckled about the different ways that they could wind up Joyce and also how much Thomas was likely to do the same the minute he learned to speak.

Back in the house the conversation was formal. Joyce and Cynthia weren't about to let any fun get in the way. After a while the two Davids walked back in and sat down to form part of the semicircle that now looked in baby Thomas's direction. No one spoke for almost five minutes as they all took in what was now part of their family. But the peace wasn't likely to last. David senior was now on his fifth can of Foster's.

"Are you sure you want to call him Thomas? It's a bit boring, ain't it? Why don't you call him Steve? That's a bit more dynamic, or …"

"Will you just … please … stop, Mr Joyce? Oh, and now I'm having a turn. Well, thank you very much."

"You're very welcome, Joyce."

4. Seven Years Later – Music Discovered

I can't really remember a time before music. It had come into my life at such an early age that it would be surprising if I did. My name is Tom, or Thomas, as only my mother called me, and only when she was angry with me, which was pretty much the only time she felt the need for us to converse.

I do remember when it started, though. I was seven years old. My cousin had been a sergeant in the army, and in his spare time, he had also been a DJ with a slot on the local radio between ten and eleven on Tuesday nights. When he'd go away on a tour, he would leave me with his prized box of records.

At the time, my parents had just purchased a new stereo system and thus had handed their old wooden turntable/radio combination to me. It had spent many years doubling up as a sideboard and had lots of dark round circles on it where they'd displayed the various ornaments they had collected on their travels around England—not abroad, mind you, as they had been averse to the idea of flight. They'd once travelled to Switzerland by boat, long before I was born, but had failed to return with anything worth displaying.

So at the age of seven, mid-1978, I'd had access to records by The Jam and The Sex Pistols along with swathes of Motown, ska, and funk music.

Within no time at all, I'd had my favourites. The most played had been the double A-side of "Jimmy Mack" and "Third Finger Left Hand" by Martha Reeves and the Vandellas. I had been attracted to this particular seven-inch, as at the time, I had been at school with a lad called Reeves.

That had been the way I'd decided on what I liked at that age. A similar instance had been when Steve Coppell had become my favourite footballer during the lead up to the 1977 FA Cup Final after I'd noticed that his birthday was on the same day as mine.

When my cousin had returned from wherever the army had taken him, he had come and retrieved his box of singles. We would sit and discuss what I had been listening to. He had always been very impressed with how well I'd looked after his records. He had said that it would have been a shame if they hadn't been listened to while he'd been away. He'd described it as them fulfilling their destiny of being played and enjoyed. I had always been transfixed by how he had talked about them in that way, like they had been people with emotions and needs.

This had gone on for several years, and I'd become a firm favourite of his, and he mine. Each time the box had been delivered to me, it had contained more records. He had left the new ones at the front so I had been able to listen to them first to let him know what I'd thought.

I hadn't been allowed to stay up and listen to his show, and my wooden box of a record player/radio/sideboard hadn't been able to pick up the local radio for some reason so I had not even been able to sneak a listen when my parents had thought I'd been asleep.

They hadn't listened to it either as he never played any Mantovani or James Last, as had been their musical preference, which, until the box of records had arrived, had also been the only music I'd had access to. The image of the silver-haired, bearded James Last on the front cover of his albums, surrounded by scantily clad women, had been one that would never leave me. What had been worse, though, had been the sound they'd made. Really awful.

After a few years, the inevitable was bound to happen. It was about a year ago now. I had been fast approaching my teenage years, and my cousin was about to leave the army.

This had meant two things. One, he would retrieve his records on a permanent basis, and two, I had been about to become the miserable, hormonal thirteen-year-old that I was now.

We still had conversed about music for a while, but once puberty hit, we had fallen out. I could pinpoint the time it actually happened. Probably not as well as he could, though. He had taken a fancy to a friend of my sister Tracey and, one day, was attempting to get some time on his own with her. But I had not let that happen for some reason.

After several times purposely walking in on them while they had attempted to get it on, he unsurprisingly had become extremely frustrated. He then shouted very loud at me, and the kinship was over. But more importantly, the record box stopped visiting, and the music chats dried up.

For a while I'd seen this as a most terrible thing to happen, made even worse by the fact that I had known it was my fault. But then it had started to have a positive effect, namely, that it had forced me to discover my own music and build a collection I could call my own.

At this time, like I said, about a year ago, I had counted myself as a big fan of Motown, punk, and, in particular, The Jam. I had also begun to pay a lot of attention to the way Paul Weller, the lead singer and principal songwriter of The Jam, dressed and acted. I had also started to listen to the lyrics of his songs intently. "Life is a drink, and you get drunk when you're young" had been one lyric I loved to repeat to myself.

I'd had a very limited experience of drunkenness, mainly just from watching various members of my family after a few drinks but also once sneaking two cans of beer up to my bedroom on Christmas Day. However, I had totally got the metaphor, I'd thought.

My own experience with the two cans hadn't been much fun as I'd thrown them back up almost immediately. But others that I had seen drunk had seemed like they'd been having fun. So the conclusion I had come to was that Paul Weller had indicated that life should be fun when you were young.

The lyric had had a strange effect on me, mainly because I hadn't really been having fun. Even thinking back to the days of the record box, which I'd enjoyed immensely, the rest of my life had seemed quite unpleasant. I had spent my days being pushed around and unfairly judged by people of my own age, none of whom seemed to like me much. The only thing that had put a smile on my face had been music, the contents of the record box in particular.

I had no music collection of my own as I couldn't afford it due to my meagre weekly pocket money allocation. Money that was primarily allocated to the purchase of Aero bars, sweet cigarettes, and Snap-its. And so I knew that I had to get some work.

It wasn't long before I managed to get myself into my first piece of gainful employment, a paper round for a mate of my dad. This meant getting up extremely early six days a week, rain or shine, and delivering papers so that on Saturday morning I could collect my pay and make my way to the local record shop to relieve myself of it as soon as possible.

My local record shop was located approximately halfway down my local high street. It was called Osbourne's. Strangely, I had never been in there before. Many times I would stop on my way somewhere else, more often than not accompanied by one of my parents, and manage to grab a fleeting glance through the window. This time, though, on the first pay day of my new paper round, I was on my own, and I had intention. But more importantly, I had £1.50 in my pocket, earmarked for music.

The first thing I noticed as I crossed the threshold of the shop for the first time was a huge poster with a picture of Paul Weller on it. But instead of having the words "The Jam" written on it, it said "The Style Council". I was confused. I approached the counter and worked up enough courage to ask the shopkeeper what was going on.

"Hello," I said in my timid and somewhat high-pitched voice, just about managing to peer above the level of the counter. He didn't seem to notice me. He was serving someone else. Fair enough.

"You want the new Style Council single?" he said to the customer.

I looked at the man buying the single and looked back at the poster. He had the same haircut as Weller, which had changed considerably from the last time I'd seen a picture of him. He was also wearing very similar clothes. *Brilliant*, I thought. I couldn't take my eyes off him.

"And what can I do for you, young man?" he said to me.

"Can I have the new Style Council single, please?" I asked, still glancing at the Weller lookalike to my left.

"Course you can, young fella. That'll be £1.50, please."

He turned and picked a copy of the single from the shelf behind him, placed it in a seven-inch-sized, heavily patterned paper bag, and handed it to me. I gave him my earnings in exchange and turned to leave.

"Not as good as The Jam, mate," said the Weller lookalike to me. "Can't believe they've split up. Anyway, enjoy, mate."

He nodded at both the shopkeeper and me and turned to walk away. I was transfixed by him. I followed him out of the door and down the street. He turned to look at me. "Something you want, mate?" he asked with a smile.

"No, mate, sorry," I replied trying not to make eye contact with him. Then a sudden surge of courage came over me. "Actually, mate, what happened to The Jam? Why did they split up?"

"Not sure, mate. Fucking stupid if you ask me. Anyway, mate, I've got to go. Enjoy the single, yeah." He gave me a quick ruffle of the hair and headed off.

"Yeah, thanks, mate. You too," I said to him as he went. He turned and gave me a quick smile. I watched him as he disappeared around the corner and out of sight.

Two things were now clear to me. One, I had to keep up with music news or this sort of thing might happen again, and two, I wanted a Paul Weller haircut.

I rushed home with my purchase in hand, running most of the way. I had to stop when I got to my front door as my parents still didn't trust me enough to give me my own key, so I had to knock and wait every time I came home as if I were merely a visitor. When the door opened, I was confronted by my mum with that look on her face.

"What's that?" she said, pointing to the seven-inch-sized paper bag in my hand.

"It's a record. I just bought it with my paper-round money," I said as if accused of something terrible.

She grabbed it from my hand and took out the contents. She stood staring at the shiny black cover with "The Style Council" written in gold lettering in the top right-hand corner. She really couldn't have looked any more contemptuous if she'd tried.

"What's The Style Council?" she asked.

"It's Paul Weller's new band," I replied. "The Jam have split up."

"Who?" she said. "Sounds ridiculous. Who calls a band that?"

"Can I have it back, please?" I said.

She smiled and handed it back to me. I then ran past her, up the stairs, and into my bedroom, firmly shutting the door behind me.

As I sat on my bed, eager to hear my new record, my mum shouted up to me that I was not to play it too loud. I replied that I wouldn't. I didn't want anything to get in the way of my listening, so I decided to appease her request. And besides, my wooden record player was hardly capable of being too loud. The new stereo downstairs with its separate speakers was able to make a right racket, especially when James Last was pumping out of them, which was, up to that point in my life, the most horrible sound I had ever heard.

I sat looking at the cover for a while. The back featured a picture of Weller wearing a long mac and dark glasses, walking down a street, talking to a similarly dressed bloke with a fuzzy blonde haircut.

To the right of picture was the name of the song, "Speak Like a Child". And below that the name of the B-side, "Party Chambers". Below those words there was a passage of writing with the words "The Cappuccino Kid" written at the bottom and, finally, a list of credits. It said, "The Style Council is: Vocals and Guitar, Paul Weller. Keyboards, Mick Talbot." And so I learned my first piece of music information. The name of the bloke with fuzzy hair was Mick Talbot.

I lifted the creaking lid to my record player, placed the single on the turntable and the stylus arm onto the record.

It began with the rasping sound of keyboards accompanied by trumpets. *Blimey, he's good, this Mick Talbot*, I thought. Weller began to sing. I couldn't really make out the lyrics. It sounded like "your hair hands are gonna step surer". I knew this couldn't be right, or could it? Who was I to know? The first lyric I could make out was, "You believe you're above it, and I don't really blame you." Who believed they were above it, and why shouldn't I have blamed them?

It finished. I played it again, then again, and again, each time turning the volume dial up a bit further. Eventually, the inevitable happened. A bang at my door accompanied by an over-the-top "turn that down" overtook the sound of "Speak Like A Child". I did what I was told; I didn't want to lose access to my new single so soon.

After a few more listens, I flipped it over to listen to the B-side, "Party Chambers". Once again the sounds of Mick Talbot's keyboards rang out. *Wow, amazing.* This time I could make out the opening lyrics: "Back in the party chambers, laughter echoes out", but the second line sounded like "I guess my kiss a war a demma miss me for a while." That couldn't be right.

I played both sides, one after the other, for the rest of the day. Periodically, I paused to turn the sound down as per the instructions that followed a banging on my door. It was nearly evening by the time I managed to turn my record player off. My tea was on the table, and hunger had taken over my need to hear the songs again, but the thought of them was still firmly at the front of my mind.

"What was that racket?" my mum asked accusingly as I tucked into my fish fingers and baked beans.

"That's the record I bought today," I said proudly. My dad looked up at me and shook his head. He didn't say much at the best of times.

"It sounded rubbish," my sister said, looking at me like I was the irritation to her that I was always trying so hard to be. "What is it?"

"I thought you liked The Jam?" I said to her.

"I do. They're my favourite band actually," she replied with an embarrassingly large ration of contempt.

"Well, they've split up, and that's Pauls Weller's new band, actually," I replied emphasising the "actually".

"That's crap. How would you know? You're just a kid. The Jam will never split up."

"Well, they have. Paul Weller is in The Style Council now, and that's their first single. Like I said."

"Don't speak to your sister like that," Mum said firmly and about four inches from my face.

"But she just said crap," I said in search of reason.

"David. Did you hear what your son just said?"

"No, I didn't," he replied dismissively. "Can you pass the red sauce, please, Tom?"

My sister's name is Tracey, and she really, really, really annoyed me. And me her. Only I did it on purpose. She, however, was just naturally annoying.

This was the first time that I had clearly managed properly to get the better of her on her level – and without the need for any childish pranks. I had outdone her musically for the first time, and she hadn't even known it. Ha. Idiot.

She had yet to discover the demise of The Jam and had to learn it from her annoying little brother. It was clearly an extremely painful experience for her. She looked at me with a mixture of confusion and hatred that I had never seen in her before. I could tell that she was eager to go and find out if what I had said was true. And clearly, for the sake of her own ego, she hoped that it wasn't, not because she loved The Jam dearly – she did to a point. But what bugged her most was the idea of me knowing something that she didn't. I could understand that. In fact, I was relying on it.

That evening as I played the single several more times, a knock came at my door. This time, it was a calm knock as if to request entry, very unlike the banging from my mum which was intended to stop the sounds coming out of my room. It was Tracey.

"What?" I asked without opening the door.

"Let me in," she said.

"No," I replied, "I'm busy." With that, the door opened, and she walked in anyway. "I said no, actually." She ignored me and sat down on my bed. She had a look on her face that made me feel uncomfortable, one that I hadn't seen before.

It was almost as if she was trying to be nice to me, and with a tinge of admiration thrown in. Clearly she had discovered what I'd told her earlier about The Jam to be true.

I decided that maybe I should go along with it and see what happened. You never knew; it might have worked out well for me. I sat next to her on the bed, both of us in silence as the final bars of

"Speak Like a Child" rang out of my crap record player. The silence remained as I flipped it over to play "Party Chambers". Her eyes lit up, and she looked at me and smiled. At that point in my life, it was by far the most uncomfortable I had ever felt.

"That's brilliant," she said as "Party Chambers" ended. Then she stood up to leave the room, quietly closing the door behind her, a far cry from the slam of the door she would usually administer when leaving my room in the past, usually after admonishing me for whatever prank I had played on her that time.

My favourite was to sneak into her room and change the time that her alarm would go off in the morning. She had recently started full-time work, having now left school. Making her late was extremely amusing to me. Not to her, though.

Once, in a vain attempt to combat this, she placed a series of hairclips on top of the buttons of her new digital alarm clock that my dad had bought for her as a well-done for getting a job, so she might know if I had been at it. As if she thought I wouldn't be able to put them back exactly as she had put them on there in the first place. Silly girl. She'd never been that smart.

That night I fell asleep with a big smile on my face. Not only had my record collection begun, but I appeared to have put one over on Tracey, and she knew it. However, that smile had a tinge of fear to it as I was still feeling uneasy about the pleasantries she had shown me. Something was bound to happen to ruin this new feeling, and it was bound to come from her direction.

5. Music Discovered, Part 2

"Where is it? *Where ... the fuck ... is it?*" I screamed the next day.

'Speak Like A Child' was missing, and I knew full bloody well where it was, because I could hear it coming from Tracey's bedroom. This was a disturbing revelation. I realised for the first time that I had never owned anything she had wanted before, and, therefore, she couldn't have really gotten to me, only me to her via the medium of her records or her alarm clock. I knew this could be used in my favour but also against me. We were entering a new phase, full of unknowns.

I made my way to her room and banged on the door. It was answered by a tall bloke with a little bit of wispy facial hair. He didn't look too pleased.

"What do you want?" he enquired, seeming to know who I was.

"I want my record back," I replied. "Now." I added with a level of courage that I had never displayed before.

He stepped out towards me, quietly shut the door behind him, and slowly kneeled down in order to be at my physical level. "You'll get it back when were finished with it. OK, mate?"

"No, mate, not OK. I want it back now."

By now he had a look of derision on his face and was openly scoffing at my despair. Suddenly the door to Tracey's bedroom opened again, banging into this bloke's backside and nearly knocking him into me.

"Leave him, Trevor," she said. "Here, here's your record, just wanted to borrow it, soz." This was weird. I didn't know how to react. Now she was sticking up for me and apologising.

"Seriously, your name is Trevor? Trevor and Tracey? Do you drive a Capri?"

Clearly that wasn't the correct way to react. However, it was too late. He clasped his hands firmly around my chin and pushed my cheeks together seriously hindering my ability to speak coherently.

"Sherioshly, mashe, tashe yer fushin hansh of my faish," I said.

"Stop it, Trevor. He's half your size. Just take the record and fuck off."

And so I did just that – took the record and fucked off. Trevor didn't look too happy, and for the next few minutes, I could hear shouting coming from Tracey's bedroom as they discussed their disagreement. The shouting may have gone on for longer, but by now I was basking in the glory of the opening chords of "Speak Like a Child" and couldn't really hear anything else.

Despite having the record back and listening to it happily, I was still disturbed by Tracey's reaction. She had openly defended me, and in front of one of the people that I imagined being considered quite cool in her world. When she sat on my bed the day before, there was no one there to hear her be nice to me, so I could understand that, to an extent anyway. But this was weird. *Never mind*, I thought and got back to the record.

The following Saturday, just as I was about to enter the record shop to spend my wages, I noticed Trevor heading up the street in my direction. I quickly ran into the relative safety of the shop and hid in the funk section. I watched as Trevor walked in. He didn't look particularly unhappy. He was clearly looking for someone, and that someone was likely to be me. I continued to hide amongst the funk, but as he moved, I was forced to do the same in order to maintain my cover. By the time he headed for the counter, I was deep in the prog rock section.

"What you doing down there?" said the shopkeeper. "You like prog, yeah?"

"Yeah … I mean, no."

I didn't really know what prog rock was but had heard it talked about quite negatively once on a programme about punk. And I like that, so I didn't like prog.

"I'm hiding from that bloke; I think he wants to punch me."

"What? That bloke there?" he said pointing. I confirmed the identity of Trevor.

"That's Trevor," he said.

"I know. I think he wants to punch me. He's going out with my sister, Tracey, and I think he might be a bit upset with me."

"Seriously, Trevor and Tracey?" He laughed as he said it, as did I, still crouched down. Trevor heard us and made his way over.

"Trev, this lad thinks you're gonna punch him. You ain't gonna punch him, are you?"

The shopkeep seemed incredibly amused at the idea of me being punched by an oaf twice my size.

"Course I'm not," Trevor said. "We had a minor disagreement outside his sister's bedroom the other day, didn't we, Tim?"

"Tom," I said.

"I know," he said, laughing uncontrollably to himself. This forced me to stand up and lose my cover, which was pretty much gone anyway. The hostilities seemed to be over.

Trevor put his arm around me and led me to the new wave section. His attitude was completely different from our first meeting. I felt immediately suspicious of this, given his association with my sister, but decided to play along and see what would transpire.

He began to talk in depth about his love of music. I was fascinated. He told me how he had seen The Jam play live twice and The Sex Pistols once but that the set was cut short due to a fight in the audience that he was not involved in. But I could tell that he was involved. It was obvious.

It seemed unlikely considering our brief and turbulent history, but I was really beginning to like Trevor. However, there was still something in the back of my mind that told me that he was likely to punch me at any minute. But as the minutes passed, it seemed less and less likely until the point arrived where I didn't think it at all. It was a relief, as he was quite a sizable chap and, at the end of the day, also had access to my house.

We conversed about music all the way to the counter. Turned out that he also wasn't aware of the demise of The Jam and subsequent formation of The Style Council, which was strange, given the stories he had just told me. You would have thought he would have known that. Anyway, we were now friends. I was pleased. He was pretty cool. Well, cooler than me anyway.

At the counter, the two of us perused the chart listings for the week. It was time to decide what single to buy. The shopkeeper, who I had now found out was called Bob, was only too keen to help me select my purchase. He played me several songs based on what he knew about me from our musical discussions so far. I liked most of them, but it was "The Lovecats" by The Cure that I was most taken by.

It had entered the charts that week, but I knew nothing of them. The record box hadn't contained any songs by them despite Bob informing me that they had been around for a little while now. This made me think for the first time that maybe my cousin wasn't as up on things as I'd thought he was. And it also made me think that maybe I was.

The front cover was colourful, and it had the name of the song and the band emblazoned upon it, along with a picture of two cats dancing, brilliant. It was a far cry from the plain blackness of the "Speak Like a Child" cover which didn't even feature the name of the song on it. The song itself also had a very different sound to it. The vocal amazed and scared me in equal measure. The overall melody of the song was unmistakably my sort of thing. I bought it, bid farewell to Trevor and Bob, who seemed to quite like me as did I them, and made my way home to listen.

That night, after several listens to "The Lovecats" and almost as many listens to the B-side, "Speak My Language", the abrasive call came from the bottom of the stairs to inform me that dinner was ready. I carefully removed the playing arm from the vinyl, lovingly placed it back in its sleeve, and laid it on top of "Speak Like a Child". At that point, I decided that I would need to come up with a better way of storing my records. The box I had from my cousin would have been ideal, but he had taken that back. I needed my own box.

"Why have you given me peas, Mum? I don't like peas. I've said that before, haven't I?" I didn't like peas. She knew that.

"Eat them," she barked, accompanied by a long and firm stare. I looked to my dad for support. He glanced up at me, but without moving his head, clearly not wanting my mum to realise he was making contact.

"Well, can I at least have some red sauce on them?"

Mum picked up the red sauce and thrust it down onto the table in front on me. The top was off; she obviously didn't realise. The force of the bottle hitting the table caused a large lump of it to propel itself onto the nice, clean white tablecloth.

"Now look what you've made me do," she said.

"How did I make you do that? I only wanted the red sauce; I didn't ask for a drum roll."

"How dare you?" she said. "David, a little support here, please."

Dad looked up, this time moving his head and wiping the smile off his face before he was told to do so.

"Don't be rude to your mum, Tom," he said. "And eat your peas; they'll make you big and strong."

I looked down at my peas and tried to work out how the little green balls that tasted like feet were likely to have that effect on me. I couldn't come to a reasonable conclusion, so I just doused them in red sauce and ate them as quickly as I could. Disgusting.

Back in my room and with a belly full of peas and butterscotch Angel Delight, I noticed one thing and one thing only: "The Lovecats" was missing. I definitely put it on top of "Speak Like a Child", but now all I could see was "Speak Like a Child". There was only one place it could be, and that was with Tracey and Trevor.

I made my way to Tracey's bedroom door where I could hear the faint sounds of the song. How could this be happening again? Was I from now on going to have to carry my records around with me? Actually, I quite liked that idea, but it wasn't practical, and I knew it.

I also wanted to have my records on display at all times and make them as easily accessible as possible. This was a dilemma, and I didn't know the answer. It seemed that there was no choice; I was going to have to make a deal with her.

"Can you let me in, please?" I said while simultaneously knocking on the door. It was light knock, as I wanted to avoid any hostility, but at the same time firm enough to let her know that I meant business.

"Go away," she said.

This time, I knocked more firmly and added some reasoning. "That's my fucking record, you dick." She didn't respond well to the reasoning, flung the door open, and hurled a tirade of abuse at me. By this time, I didn't care; I was all angry and stuff.

My love for my record had taken over my reasoning and also my sense of self-preservation. I pushed my way past her and made my way to her record deck, which was much better than mine, by the way. I didn't get to it though, as Trevor had now entered the struggle. He grabbed my arm, but instead of using anger to get his way, he, like me, was clearly up for making a deal.

"Tom, mate," he began. "I know we shouldn't have taken it, but I'd only heard it that one time in the shop earlier, and I wanted to hear it again. Cracking tune, ain't it?"

"Well … yeah, it is, but … Trevor, you know, it's mine, isn't it?" I said, adopting Trevor's amenable attitude.

Post our interaction earlier that day, coupled with his new attitude towards me, I definitely liked Trevor, and he definitely liked me. Of course, not as much as he liked Tracey, but I was not in a position to be offering him what she was able to. I didn't like Tracey and never had, despite her being my sister. Well, adoptive sister anyway. Plus, I was pretty sure that if she were ugly, Trevor wouldn't be in her bedroom. But apparently she wasn't, and therefore, he was. I suppose what really mattered was exactly how dedicated to his love of music was Trevor. "Tits or tunes" was the question I needed Trevor to answer, but now wasn't the time or place. I just wanted my record back.

"Here you go, mate. What you gonna buy next week?" he asked with a smile and a look of genuine interest.

Trevor had clearly cottoned onto my record-buying routine before it had even had a chance to develop properly. I was only two weeks and two seven-inch singles in, but already someone much older and experienced than me was awaiting my next move. It was a good feeling. I definitely liked Trevor. Tracey was a dick, though. I knew it, and I think Trevor knew it, but the guy was only doing what blokes do. At the age of twelve, I was starting to get those feelings and could only imagine what someone a few years older like Trevor must have been going through with his emotions. I decided to cut them both some slack.

"Don't know, mate. I'll be in the shop next Saturday if you wanna come with," I said. "I'll finish my paper round about nine, so meet you outside quarter past, yeah?"

"Yeah, mate, sounds good. See you then."

I think it was safe to say at this point that the previous hostilities were officially over, and this new relationship between Trevor and me was here to stay. Tracey didn't seem too happy about it. She looked very confused during pleasantries. There was no doubt that she would happily return to the air of hatred we lived in previously, but one thing that I wasn't considering was that she was just as in need of what Trevor could offer her as he was of her.

The next Saturday, Trevor, good to his word, was waiting outside the record shop for me when I finished my paper round. I had no idea before I got there just how important this visit to the record shop was going to be.

As usual I perused the chart listings, searching for this week's purchase. I was only two singles into my collection, but already I was thinking about albums. I knew that The Style Council were due to release their debut LP early in 1984. I had formulated a plan of how I was going to afford it. I would, through a façade of good behaviour, attempt to get my pocket money increased and at the same time try and save 50p a week from my paper round. I also planned to request a pay rise from the paper shop owner. I was only too aware that it was not likely to go well as he was a particularly horrible man who seemed to relish having people in his charge. Nevertheless, I was going to do it. Even if it didn't pay off. As long as he didn't sack me, I should be able to collate enough money before the album's release to buy it.

What I didn't see coming up was an event in music that was likely to have a lasting effect on the rest of my life was occurring.

In my cousin's box was a song called "She's Lost Control" by Joy Division. I loved it. It had an effect on me that no other song ever did. It didn't necessarily have the sort of melody, singing, or structure that I adored in so many other songs. It did something else. Without knowing it, it was the first time that I had loved a piece of music for more than just the sound. The vocal transfixed me, but I didn't really know why. The drum pattern was as familiar to me as my own heartbeat, and the guitar I just couldn't explain. But the one thing that confused me the most about the song was that despite knowing that it was in no way my favourite song, it was most certainly my favourite to listen to.

Each time I would put a record on from the box back in the box days, it would be a split-second decision, usually between two songs, sometimes many more. But with "She's Lost Control", I would plan in advance to listen to it. I would go through a range of emotions during the prelude to actually putting it on that would include fear and trepidation.

I didn't really know much about Joy Division. Just that the lead singer had committed suicide, which made the song scare me even more. Sometimes, with some of the records from the box, my consciousness could drift away from listening intently to the song but with "She's Lost Control", it was never the case.

I would never say that any song I listened to, and no matter how many times I heard it, could ever be described as being on in the background but with this song, I was actually afraid to take my attention away from it – almost like it might jump up and kick me in the bum if I lost concentration at any point.

"So what are we buying today then, young Tom?" said Bob, the shopkeep, as I approached the counter that Saturday morning. Trevor stood by my side and seemed eager to hear my decision. Bob looked at him and back at me, clearly remembering that the last time we'd met I'd been expecting a punch in the face from Trevor, and not really knowing if the issue had been resolved.

"Not sure. What would you recommend?" I asked him.

"Well, you could wait a week and get the New Order twelve-inch," he said.

"The what?"

"New Order released a song on twelve-inch only a while back. We sold out but I've got some more coming in next week," he informed me excitedly. It wasn't that I didn't know what a twelve-inch was – far from it. It's just that I hadn't bought one before, as to be able to afford it would involve not buying a single one week. Also, my cousin's box was not built for their size. It was specifically designed for the seven-inch single and his job as a part-time DJ was all about the seven-inch. A twelve-inch would take up too much air time and not leave enough time for idle chit-chat.

"How much is that going to cost?" I asked Bob. He was only too aware, even so early on in my collection, how much I could afford, week on week. It was good for me to know that he was taking that much interest.

"Two weeks wages, mate. Seems to me that you should ask for a rise." Bob was right. I knew of many paperboys who worked for other shops that were paid far more than me. And some of those didn't have to get up each morning to make their deliveries. They had evening rounds. Some of them delivered those free papers that nobody actually wanted. So even without any profit on actual paper sales, they were still being paid more than me.

I decided quite quickly that I would save up for the New Order twelve-inch. I had so many questions about them but was afraid to ask and thus look ridiculous. Luckily I didn't need to ask, as Trevor was only too happy to offer up the information via a discussion with Bob that I was listening in on.

"I've heard this is the biggest move away from the Joy Division sound they've done," Trevor said to Bob.

I looked at Bob.

"Not sure Ian would have liked it to be honest, mate," he continued.

I looked back at Trevor. Bob and Trevor were getting on extremely well. They both periodically glanced at me as they exchanged views, clearly keen for me to be involved. And I was involved, only more in an observatory capacity at this stage.

"I think Ian would have loved it," Bob replied. I looked at Bob. "In fact, I think, should he not have killed himself, Joy Division would have progressed to sound like that by now."

OK, so now I was getting the story. I had already ascertained that New Order were made up of three members of Joy Division and had a different singer due to Ian having committed suicide. I needed that twelve-inch single.

"Bob," I said confidently. "I shall see you at the same time next week, and I shall be purchasing that New Order twelve-inch, so can you keep me a copy, please, mate?"

Bob looked at me with a strange sort of admiration that manifested itself via the medium of a slightly upturned left-hand corner of his mouth. He tilted his head towards me and glanced up at Trevor while simultaneously nodding at him. I took this as a sign of respect and decided that I would spend some time in front of the mirror practicing the move myself.

"Course I will, mate," Bob said. "You sure you'll be able to get through this week without a new single?"

"Should be OK, Bob. I've got a fair bit to keep me going," I replied decisively.

It was like I was a new person, brimming with the confidence that my love of music coupled with my relationship with Bob and Trevor had given me. It felt good.

"Actually, Tom, ain't it about time you bought an album?" Bob enquired. I had thought about this many times. He was right. It was time for me to buy an album. "You know The Style Council album comes out early next year, don't you?" I did know this.

"Yeah, course, Bob," I said. "Was thinking that will probably be my first album purchase. What you reckon?" Bob agreed. So by early next year, I would potentially have in my possession all three vinyl formats.

By then the seven-inch collection was likely to number as many as ten, maybe more, and who knew how many twelve-inches. Of course, I would have to save up for the album, and who knew how many twelve-inch singles I might want from now until then. It was difficult to predict. All of it depended on money. It was time to ask for a pay rise, not only from my employer at the paper shop, but also from my parents in respect of pocket money. This was going to be a difficult week.

6. Finances and Improved Potential

I decided that I had to start my efforts to improve my record-buying capabilities as soon as possible. The next morning I planned to speak to the paper shop owner about my wages, and then depending on how that went, i.e., whether I still had a job or not, I would speak to my parents that night about an increase in pocket money.

I walked into the shop at around 7.30 a.m. Mr Penbury, the owner of Penbury's Newsagents, was standing behind the counter, looking as charming as ever. He had a comb-over hairstyle that was less than convincing. On his face, he sported a large, thick pair of glasses that resembled those of Deirdre Barlow in *Coronation Street* and an even larger, thicker, moustache.

It was early morning. Neither of us was happy. The difference was that he was the employer and, therefore, had the upper hand. I had no bargaining point whatsoever, other than a promise of my continued service, which I was banking on him wishing to maintain.

I had always managed to deliver the papers he had asked me to. But as far as I knew, I didn't do it to any greater degree of expertise than anyone else in his charge.

My dad belonged to the same Rotary club as Mr Penbury. I was hoping that this would give me a bargaining point, but I had no real idea if it would work in my favour or not – knowing my dad as I did, probably not. Not always the easiest bloke to get on with was my dad, and since suffering a stroke a few years back, he had developed an unpredictable and sometimes irrational temper.

"Morning," I said professionally. Mr Penbury didn't answer; he simply thrust a sack full of papers and magazines in my direction. "Thank you," I said. He looked at me like the last thing I should consider doing was asking him for a favour. But that was exactly what I was about to do. The end result of more record-buying power was far more important than anything else. It was worth the risk.

"Don't … even … think about it," he said firmly, not even looking up from the magazine he was reading before I had the opportunity to speak. "I know you're going to ask for a pay rise." How did he know that? Did I have that sort of look about me? Had he seen that look so many times because he was such a tight-fisted wanker that he could read it in any face that looked at him? Or had he heard my conversation with Bob and Trevor in the record shop yesterday? Unlikely.

Predictably, it was the first one. He had, for obvious reasons, i.e., being a tight git, seen the look many, many times before. But I was still determined to ask and get the required response.

"So what about it then?" I asked. "Most people I know who do paper rounds get twice what you pay me." Judging by the look on his face, the vein protruding from his neck, and the redness beaming through his extremely thin white shirt, it was quite clear that he was not taking this well. He stared for a while and then gestured to me to leave, or at least that's what I thought. I turned to leave, paper bag over my shoulder.

"Where do you think you're going with that bag?" he barked aggressively.

"I'm going to deliver the papers."

"No, you're not. You're fired." This was alarming news and somewhat unexpected. All I had done was ask for an extra quid or two per week. Three tops.

"I was only asking," I said. "Now you've said no, I'll continue as before."

"No, you won't. You're sacked. Put the bag down and go." He was quite adamant. The vein was now quite prominent and zigzagged across his neck. It looked like the coastline of the south-east of England as seen from space. Very alarming, it was.

"Twat," I said under my breath.

"What was that?" he replied.

"I said I'll be back."

"Is that a threat?" he asked.

It took me a while to work out how he could possibly see that as a threat. I presumed he thought I might come back and rob the place. That was hardly me, but he wasn't to know that. I decided not to respond and leave him guessing. After all, I was no longer under his charge and, therefore, he had no hold over me, so I could say what I wanted.

As I slowly walked out of Penbury's Newsagents, the enormity and full implications of what had just happened hit me right in the face. There were positives to be taken. No longer would I have to get up ridiculously early for a pittance of pay, no longer would I have to endure Mr Penbury's miserable face, and no longer would I have to see his nipples through his cheap shirts. But I had now lost my ability to purchase a single per week. My only hope was to get myself a new paper round or get my pocket money increased. This also threw into serious doubt my impending ownership of the New Order twelve-inch single. Things were bad.

"Dad?"

"Yes, son?"

"Can I have an increase in my pocket money?"

"You better ask your mum."

"So, no, then."

The look my dad gave me was both derisory and somewhat helpless. He knew full well that he didn't have the authority to hand out pocket money increases, despite the fact that it was he who earned the money in the first place. He also knew that I didn't stand a chance with my mum and, at the same time, had completely devolved himself of any responsibility with regards to a possible increase. Clever man, my dad. A man of experience. A man who knew full well that he had married the wrong woman. A foolish man maybe?

I wanted to say to him that he needed to stand up for himself and get Mum used to him being in charge pretty sharpish, or this would be the way things would go for the rest for his life. But I was not in a position to be handing out that sort of advice. And besides, I was only twelve-and-a-bit years old and could well be wrong. Maybe he was a clever man after all. I just didn't know at this stage in my or his life.

"Mum." No vocal response came back, just a reluctant stare like I had interrupted something important. "Can I have an increase in my pocket money?" *I should add a please*, I thought. "Please," I said.

Still no response, just an increased intensity in the stare and a narrowing of the eyes. Should I ask again? Should I maintain the same tone of voice? Would that make it worse? Maybe I should soften the tone of voice, sound a bit more amiable. But that might sound OK to me but bad to her. My experience told me that the outcome of this could not be predicted. There was no right or wrong way of going about it. It was all about the mood of the recipient, i.e., my mum. I would ask again.

"Can I have an increase, Mum? It's just I've lost my paper round."

"*What?*" Oh dear. "How on earth did you manage to do that? I told you, David, he wouldn't keep that for long. That nice Mr Penbury bent over backwards for you. I told him you wouldn't be any good, but your dad managed to convince him you could do it. Sometimes I wonder what I brought up. I really do, so help me. David, are you not going to say anything? Are you even listening? My God, what is wrong with the men in my life? You try and do someone a favour, and this is how you get treated. Well, this is the last time I do anything to try and help you, so help me. You continuously let me down, and all I do is try and help you and this is how you repay me. Well, no more. That's it. David, deal with this, will you? I need to go and lie down, so help me."

OK, that did not go well. My dad and I looked at each other like we should have seen it coming. In fact, he had seen it coming; I was the one who should have.

"You should have seen that coming, you know," he said quietly so as not to incur a repeat performance. He knew as I did that although my mum was out of sight and on her way upstairs for a lie down, so help her, she could hear through brick walls.

"Sorry, Dad, it's just that My Penbury is a bit of a—"

"Dick," he said, finishing my sentence.

"All I did was ask him for an extra quid or two per week, and he just sacked me there and then."

"You should have come to me first, Tom. I would have told you not to bother. Like getting blood out of a stone, trying to get money out of that bloke. He's a dick."

This was the first time in my life that my dad and I had conversed in this way. To be honest, I had given up all hope of it ever happening. I knew it would never happen with my mum; that was a given. But I'd always hoped that one day my dad and I would end up relating to each other.

"Look, I've got an idea," he said, once again very quietly so as not to incur wrath. "Why don't you do a bit of work for me? I'll give you a tenner for a few hours, but it does mean giving up your Saturday mornings. So no more of that crap TV you watch."

I friggin' loved Saturday morning television, but not as much as I loved music. Often the two would be linked intrinsically, sometimes by my favourite bands appearing on it, but also simply due to its anarchic nature. Despite this, it was an easy choice. I accepted.

Why this didn't happen earlier, I'll never know. Why I had to spend the last few months getting up at the crack of dawn six days a week for a pittance when this was on the cards was beyond my comprehension. But no matter, now the option was on the table, I was in. *I could ask. Should I ask? No, best not.* I didn't want the decision to be reversed.

"So what do you want me to do?" I asked.

"Just do a bit of filing, post a few letters, make me a cup of tea, that sort of thing." Sounded excellent to me. I could spend my Saturday mornings in my dad's office doing that, collect my tenner, and make my way to see Bob at the record shop. Not only that, but now I could afford to buy an album each week, and have some change.

In the space of a few hours, I had gone from being sacked by a dick with a comb-over and being ranted at about my inadequacies by my mum to getting a job that was four and a half fewer days a week, in the warm, and paid five times as much. Something had to go wrong.

7. Blue Monday, Part 1

That Friday afternoon I decided to pop into the record shop to see Bob and tell him the good news. And also to make sure that my copy of the New Order twelve-inch would be available for me to purchase on Saturday afternoon rather than early morning due to my shift in fortunes, job-wise.

"Bob," I said, "good news, I've got a job working with my dad and can now afford to buy an album a week, maybe more." Bob was very pleased. Not only for me but also for himself, as it meant more money in his till. We were both very happy. Something simply had to go wrong.

I thoroughly enjoyed not having to get up early in the morning to do my paper round that week. Not only was it an extra hour in bed, but also I could wallow in the happiness of knowing that, come Saturday, I would be doing just half a day's work followed by a visit to the record shop.

When Saturday finally arrived, I awoke even before my dad. I was keen to see what he did at work and also where he worked. But more than anything, I was so very excited to be getting the New Order twelve-inch.

I made it through the morning with ease. I filled documents in a filing cabinet, I put stamps on envelopes, I made tea, and then at around twelve o'clock, the words I had longed to hear came from my dad.

"OK, let's go, Tom. Here's your tenner. You've done well today." He was very pleased with me, and we had another moment of closeness.

His office was just 'round the corner from the record shop, so I turned down the offer of a lift home and told him I was off to buy the record. He wasn't as excited as I was. I didn't really expect him to be. But he seemed happy that I was happy, and that was good enough for me.

"Bob, you OK?" I said as I approached the counter, tenner in hand.

"Hello, young Tom, yeah, I'm good, thanks. Trevor not with you today?"

"No, mate. Just finished my first morning working with my dad."

Bob could see I was struggling to get my words out due to the excitement. So instead of making me do so, he reached under the counter and produced a twelve-inch-sized colourful paper bag, stapled at the top with a label on it reading, "New Order – Blue Monday 12 - Tom – Saturday PM".

I thanked Bob. He patted me on the head and simply said, "Enjoy." I had every intention of doing so.

"Thanks, mate. See you next week."

I didn't really want to leave the shop, but Bob was pretty busy putting labels on things. We could chat later.

I began to make my way home with my head down and one eye firmly on the bag in hand. Bob chose to use paper bags for his customers' wares. I imagine that was a financial decision on his part. It didn't exactly fill me with confidence that there wouldn't be an accident, though.

As I approached the top of my road, I began to periodically break out into a series of small runs. I was getting closer to my record player all the time, but it seemed like an age before I made it to my front door.

When I finally did arrive, I rang the bell, as, of course, I was not allowed to have my own key. My mum answered and looked quite happy, which was strange. She didn't even give me any instructions with regards to volume. She just let me in and watched me as I made my way upstairs. All was good. I still waited for something to go wrong.

I sat on my bed, carefully removed the two staples from the top of the bag, placed the label on my bedside table as a keepsake, and pulled out my new twelve-inch single.

It was a thing of beauty and made to resemble a computer floppy disk with no mention of the band or song name anywhere on it. I lifted up the creaky lid to my record player/sideboard, carefully placed the vinyl upon it, the needle on the vinyl, and sat back to listen.

Dum dum dum dum, dumma dumma dumma dumma, dum dum dum dum, dum dum, dum dum, dum dum. It took me a while before I realised that the intro was going on for too long, even on a song that I hadn't heard before. I approached the record player and watched as the needle got to the second lot of dum dums and kept shooting back to the beginning, thus repeating the same dum dum, over and over. So this was what was going to go wrong. The record had a scratch. *Bollocks. Not good.* My day was ruined.

All the anticipation of the last week or so seemed to be pointless for that brief moment. *No matter*, I thought. *I'll just go and get another copy. Bob would oblige.* I closely examined the record and could see that, right near the start, there was a small line that looked out of place in the otherwise shiny-looking piece of vinyl. I decided that I would go and try it on my parent's record player.

The scratch, although visible to the naked eye, had no effect on their turntable at all. Mine was incredibly old and, let's face it, up till the days of the record box had only had complete shite played on it, so it was probably still harbouring a bit of resentment.

I briefly looked at my parents' collection of god-awful records. Several of them by James Last, others by Mantovani, and an Abba album. All of the J. Last albums featured dubious-looking pictures on their covers, a far cry from the artistic nature of all the records I owned. I thought it might be amusing to put one of them on for a few moments. It had been at least a couple of years since I had heard any of them.

My God, what is this crap? I quickly removed it and decided to get myself back down to see Bob as soon as possible, but first off, I needed to return to my bedroom to listen to "The Lovecats" as the mental residue from that few seconds of James Last had to be removed from my mind before it had any lasting effects.

"Bob," I said. He looked worried.

"What's up, Tom? You look like you've seen a ghost."

"The record, Bob ... dum dums ... it's scratched. I can't get past the second set of dum dums," I said, breathing erratically.

Bob took the record out and placed in on the in-house record shop turntable. It made it past the second set of dum dums without a problem. This was alarming. The only realistic conclusion that could be reached was that my turntable was not capable of playing it, which of course I already knew.

"The only conclusion I can reach Tom is that your turntable isn't capable of playing it," Bob said. I knew that.

"Yes," I replied "That seems to be the case. Er, leave it on anyway."

"How does it feel,

"To treat me like you do,

"When you've laid your hands upon me

"And shown me who you are?" it went.

What ... the fuck ... did that mean?

About halfway through, I turned 'round to see everyone in the shop looking towards the counter in total awe of the song. It was like a spaceship had landed near the chart listings. But it hadn't. It was all down to the amazing tune.

As it faded out and the shop patrons went back to their businesses, the world didn't seem the same anymore. Before the song started, there was an audible murmur in the shop as everyone chatted about music, but during it, the shop became bathed in silence, everyone just trying to take in the new sound that planet Earth and its inhabitants had made.

"That, Bob, is the future, is it not?"

I was hooked. I immediately thought back to the James Last album that I heard a few seconds of before I'd left my parents' house. How could anyone produce music like that when music like this existed? Incredible.

"So, can I have another copy to try, please, Bob?" I enquired.

"Don't see why not. I can still sell this one."

I chose not to mention the visibility of the scratch that caused my record player to seem so inadequate. He would find that out himself, or at least the next owner of it would. Not my problem. In any case, it didn't make a difference on his player or my parents', so as long as someone didn't buy it who had as shit equipment as I did, it shouldn't be an issue. I did feel bad, though. Bob had been good to me, and I wanted to be good to him, but I wanted a working version of the record more, especially now that I had heard it and was quite literally addicted to it.

Back in my bedroom and the new copy worked like a dream. I had to get used to the fact that it sounded a bit shit on my record player compared to Bob's and my parents', but it was better than not hearing it at all. And it taught me a valuable lesson. Well, two actually—one, that I should never go anywhere near my parents' record player again, as it made mine sound shit; and two, that New Order are the best friggin' band I had ever heard in my life. I was set. I was only in my early teens, and I was set. Life was good.

Over the next few months, my collection grew and grew, as did my respective relationships with Bob and Trevor. It actually got to the point where Trevor would spend more time in my bedroom listening to records than he would in my sisters' room doing whatever they did. I was pretty convinced after a while that he was only going out with her to spend time with me. All they seemed to do was argue with each other.

So with my newfound wealth due to the job working with my dad on Saturday mornings, I was able to fill out my New Order collection and also keep up with the new singles that took my fancy.

I also purchased my first albums, both by New Order. First came *Power, Corruption & Lies*, released in the May of 1983. And then I purchased their first album, *Movement*, which was released two years earlier in 1981. Both completely brilliant in every way.

I now started to use my memories of those few seconds listening to that bloody James Last album to my advantage. I realised that you really couldn't get much further from that hideous sound than the two New Order albums I had purchased. And so I started to use James as a benchmark for shitness.

Many singles were added over the next few months, by both new and old bands alike. I was quite enamoured by the whole new wave of artists that occupied the charts. The synth pop bands really did it for me. But as was usually the case there was a yang to the yin. Fortunately though, since the incident with the James Last album, I now knew how to use it to my advantage.

Bands like Wham and Spandau Ballet, coupled with solo artists like Lionel Richie and Phil Collins became my new benchmark for what was good and what was not – them being the not good, of course. Really awful.

So within not too much time at all, my collection was ready to be housed in a box. I still had mainly seven-inch singles, a few twelves, and the two New Order albums. I had also discovered the joys of smoking fags during this time, so that was taking up some of my music money, but I was too young to appreciate how bad that was likely to turn out.

Far too many of the musicians I was into looked cool smoking, and I wanted to be a part of that. And besides, the TV adverts seemed to think there was nothing wrong with it, quite the opposite. It seemed very likely to me at that time that the more I smoked, the more good things would happen to me. And also most sports seemed keen to advertise smoking, so it couldn't really have much of a negative effect on your health, or they wouldn't do it, right?

By Christmas 1983 the collection was looking as healthy as it could be. I also managed to get my parents to buy me a box for Jesus's birthday. I couldn't wait. When the day arrived and the box was mine, I filed the singles in alphabetical order, made a little label to go on the front, and sat the box proudly on top of my record player/radio/sideboard. I then immediately removed them all and refiled them in chronological order and then straight back to alphabetical. The box was big enough to grow into for the foreseeable future but also full enough to make it worth having. Perfect.

As at 25 December 1983, the box contained following (not shown in box order but chronological, as I would go back to eventually, and then back to alphabetical, as it proved impractical when in a hurry to find a particular song while not in a compatible emotional disposition or idiom):

- The Style Council – "Speak Like A Child" b/w "Party Chambers"
- The Cure – "The Lovecats"
- Tears For Fears – "Change"
- Siouxsie and the Banshees – "Dear Prudence"
- Howard Jones – "New Song"
- U2 – "New Year's Day"
- Aztec Camera – "Oblivious"
- REM – "Radio Free Europe"
- Madness – "The Sun and the Rain"
- Heaven 17 – "Temptation"
- Duran Duran – "Rio"
- The Smiths – "Hand In Glove"
- The Cure – "The Walk"
- The Thompson Twins – "We Are Detective"
- Kajagoogoo – "Too Shy"
- Tears for Fears – "Pale Shelter"
- Echo and the Bunnymen – "Never Stop"
- Depeche Mode – "Everything Counts"
- Dexy's Midnight Runners – "The Celtic Soul Brothers"
- The Style Council – "Long Hot Summer"
- Blancmange – "Blind Vision"
- Joe Jackson – "Steppin' Out"
- The Smiths – "This Charming Man"

And, of course, propped up against the box was the twelve-inch of "Blue Monday" and the two albums *Movement* and *Power, Corruption & Lies*, also both by New Order.

It was indeed a collection by this point, and quite a collection too.

I had no idea what the future would bring with regard to the bands I felt compelled to purchase the songs of. Would I still love them in ten years' time? Would I still love them by the end of next week? Who knew? All I knew was that, by Christmas 1983, I had a bona fide and respected collection, respected in particular by record shop Bob and also Trevor, who slept with my sister, god help him.

Another notable occurrence in the collection was the inclusion of multiple items by the same artist. This was now the case for The Smiths, The Style Council, New Order, and The Cure. It was a clear indication of how my taste would develop over time. Not only was I now a huge fan of these bands, in particular, but also their lead singers were becoming idols of mine.

The words and actions of Morrissey, Paul Weller, Robert Smith, and Bernard Sumner were starting to influence parts of my personality, something that didn't go unnoticed by my peers. Bob and Trevor loved watching me develop into a hybrid of the four of them, unlike my own group of friends who hadn't developed a love for music in the same intensely scary way, as they described it, that I had. But that wasn't a concern of mine. I didn't really like any of them anyway and spent most of my time fending them off.

There was big and little Chris. Both of whom were annoying in equal measure but for different reasons. Little Chris was just a complete gobshite, and Big Chris, well, he was a gobshite too but also big and strong so he got away with it. Both of them had the most god-awful taste in music. Although to be fair to Little Chris, he did know a lot about Bowie.

Then there was Phil, Nick and Nat who just had no relevance whatsoever, musically or otherwise. They would just go along with whatever Big Chris said to avoid becoming one of his targets. Weezel I liked, he had his own problems. Mainly that he had been indoctrinated into liking prog rock by his parents, but also because when we were very young he was a really good-looking lad and had gotten a lot of attention because of that, but then he seemed to lose his looks overnight. It affected him in a really weird way. His confidence went and he seemed to just blend into the background, whereas before he had always been the face of the group. The only one I did like was Gary, despite his crap taste in music, and although he would never have admitted it in front of the others, I think he had always felt the same way about me.

They all saw me, with the exception of Gary, as their complete opposite, as did I, mainly due to my physical size and inability/lack of concern with regard to being seen as "hard".

So there I was at the end of 1983, twelve and a half years old with a haircut like Paul Weller and a record collection to match any other that I knew of in size, and no other that I knew of in class. Apart from Trevor, that was. But his was almost identical to mine, as he had taken my lead and purchased his own copies of whatever I bought. When I found out Trevor was doing this, my proudest of moments was at that point in my life.

I didn't actually know anything about Bob's own personal collection, although I always presumed it was something to behold. He was always very impressed with my choices. The three of us had become firm friends.

I spent a great deal of time with the two of them and always in a musical capacity. What other capacity was there, really? Bob owned the shop that provided us with our music needs, material, and otherwise. Trevor was sleeping with my sister and developing musically, albeit slightly later in life, in the same way as myself. None of us ever saw a reason not to discuss music. Sometimes they would ask me about school, and I would in turn ask them about work, but within less than a minute, the conversation would always turn to music.

Everything was good, apart from the constant negativity of the judgement I was putting up with from my equal-aged peers, but that didn't really concern me. I had music to comfort me, which was much more of a friend than any of them had ever been or were likely to be.

The only thing that did concern me at this point was that despite becoming firm friends with Bob and spending pretty much all of my money in his shop, I had yet to see his legs. Not that I was desperate to see his legs. It was just strange that when I thought about him, I just saw a floating body in my mind. It didn't bother me that much, though. I was pretty sure things were as they should be below the waist. It wasn't like I thought he was wearing a skirt or had the legs of a chicken or something really weird like that. It's just, whenever I saw him, he always had a counter in front of him, and I was too short to see over it.

Anyway, at the ripe old age of thirteen, I was pretty much set and ready for what the next few years had to offer. I had a record collection to be proud of, and I had a Bob and a Trevor. Everything else was a bit rubbish, to be fair.

I had several years of being at school ahead of me and a future that was as uncertain as anyone else's was. Let's just see what happens was the way I looked at life back then.

8. Five Years Later – Talking about My Generation

Just like rock and roll in the fifties, the beat generation in the sixties, and punk in the seventies, my late teenage generation of the mid- to late-eighties was to have a movement. And in the same way that its predecessors had, it would crap the life out of the establishment and the parents of those taking part, alike.

I was now approaching eighteen years old and spent half of my days thinking of new and inventive ways to piss my parents off. The other half I spent thinking about girls and music. More often than not, the three collided, and I could piss my parents off by just thinking about girls and music. Well, when I say piss my parents off, it was just my mum really. Dad was pissed off too but mainly only because I wound my mum up so much that she ended up taking it out on him. It wasn't my intention, and he knew it, but it was an inevitable by-product of what I was doing.

Basically, the only way I could avoid my mother's wrath was if I went back in time and immediately turned into her as soon as I was old enough to think for myself. But then, of course, that was what she had always been trying to avoid happening, me thinking.

Still, the most important thing in my life was my record collection, which was now considerable in size. A couple of years ago, I had decided to sacrifice my birthday present in favour of combining it with my Christmas present and several weeks wages in order to obtain a brand-new stereo system. It was a far cry from the creaky, old wooden thing I had been using since my love of music began with the emergence of the record box more than ten years ago now.

It took up a lot less space in my bedroom and was stacked in a logical way: record player on top; below that was a graphic equalizer, which was really just a few slider switches that made no real difference to the sound; below that, a radio; and then at the bottom, a double tape deck.

I was so keen to get a new system that I failed to heed the warnings from several sources – in particular, Trevor, who inexplicably was still with my sister, and Bob, who I had now seen the legs of several times and was able to confirm that he was not a freak and had a fully functioning bottom half – that the new medium of compact discs was about to take over from vinyl.

I must admit, I thought it was a fad, and at the end of the day, they were horrible little plastic things whereas vinyl was beautiful. Nevertheless, I knew that I would eventually have to make the switch.

I still purchased all my records from Bob's shop, usually accompanied by Trevor. Unfortunately, I hadn't really gained much height during the last five years and, therefore, had gone from being a just-below-average height thirteen-year-old to being a short-arse seventeen-year-old.

Just recently a friend of mine called Gary, who as I mentioned earlier, I disliked slightly less than I disliked all of my other so-called friends, had started to attend all-night parties, or raves, if you would. I was not really interested, as the music was godawful, if you could even call it music. It was a far cry from The Smiths and The Cure. To me, it was like something that had happened by accident when someone had spilt a cup of tea in a fax machine. He played the stuff constantly whenever I went 'round his house.

I supposed you would have to say that Gary was quite a cool person really, cooler than me anyway. But I wouldn't tell him that.

His slightly feminine nature coupled with his high-pitched, whiny voice had led him to get bullied quite a lot over the years but not in the same way that I had. The reason for this was that he had always been in awe of the bullies and longed to be like them, whereas I just thought they were a bunch of wankers. But as was always the case when a group of people sit in judgement on an individual, I was too afraid to tell them.

However, he knew full well that he would never be like them, as it just wasn't in him. He was too much of a decent bloke. So he just gave them whatever they wanted in an attempt to escape their wrath. More often than not, that would involve diverting the attention onto me and then joining in. In a strange way, it had actually made us quite close friends. Well, sort of. My only real friends were Trevor and Bob, but they were both older than me and had friends their own age. Ours was a music-based relationship, the best sort. But it was also dependent on me spending money in Bob's shop and Trevor knobbing my sister.

For quite a while now, Gary had been asking me to go to a rave with him. I was not keen, mainly because of the music, but also, despite the fact that most, if not all, of the musicians I loved took a lot of drugs, I was not really up for that either. Initially, I didn't think that Gary was taking them, and for a while he wasn't, but eventually he met a group of people who convinced him to do so. It was obvious.

Every Saturday after a Friday-night rave, his eyes looked like they were almost popping out of his head, and his mood was unpredictable, to say the least. This was highly amusing, as he wasn't really capable of portraying anger effectively. He just came across like a slightly perturbed penguin.

This weekly change in his demeanour encouraged me not to get involved even more, but I knew, as did he, that I would give in eventually. It was just a matter of time.

One Sunday afternoon, he arrived at my house in his shit bright-blue Vauxhall Nova, full of stories from the Friday night before. Only this time he had something else with him, a small lump of cannabis resin.

"You should definitely start coming on Friday nights, Tom," Gary said excitedly. I knew what he meant, but it was too tempting not to misunderstand the word coming.

"That's disgusting. What makes you think I don't already come on Friday nights; you're not the only one with a penis you know. Ha ha." I really did find myself hysterical sometimes. Gary was often not of that opinion.

"For fuck's sake, why the fuck would I say that, you fucking idiot? I meant fucking come raving, you fucking dick."

Despite the fact that it was not Saturday night and not therefore during one of his comedown periods, his persistent use of Ecstasy was now starting to have a weeklong effect on him, which when you considered his use of the drug was now on a once-weekly basis, as far as I knew anyway, this made for a permanently miserable Gary, apart from, I can only presume, during the time he was actually on the drug, which, of course, I never got to see.

"So, if I do come raving with you, will I end up being a miserable twat too?" I enquired.

With that, Gary buried his foot down fast onto the accelerator of his Nova, and in the blink of a lazy eye, we jumped from thirty-seven to nearly forty miles an hour. Gary, now quite angry with me, slung the Nova down into second gear in an attempt to get some traction.

"I am not a miserable twat," he said.

"But you are miserable and also a twat. Hence, you are a miserable twat," I said.

"You're a twat," he said. The conversation ended there. Both of us content in the knowledge that the other was of this opinion.

As we approached our destination, Gary's mood changed, and he became amenable once more. I was satisfied with my work so far with regard to winding him up, so I decided to drop off and play along with his mood change.

Our destination turned out to be the car park of the rave club he had been frequenting. He seemed to be assuming that I was up for smoking his cannabis, which I wasn't, but foolishly I allowed him to wear me down. I was only too aware at that point that the moment I first placed the joint in my mouth could be the beginning of a slippery slope with regard to drugs. I was not really a fan of drinking and had a penchant for being fully conscious of whatever was going on around me at all times. This development in my life was not conducive to that thought process.

Gary rolled what I was now joining him in referring to as a "joint", and we both sat back in his Nova to what I presumed would be enjoy, the joint.

"That smells pretty gross, dude," I said, taking in a huge breath of second-hand smoke.

I would love to say that my first experience of taking an illegal drug was amazing or life-changing in some way, but it really wasn't. It just made me feel a bit tired and rendered my eyesight questionable. My opinion at that point was that if that's what they all do, then I would rather not bother.

As Gary was somewhat preoccupied with his drug intake, I managed to get control of the Nova's cassette player. I had recently taped both *Meat Is Murder* and *The Queen Is Dead* by The Smiths using my new stereo system. Managing quite skilfully to fit both them onto one C90 cassette. Gary wasn't a fan of The Smiths but had always been very aware of how much I loved them and, that day, was prepared to make allowances for this. Not a regular occurrence since.

He had several tapes of his own in his car, recorded live at raves. I was fairly positive that they would come out eventually.

I had already heard most of them. They were awful and just blended into one continuous sound to my ears. Mind-numbing, coma-inducing repetitive shite was my opinion of rave music at that time. However, I was quite fond of some of the jolly piano riffs featured on some of the tracks.

What made these tapes even worse was the MC, who shouted out ridiculous, nonsensical comments periodically throughout their duration. Usually "bigging up" various "crews" or "massives". But the worst thing by far was Gary's constant commentary about what he'd been doing during each "song". I've never been able to work out how he knew. As I said, apart from the piano riffs, it all sounded like a constant noise to me.

What I did find attractive about the scene, though, was that it was very underground and very much in its infancy, which gave it a distinctively anarchic edge. No one really knew if it would last or if it would just crash and burn within a year.

So basically, the music to my ears was awful, but what it represented excited me a great deal.

The only way to listen to rave music was to either go to one or listen to one of these tapes. There were literally no records on sale in the high street or even in most independent record stores. The radio didn't play them, and they were not in the charts. When you did hear them on television, it was usually during a news bulletin about how this new culture was ruining everybody's peace.

I think it was fair to say that, right from the start, there was absolutely no question whatsoever that I was well up for being involved in the rave scene.

It was indeed my generation's punk. And as with punk, there was a specific drug associated with it. And it was inevitable that eventually I would more than likely start taking it.

And so here I was. Sitting in a pub toilet about to leave to go to my first rave. On the other side of the toilet door, there were several blokes who had been taking the piss out of me for most of the night and were ready to deliver even more so. They were all pretty pissed now. And I did deserve everything that I was getting, but it was becoming a bit tiresome.

Like I'd said, I was about to go to I don't know what. But before I did, I think it's important for me to explain the reason why they were taking the piss.

Over the last few months, by some strange twist of fate, I was destined, due to a combination of music-related events, to get involved in a music scene that I deeply regretted and am likely to always regret.

9. Flirting with the Commercial

I had a tendency, no matter what the subject, but in particular when it came to music, to immerse myself in whatever takes my fancy at that time.

I had always taken my lead from music ever since I'd first discovered it during the days of the record box.

Also, since I had created my own collection and developed a love for various bands, I had gone out of my way to sport the haircuts and the clothes of their lead singers as well as listening to their records. The Smiths and The Style Council are the two that had led me the most, regarding the way I looked and thought in particular.

Come late-1987, both of those positive life forces demised in quite different ways—The Smiths on a high, with a well-timed, but essentially gut-wrenching split and The Council with a demise in quality.

I didn't really know what to do with myself. I still had bands like The Cure and New Order, but they didn't give me the full package. Their music was faultless, but the looks were hard to replicate—New Order because they didn't really have a discernible look, they were just cool without trying to be in any way whatsoever. And The Cure? Well, as much as I loved them and saw Robert Smith as a godlike figure to rival Weller or Morrissey, the hairdo and clothes were not for me. And even if they were, I didn't think their replication would be possible on my head and body.

So I came to the conclusion that dressing from head to foot in mod wear like Weller but having a wild mop of hair that resembled a bird's nest like Robert Smith would have been too much of a contrast. This left me lost and in search of musical and aesthetic direction.

Of course, the most ridiculous thing about this way of thinking was that although the two bands had gone, it didn't mean that everything they had done to date wasn't still there. It just felt like I needed to replace them.

At no point was any of this a justification for what happened next. It was a token effort towards reasoning, yes, but I should take full responsibility for my actions during the period that led up to where I am now.

One night, late in 1987, I met two girls called Tanya and Beth in my local pub. I immediately hit it off with both of them, Beth more than Tanya, as she was clearly interested in me.

Tanya's boyfriend was someone called Simon I knew from a few years back. We weren't friends, and we weren't not friends. But his association with the two girls – one of which, as I said, was clearly up for being more than just a friend to me – would bring us together and we could, potentially, for a while anyway, become a foursome.

Simon's haircut interested me. It was similar to the Morrissey cut but peroxide blonde. His clothing also interested me. I had always attempted to look as much like Weller as was possible for a bloke like me, but his look bore no resemblance to that whatsoever. His jeans were ripped, his shoes were chunky, and his top half, that night, was covered in what could only be described as an American flag cut into the shape of a shirt.

"What music do you like, Simon?" I asked him.

"Can't you tell?" he replied with a look on his face like I had missed something obvious.

"No, not really. Something American, I presume?" I said, pointing at his shirt.

"I'm into Bros, ain't I?" he revealed with all the pride he could muster up.

I stood and stared at him for a while. I knew I had to respond pretty quickly, or things could get awkward. And more importantly, the two girls were dressed in a similar fashion, so they were clearly of the same disposition. I didn't really know much about Bros, but what I did know, I did not like in the slightest.

"Oh right," I said. "So, er, I don't really know them. They any good?" I enquired, trying ever so hard not to sound like I knew anything about them.

"They are the best, Tom, so brilliant," came the excited reply from Tanya, choosing to speak for Simon on this matter.

I looked at Tanya for a while, knowing full well that my next comment could mean that I did or did not get to have sex with the listening-in Beth. And so, my hormones took control of my mouth.

"Oh, course, yeah, I know them. Yeah, good band."

I had sacrificed all of my musical morals in one sentence. The last ten years of pride out of the window in one foul-tasting moment. Shame on me.

Not once until this point in my life had I ever made a comment on whether I liked a band or not without first knowing their music to the finest detail. Everything I knew about Bros indicated to me that their music would be shit, but I didn't actually know what they sounded like. I rested safely in the knowledge that you should never judge a book by its cover, and despite their ridiculous look and prepubescent following, the music might actually be good. After all, I didn't like Robert Smith's look but loved everything about his music.

"They're really cool!" said Tanya. "You should get your 'air done like them."

"Yeah, you should get your 'air done like them," agreed Beth. Simon was nodding, which temporarily dislodged his Bros quiff.

"OK," I said, getting into the mood. "I'm gonna get me 'air done like them."

I was completely sucked into all the positivity coming from the three of them. On reflection, it was a massive warning.

The following Saturday morning I went to work with my dad, and when I returned home, I found Tanya, Beth, and Simon waiting for me outside my parents' house. They had a bag with them and big grins on their faces.

"We've come to do your 'air," Tanya said, flanked by the other two looking equally excited.

"What's in the bag?" I asked, attempting to sound just as excited but feeling a mixture of fear and guilt – fear because I didn't know what they were planning on doing and guilt because I was betraying my favourite musicians and my own self-esteem by willingly letting this happen. But when you were seventeen years old and had a really good chance of losing your virginity by only having to agree to like a band that you had never heard before, and then changing your look to be like them, well, what self-respecting teenager wouldn't go along with it?

I was painfully aware that I was being led in a direction that couldn't be any more different from the one I had naturally chosen thus far. I rested safely in the knowledge that my integrity was, at this point, still slightly intact, albeit somewhat hidden from view. How long it would stay hidden was part of the larger unknown that I was entering into. I was happy to see what would transpire.

The four of us made our way upstairs to the bathroom like a herd of morons, me being the lead one. At least they knew what they were doing. I was blinded by my groin.

"Take off your shirt," Beth said.

"OK," I said, feeling excited and then subsequently less so as I remembered both Tanya and Simon were there too.

I removed my shirt as instructed and sat on the side of the bath. At this point, Simon revealed the contents of the bag. It was a bottle of Sun-In, or to give it its more descriptive name, "blonde hair dye for cheapskates".

Sun-In came in a spray bottle and absolutely stunk of cat piss. In preparation for the application, you had to wash your hair – something I didn't like doing very often, as it was quite thin, and this made me lose control of it – and then spray the Sun-In on. It was always better to do this during the summer months, as, for the best results, you had to allow your hair to dry in the sun naturally. Unfortunately, it was November, and so I would have to do with letting it dry in artificial light and heat.

The smell was overpowering, but Tanya assured me that the end result would deem it worthy.

The Sun-In was starting to dribble down from my scalp. A burning sensation developed on my forehead, and the dribbles began to dry onto my face. They formed a solid block of yellow on my forehead and further trails of yellow led down my nose and cheeks, meeting at my chin to form what looked like a piss-stained chinstrap. For one brief moment, I looked like I had a bright ginger fringe with the rest of my hair, jet black. How was I allowing this to happen? It was alarming, to say the least. But then I quickly remembered the whole virginity-losing prospect.

"It's starting to sting a bit," I said to Tanya.

By now the drips down my face meeting on my chin were starting to fall onto my jeans. I wasn't concerned, as it seemed pretty certain that eventually I would have to buy some like Simon's anyway. And if I couldn't get my parents to fork out for pre-ripped jeans, then the location of the yellow stains would provide an ideal place to start ripping them myself.

After a few hours of allowing my hair to dry, interspersed with bouts of panic regarding how much it was starting to look ginger, I suggested that we recoat the hair in an attempt, or rather gamble, to make it look more blonde than ginger.

"No, you should stick with it," Beth eagerly replied. "It will be well worth it when you look just like Matt Goss."

At this point, I should definitely have backed out of the whole thing, but it was too late. My hormones were one hundred per cent in control.

"Do you really think I look like Matt Goss?" I enquired.

What was I doing? I knew full well how wrong this was, and I knew full well how much I would probably never be able to live this down.

Why, oh why, are hormones so uncontrollable in humans at that age? It made no sense at all. The last thing you should want when you are in your mid- to late-teens is a level of intelligence that is not capable of realising the implications of promiscuity. And a groin that constantly wants to nestle itself somewhere that will make that lack of intelligence likely to have those implications. Surely it would make more sense for humans to reach sexual awareness closer to thirty than sixteen.

"That ... looks ... fucking ... stupid," Gary said as I answered my front door sporting my blonde, quaffed-up hairdo. Tanya, Beth, and Simon were all still upstairs in the toilet, congratulating each other on making me look like a twat, although they didn't see it that way. They were very proud of their work. You couldn't blame them really; they had done a good job. What was in question was my judgement, not their hairstyling skills.

"You won't be saying that when I'm getting my way with Beth," I said.

"Beth who?" Gary asked, still sporting his quizzical look from the previous question.

"Beth Simpson."

"Bit of a dog, ain't she?" he said.

"She's upstairs, dude, fuck's sake," I said quietly, stepping down onto the doorstep and pulling the door to behind me so the poor girl wouldn't hear him. "That's Beth Norman you're thinking of. Simpson's got the minerals."

"Oh yeah, she has, ain't she? Don't she like Bros, though?"

There was a pause while Gary put two and two together. "Ahhhhh, ha ha, you've done yourself up like Brosette, ain't you? You bellend, ha ha ha ha ha."

There was nothing I could say. I just had to take it on the chin. He knew full well that this move could end up with me having sex with Beth, but he also knew, as did I, that I didn't really need to go that far. I could have just opted for the jeans or one of their jackets, but instead I had gone for the hair.

"What the fuck is that on your hair? It looks ginger," Gary asked, still in fits of laughter.

"It's Sun-In, ain't it?" I replied.

"Sun-In? This is classic. Oh my god, this is friggin' hilarious." Just as Gary was beginning to calm down a bit, Beth appeared at the door.

"Hi, Beth," he said pathetically.

"Hi, Gary. Don't you think Tom looks amazing? I could just eat him up. Looks just like Matt," she said excitedly.

"Yeah. Matt," Gary said trying to stifle his laughter.

"You should do yours like Luke, Gary. It would really suit you. You would look amazing." Just as Beth said that, Gary's demeanour changed and he suddenly seemed keen.

"Yeah, Gary, you'd be a dead ringer for Luke," I said. "But then it's not really you, is it, mate?" I continued accusingly.

"Well, no, no, no, hang on a bit. I could give it a go." I looked at Gary and disapprovingly shook my head.

"Yeah, you give it a go, Gary. I would say now is as good a time as any. You got any of the Sun-In left?" I asked Beth.

"Plenty," she replied.

"Let's go then."

Beth turned and made her way back up the stairs to the toilet. I positioned myself behind Gary and pushed him in the same direction while simultaneously whispering in his ear that he was a massive cock. Although I think he already knew that.

10. Flirting with the Commercial, Part 2

A few weeks later, one Sunday morning, I was rudely awoken by my mum screaming at me that Gary was at the front door.

By now, Gary had taken to his new look rather well. It did suit him actually. But his lack of displeasure about it was by now more directly linked to the fact that he was now having regular sex with Beth. It was no surprise really. He was much better looking than me and had a distinct height advantage. I didn't take it badly. Not that bad anyway.

"What the fuck do you want, bird thief?" I enquired.

"You said you weren't bothered," he replied.

"I'm not. Anyway, what do you want? I take it you are aware that it's Sunday morning?"

"I've got the eighteen-minute version of 'I Owe You Nothing'. It's got fuck all on the B-side," he said.

'I Owe You Nothing' was the new single by Bros, and apparently Gary had procured a version of it that went on for eighteen minutes.

"What?" I said.

"I've got the eighte—"

"Yes, Gary, I got that, you dickhead. What the what is, is what the fuck are you doing on my fucking doorstep telling me this now?"

"I'm on me way to work," he replied.

"But I don't fucking work on Sundays Gary."

"Well, I fucking *do*."

With that, Gary turned 'round and steamed back up the driveway, apparently displeased with my reaction to his purchase. He then got back on his shit bike - as his shit Nova was undergoing repairs, and with his twelve-inches under his arm, off he went.

I stood on the doorstep for a while trying to work out what had just happened, when I heard a familiar sound coming from the television in the front room. It was Bros, miming to the new song. I sat and watched for a while and then had an epiphany. What in the name of all that was holy was I doing?

I quickly turned the channel, put my head in my hands for a few seconds, and then made my way upstairs to the toilet and locked the door behind me. I stared in the mirror for several minutes in horror. I had the most ridiculous hairdo. My jeans had holes in them, and I had a best mate who thought it appropriate to knock on my door early on a Sunday morning to show me a fucking Bros twelve-inch. Things had gone bad. It was time to get back to reality.

The first thing to do was to get rid of this ridiculous quiff. I pondered for a while getting some dye to cover up the effect of the Sun-In, but as it was already starting to grow out a bit, I decided to leave it and make it look as Weller-like as was possible.

What was very alarming was that during this period of Brosness, my record collection hadn't grown at all, as all my money had gone on Sun-In and second-hand jeans, both of which were now of no use to me whatsoever. Sewing the jeans up was an option, but you would always be able to see that they were once ripped. It would be like having a terrible scar that had healed as much as it could but was still obviously once there.

I was fairly sure that the psychological scar of this period would be with me for some time to come, and so I was keen to cover up any physical ones as soon as possible.

The only thing that could have possibly saved me from the inevitable ridicule was the fact that Gary, who was, after all, relatively popular, had gone down the same path. In fact, he had gone down an even worse path, because he had much further to fall than me. People expected me to do stupid things; it was what I did. The problem was this was a music-related issue, and I was known as the go-to bloke when it came to musical issues. I really should have known better.

Yep, I was pretty sure from the off that Gary would get away with this, and I would take the brunt of the abuse. Oh well, just another reason to not want to get up in the morning. But more importantly, another reason to immerse myself in the music I loved.

After a while, Gary had inevitably started to piss Beth off and vice versa. It was destined to end up that way, as the only thing their relationship was based on was the love of a really bad pop band who, of course, would only last so long themselves.

Cracks were already beginning to show in the Bros armour. The "other one", whose name was Craig, was drifting away from the main body of the group, that being the two brothers, Matt and Luke Goss.

When they'd started, I think it was fair to say that part of their attraction to the masses was their music, but it wasn't long before it was just about hairdos and jeans.

The brothers Goss disappeared up their own backsides, and then Craig left and so on, etc. Not that any of it mattered anymore, or even then, to be honest. Like I said, initially it might have been music-related, but eventually it was just a bunch of crap.

Just two weeks after the whole eighteen-minute Bros twelve-inch, Sunday-morning-intervention situation, Gary was back on my doorstep, this time at a far more amenable time, sporting a new haircut and a look of someone who had something to apologise for. I knew what that was, of course. He felt guilty about the whole Beth thing, but I really didn't give a shit. Not that I was about to let him know that.

He also now had his transport back from the garage, which he parked proudly, about three-quarters on and one-quarter off the path outside my house.

"Alright," he said, looking sheepish and failing to make eye contact for more than a second at a time.

"Yep, good, you?" I replied, maintaining eye contact throughout.

"Yeah. Look, soz about the whole Beth thing, Tom," he said, maintaining his previous demeanour. "It's just, you know, she was well up for it and, like, well, I'm only human, eh."

"Well, Gary, like Albert Einstein said, two things in life are infinite, the universe and human stupidity, and I'm not so sure about the universe. What I'm saying, Gary, is that you are stupid."

"Aw, man, I'm really sorry, mate."

I then decided to interrupt him and put him out of his misery. I couldn't stand to see that daft look on his face for one more second.

"Really couldn't give a shit, mate. As long as you don't turn up on my doorstep with another Bros twelve-inch. I mean, what the—"

"Yeah, what the fuck was that all about?" he asked rhetorically.

We proceeded to discuss it like neither of us were even there or in any way responsible for our actions. Both of us were driven by our carnal lusts and, therefore, could not be held accountable for what had happened.

"Exactly how many people have actually seen us dressed like Brosettes, Gary? I fear it may be too many."

"To be honest, I don't think it matters how many, Tom, mate. One is too many. Plus, it's more about who has seen it. And the news on that one ain't good, as you well know," Gary said reassuringly.

I held his gaze for a few seconds and watched the fear in his eyes multiply. I started to sweat; a thin sheen of it had now formed over my entire face. I knew full well what he meant when he said "who".

"Little Chris saw it, mate." Gary was right. Little Chris had seen it.

"Oh dear, this isn't gonna be forgotten in a hurry. Please tell me he didn't get a picture."

"No, I think we're good there, but you know full well that he will make this sound worse than any picture could look. At least if there's a picture, there might be a chance we could make it sound a bit less gay than the nightmarish view that little twat will conjure up. Nah, mate, we're fucked." Gary was right again. It was time to face the music.

Little Chris, as his name would suggest, was in no way physically threatening. But he had the ability to destroy us both.

First off, he would seek out everyone from our peer group and make sure they all had the same view of the situation as he did. Then, once the group was together, he would use his primary weapon, his massive gob. The only way we could avoid this would be if one of us were to physically threaten him, and that was just not going to happen.

Despite Chris's size, he was a very popular member of our peer group as he was extremely funny, and, therefore, had full backup. Any one of our group who was labelled "hard" would easily take his side over mine or Gary's.

"Do you really think it's a good idea to go down to the pub together?" Gary asked later that night as he called for me on the way. I knew what he was doing. He was trying to get there first and offload the blame onto me. I wasn't having that.

"Yeah, I think we should go together. There's nothing we can do to avoid this. Strength in numbers and all that, ain't it?" Gary agreed, and we set off.

He would have been better off if he hadn't called for me. He missed a trick there the idiot. Actually, I would have been better off if I had left before he arrived. Bollocks.

As we entered the pub together, sitting in the usual corner was our group of friends. One of them, of course, was Little Chris. We exchanged pleasantries and ordered a drink from the bar.

I could tell immediately that there was an air of disappointment as they all realised that the whole Bros thing had come to an end without any of them but Chris seeing it. There was still a chance at this stage that this could work slightly in our favour. But what was also very clear was that Chris had passed his version of events on.

So, as we had already ascertained, the truth was not to be a factor in this. Chris's version of events would be the one they went on.

"Two Cokes, please," I said to Gordon, who owned the pub.

Gordon was once an extra on the seventies TV drama *Triangle* and also once appeared in the audience on *Top of the Pops* dancing to the Bee Gees. But he looked more like he played the lead role in *The Singing Detective*. His skin was like the surface of the moon, and his hair made him look like a cartoon dog. Despite these things, he was good fun and actively sought us out to have a laugh with, much to the displeasure of his wife, Barbara, who looked and acted like she was once a pretty serious heroin addict.

"I told you about me being in *Triangle*, didn't I?" Gordon asked.

"Yes, Gordon, a number of times. It's a good story, mate," I replied cheerfully.

"D'you know what I used to think when I was playing those extras roles, Tom?"

It was unusual for Gordon to ask so many questions, but it was always good to talk to him, and I was happy to hear the *Triangle* story again. Gary had by now turned 'round and was watching the group in the corner who were all looking down at their drinks and sniggering.

"What did you used to think, Gordon?" I asked.

"No, don't ask, Tom!" Gary added with a great deal of concern in his voice.

"I used to think—"

And then at that moment, the group in the corner led by Little Chris stood up and joined Gordon in loudly singing, "When, will I, will I be famoooouuuusss."

"I told you not to ask," Gary barked at me.

I couldn't help but crack up as they all went into their own little Bros-related moves and sounds. Little Chris continued with the hook line from the Bros song "When Will I Be Famous". Weezel made the noise that comes after that line in the song, which sounded like he was having a painful yet sexual experience. Nat, Phil, and Nick formed the Bros emblem, which consisted of Phil standing with his arms in the air and legs apart like a big X, flanked by Nat and Nick with their hands on their hips and their legs also akimbo. Big Chris said and did nothing, as he had no sense of humour. Although he did seem to recognise to an extent that it was an amusing situation.

Big Chris was the hardest in our little band of warriors and, therefore, was the leader by default. No one had appointed him. He'd just assumed the role, and no one was about to stop him, hence why he was the right choice. He had a younger brother called Mark who was also hard but nothing like Chris.

Mark had always secretly longed to be one of the lads proper but knew deep down that no one would ever dare be honest enough with him for it to come true, something that was now being backed up by the fact that, along with his brother, he stayed seated.

"Ahhhh, you couple of twats," Little Chris belted out.

There was nothing we could do. He knew as well as we did that we were a couple of twats. Gordon had by now poured our Cokes and stopped laughing uncontrollably, which was replaced by a slight titter and his customary shuffle of the shoulders like Mutley, the dog from *The Wacky Races*.

"It's not as bad as he's making out," I said in an attempt to diffuse the situation.

"Come on, Tom. It is."

"What … the fuck … are you doing, Gary?"

I couldn't believe it. He was taking their side. Hang on. I knew what he was doing. He was trying to make me look like I was the one who had something to hide. I decided to play along.

"I suppose so really." I contemplated bringing up the eighteen-minute-long twelve-inch story but decided against it. Gary would always have the fact that he got a couple of weeks' worth of sex out of it, which would excuse most things but maybe not this, whereas I had no excuse. Besides, it was all quite jolly really. Until Big Chris spoke, of course.

"Exactly what did you think you were doing?" Big Chris said in his usual sneering manner. Suddenly the mood changed. The previous rapturous laughter was replaced by a heavy feeling of judgement.

Big Chris generally tended to have that effect on the group for several reasons. One, most of those who surrounded him didn't want to become a target of his judgement and therefore just went along with whatever mood he adopted. Two, Gary was in awe of Chris and wanted more than anything in the world to be just like him. And three, he had to maintain his demeanour as the strong silent type or risk losing it. If Mark wanted to, he could have brought an end to Chris's reign, but even he, like his brother, couldn't see the point.

Mark was hard; that was for sure. Maybe even harder than Chris. But what kept Chris at the top was that we were all at least three years younger than him.

We all knew the story. Basically, Chris started school and everyone in his year thought he was a dick. Mark then started at the same school when Chris was in the fourth year and, therefore, gave him a social outlet. Mark was popular and, up to the point Chris came along, was firmly one of the lads. Chris then put paid to that as soon as he arrived.

He was after revenge on those of his own age who had thought he was a dick. Like I said, Mark was very popular, despite having to fit in with his brother, but he couldn't let him down and, therefore, had no choice but to allow him in.

The evening continued along the same lines. Little Chris and the others, excluding Big Chris, would make references to Bros continuously. It was deserved and extremely amusing. It would only stop when Big Chris got involved. I think he was trying to play along to an extent, but the natural reaction he drew from the rest would make it seem increasingly unpleasant.

I did actually feel a bit sorry for him. It was obvious that Mark was keen to join in, but Chris just couldn't do it. To be fair to him, it was not totally his fault. If we'd all stood up to him, then he might have chilled out a bit. But it was too late now. He had played the bad man too often, and his voice had become synonymous with aggression.

As the clock approached closing time, Gary was starting to get a bit annoyed with the constant Bros-related digs and leaned in to ask me a question.

"So, shall we go to this rave tonight then, Tom?"

"Yeah, OK, let's give it a go."

"I'll warn you now, mate. I am going to be doing some pills," he informed me.

I looked at him for a while. I couldn't really come to terms with the idea of doing a drug like Ecstasy. All my knowledge of it so far was fairly negative. Gary had become far more temperamental since he'd started taking it, and the news reports depicted what looked like a bunch of morons dancing in clubs and warehouses or in the middle of a field. But what concerned me most was the possibility that I might end up liking that godawful racket known as rave music.

"Not sure I'm really up for doing that, mate. What's it like?" I hadn't actually seen Gary or anyone else on Ecstasy, and I wasn't sure I really wanted to.

"It's called Ecstasy, Tom. What the fuck do you think it's like?" He was right; the name did say it all, I supposed. But then other things had positive names but weren't always good. Take heroin, for instance, the name for a heroic lady but also something that makes you look like Gordon's wife.

"Do I have to do it? I mean, am I going to look a dick if I don't?"

"You're more likely to look a dick if you do, to be honest, mate. But then everyone else will as well, so it won't seem so bad."

"I think you're just trying to avoid looking like a dick yourself by making me look like one."

"Well, don't fucking come then." There it was – Gary's newfound short fuse.

"I'm just saying, mate. It's like you look like a dick anyway, so whatever happens tonight ain't gonna make any difference to me." I said this in jest, but there was an element of truth to it. I quickly decided that I might as well have a go. "OK, I'll have one. Do we do it now?"

"Yes, Tom, you're very amusing. I also think you look like a dick, so we'll be in the right place, eh? And, no, we don't do it now. The bouncers will be able to spot if we're out of it when we get there."

"But I thought that was what raves were all about, doing drugs and that."

"Well, yes. But not officially. They're still illegal. You can't buy them at the bar."

"There's a bar?" I enquired. "Selling what? I thought you said people don't drink at raves."

"They don't drink alcohol, but you have to drink something, or you'll die, Tom. Especially a sweat monster like you. You'll have to replace all that liquid that comes out of your forehead." Gary was starting to get agitated by my questioning. "Look, you'll find out. Come on. Let's go."

With that, we stood up and bid our farewells. We didn't ask anyone else to come, as they had already made it quite clear that they thought the whole thing was ridiculous, which, of course, so did I, really. But anything was better than sitting listening to the same joke over and over again about Bros.

"Don't forget, lads: you need to find out when you will be famous," Little Chris said for the seventeenth time.

"Very funny, Chris," I said. "That's the seventeenth time you've said that now."

"Still funny, though," he said.

"Still?" Gary replied.

"Hang on. I need a wee first," I said.

"Hurry up then."

11. Raving

We pulled up at about 11.00 p.m. in the club car park. Gary parked his shit Nova fairly centrally and turned off the engine, which also disengaged the tape deck, thank fuck. The relief was palpable, by me, anyway.

However, I did realise that although I had this brief respite from the repetitiveness, I was about to enter a room playing it for the next seven hours. Not only that, but also I would be surrounded by what I presumed would be hundreds of people who thought it was brilliant. And those people would, I also presumed, be completely off their heads on Ecstasy.

At this point, I was not looking forward to this, but I was here now, and I thought I should at least attempt to be positive.

Gary was on a completely different level. He was buzzing. I didn't think I had ever seen him like this. I didn't know what to take from it really. The difference was definitely a positive one, but it was alarming me equally. I supposed, to be honest, and it was a shame, but I didn't really like seeing him this happy.

"Come on, Tom, mate. What's up with you?" Gary said somewhat accusingly.

"What's up with me? What's up with you?"

Everything about him had changed. Even his voice had changed. It seemed like he was speaking under his breath. Almost like he didn't really want me hear what he was saying.

"What? There's fuck all up with me."

"I can't hear you, mate. You've gone all quiet. You sound a bit like a gangster."

"Tom, mate," he leaned in close and gave me a look like he had something important to tell me. "You, Tom, are about to enter a different world, mate. You know how much you love punk. Well, this is our generation's punk. Let me ask you a question, yeah? What do you know about raves? And how do you know what you know?"

Gary now looked quite serious, another twist in his personality that I wasn't ready for.

"All I know is what I see on the news. And those shit tapes you keep playing," I said, taking on Gary's current style of communicating but genuinely not taking the piss.

"Exactly, mate. What you see on the news. Not what you see on *Top of the* fucking *Pops*. The news. That, Tom, is because this is news. You're always telling me about how punk grew from the underground and completely shit the life out of society. Well, this is the same. If you are going to enjoy this, mate, you need to understand that. Are you with me, mate?"

Gary put his hand out to shake mine. I looked at it and then back at his face. I realised in that second that not only had we never shaken hands before, but there had actually never been any physical contact between us, or anyone else from our group of friends. I took his hand firmly, and we held for a few seconds and looked at each other intently.

I was starting to get it. This was like nothing I had ever seen before. It wasn't just about the music, although that was the driving force. It was a feeling. Like it was something to belong to, something that may have even eventually identified me as a person, like it clearly did Gary already.

I also noted that Gary managed to keep this away from the rest of the group. I must also learn to do that. This would be our thing, our own little post-Brosette movement, bit like therapy.

Inside the club, it all hit me again. I had been here before but only at a finish at two o'clock, full of pissheads, fights-going-off-every-few-seconds type of way. Tonight the décor was different, but that wasn't it. There was something else.

"What is that smell?" I said with a look on my face like I had just turned up at the last known location of the Holy Grail.

"What does it smell like to you?" Gary asked like he knew that I wouldn't be able come to terms with what it actually was.

"Smells like Vick's VapoRub. What the fuck?" Gary put his arm 'round me and laughed.

We walked towards the bar, which on a usual club night was always at least ten people deep and a bit shouty. But now, it was empty and looked somewhat superfluous, unlike the dance floor which was heaving with bodies. On a normal club night, there would be a few people, beers in hands, spilling them, dancing to something really crap. What the punters were dancing to tonight was beyond my comprehension. It sounded like the entire contents of one of Gary's tapes condensed into one sound bite.

"There's my mates; I'll get them over." Gary pointed to a group of revellers pumping their arms furiously in the air, perfectly in time with the "music". They saw him, and their faces lit up like they had also heard the Grail resided here.

"Dude, how's it going, mate? It's fucking banging tonight, mate. Carl Cox is on at three. You sorted, yeah?" one of them said.

"Nah, mate, can you sort me out?" Gary asked in that gangster voice he was doing earlier, which was now almost completely inaudible due to the current noise. "This is Tom; it's his first time."

"Tom, mate," the bloke said, flinging his arms around me like we were old buddies from way back. "This your first time? Fuck, man, I remember my first time. You're gonna love it. You want sorting too?"

I looked at Gary. I presumed this bloke was asking if I wanted to be sorted with some drugs, but I couldn't be totally sure at this stage.

All of a sudden it fully hit me how I was completely at Gary's mercy. He was like my guide through a rough town, and without him, I would almost certainly be killed. But this was the opposite. I needed him to take what was already a rare experience and make it something even rarer.

Gary leant into me again. "So, Tom, this is the decision we talked about. Are you gonna do an E?"

Gary and his mates stood 'round me in a semi-circle, waiting for my response. It was weird. I did, but also didn't, feel any pressure. Gary had already told me that I might as well experience tonight and then decide if it was for me before I took a pill. But I had already decided.

"Yeah, OK, I'll do one." The group cheered and all scrambled to be the first to put their arms around me.

I really didn't know what to make of any of this. I had clearly made the choice that they were all hoping for. And to be honest, I was already loving this rather a lot. A genuine air of positivity came over me, and a warm feeling moved through my body.

I told Gary this, and he said, "You think that now, just wait and see how you feel in about thirty minutes."

"So what's your name, mate?" I said to the bloke who seemed like the leader of Gary's ravey friends.

"I'm Mick. This is Dave, Clarkey, and One Eye, but we tend to call him One, like the number, y'know? One? But everyone thinks it sounds like Juan. You know, like the Spanish name – Juan? Yeah, mate, but it's One, the number."

I think it was safe to say that I liked all of them, and they seemed to have taken to me also. They didn't know my backstory or me theirs. We were all starting on a clean slate. Gary could easily have made me look a dick if he wanted to, as he had done so many other times in our lives. But he clearly didn't want to in this situation. I suppose really all these people knew about me is that I was Gary's mate, and it would, therefore, have reflected badly on him if he'd made me look a dick. Besides, they could work that out on their own, given enough time.

Mick had your standard raving hairdo, much like Gary's. It was long, parted centrally, and almost reached his shoulders. Dave and Clarkey had hair similar to mine. They were clearly in awe of Mick, much as I was in awe of Gary at this point. It was strange really. I had always thought of Gary as a bit of a dick. But in this situation, I had to hand it to him. He had created a world away from the one I knew him in, one where he was held aloft as a bit of a hero by people that I had never met.

Mick, like I said, was clearly the leader of his gang and had latched onto Gary's similarities to him, of which there appeared to be many – the hair for one, and the gangster voice for another.

One Eye was a bit different. He stood about my height, close to five foot seven–ish, didn't dress particularly well, and had a look in his eye like anything could happen. I didn't know. Maybe that was why they called him One Eye. I decided to find out.

"So why do they call you One Eye, mate?"

"Mainly because they think they're funny. I'm used to it now, though," One Eye replied. Mick laughed and put his arm around him.

"Well, that's not his full name. His full name is The One-Eyed Wye. Reason being that when we were kids we went swimming in the river Wye, and he got conjunctivitis. He only had one eye open for nearly three weeks. It was friggin' hilarious," Mick informed me.

"I actually didn't find it that funny, Mick," One said. "There was all this fucking goop coming out of my eye. I would wake up in the morning with a big, green, scabby eyepatch. I genuinely thought I was going blind."

"Yeah, but you have to understand though, One, that that was extremely funny for us," Dave intervened.

"How is my possible blindness in any way amusing? For a start, who would have driven you here tonight? Or any other night for that matter."

One's mates all laughed, as did Gary and I. Then they all agreed that his vision was just as important to them as it was to him, which made him very happy. Mick put his hand into his pocket and pulled out a small bag containing pills. He handed one to me and one to Gary. We both paid up fifteen pounds each, which seemed like a huge amount of money to me for something so small. But Gary assured me that it would be worth it. He handed me a bottle of water and instructed me to swallow it. We both nodded at each other in agreement. Mick and the lads made their way back to the dance floor, leaving the two of us stood propping up the bar.

"Don't worry, mate. I'll stay with you while the pill comes up. Don't try and presume what it's going to be like, because it won't be like that," Gary said reassuringly.

"I'm not even sure what that means, Gary."

"You'll see," he said with a knowing smile.

Thirty minutes went by and nothing. Maybe it was a dud? I decided to persevere. I looked over to the dance floor at the location of Mick and his mates. Their demeanour had changed. Before, they were pumping the air furiously to the music, but now they were all slightly out of time. Mick periodically looked to the heavens, his mouth wide open like he had spotted something stuck to the ceiling that he wasn't expecting to see there. Then he looked over at us and seemed to be mouthing the words "fucking hell", but was elongating the vowels to make it look like he was saying it in slow motion. He then began to make his way back over to us, again in slow motion. He also seemed to have acquired a faint glow around him and a slight trail that increased with each movement. I looked to Gary in search of some reasoning. He was already looking back at me and grinning from ear to ear.

"What the …" I couldn't finish my sentence.

I closed my eyes for a few seconds and watched the kaleidoscope of colours in my mind as they danced in front of me. When I opened my eyes, I knew what was happening. Then I didn't. And then I did again and so on.

"You up, mate?" Gary asked, his eyelids drooping down over the tops of his pupils. His face was contorted, and his mouth moved as if out of control but strangely in control.

I didn't really know what to make of any of this. How was I supposed to respond to Gary's question? *Am I up? Up where? What did he mean by up?* I was certainly not down, but I felt like I needed to be. *Sat* down, that was.

"I think I need to sit down, mate."

Gary beckoned me over towards some chairs. I watched him intently as he made the suggestion but couldn't quite work out what he was trying to say.

I could see chairs, and as I had just told him that I wanted to sit down, it seemed to make sense that he wanted me to go in that direction. It was too late, though. I decided that the piece of floor currently accommodating my feet would now suffice in accommodating my rear end. I sat down. Gary tried to pull me up but was laughing too much. Or at least I thought he was laughing. His mouth was moving even faster than earlier, but slower at the same time. His eyes seemed to be pointing at me. He looked for all the world like a sad cat.

"I'm OK here, mate. Why … why … why …" I couldn't finish again. And by the time I felt like I could, I had no idea what I was going to say.

"Why what, Tom?"

"I don't know, mate. Just why."

"There is no reason, Tom. You don't need a reason."

"Hang on. I remember now. Why don't you sit down here with me? It's really, really, really comfy."

I could suddenly feel my own smile. I could feel pretty much everything. I didn't think I had ever been so aware of my legs before.

"I can really, really, really feel my legs, Gary." Gary sat next to me on the floor, both of us with our backs against the bar.

"What about your arms, dude? How do they feel?"

Gary was entering into the spirit of things. He seemed interested in the new elements of reality I was going through. He grabbed my left arm and hoisted it above my head. I looked at him and smiled the biggest smile I had ever smiled.

"What are you doing Gary?"

"Your arms, dude."

"Yeah, totally. Let's get up, yeah."

Mick stood in front of us, smiling manically. "How's it going, Tom?" he asked.

"My legs and arms are really, really, really there, Mick. I'm so aware of them."

He grabbed my left arm and Gary my right, and they hoisted me to my feet. My god, I could really feel my feet. My shoes were so comfortable. And my jeans fit really, really well.

I had Mick on one side of me and Gary on the other as we approached the seats. I sat down flanked in the same way as when I was on my feet. One and Dave then joined us. I could see Clarkey in the slight distance. He was going pretty mental on the dance floor.

"Here, Tom. Have a sniff of this." One passed me a small bottle with a yellow lid. I stared at it for a while and then handed it back to him.

"Don't you want it, mate?" he asked.

"What?" I replied. One then took the lid off and handed it back to me.

"Take a sniff, mate. You'll love it." Gary and Mick both looked at me and nodded, clearly wanting me to follow One's instructions. I took a sniff.

"Wha ... whoa, I can't ... where ..."

Whatever it was that I was feeling after my first E came up, which I still couldn't work out, could never have prepared me for this. The elation was indescribable, only punctuated slightly by a small amount of fear that it might never stop. That would be bad; I didn't think I could take this for long. My head heated up to an alarming level. Every part of my body felt more relaxed than I thought was possible. The vapour trails I was seeing earlier stretched out in front of me and into the distance until I couldn't see their end. And then as quickly as it started, it stopped, and I was back down to whatever level I was at before I took the sniff.

I knew immediately why they had given me this. It had an amazing effect while it was happening but also an incredible levelling effect on me. Suddenly I could make a bit of sense of what the E was doing to me, as although the effects of the Ecstasy are indescribable, what just happened was several levels above that.

"What was that, dude? I don't ... I don't know what ... what to make of what just happened."

Gary, Mick, and One smiled and put their arms 'round me once more like I was now part of whatever it was that was going on here.

"That's was poppers, man. Amyl nitrate. Takes your head off, don't it?" Gary replied.

"Yeah, that was amazing. This is amazing," I said incredulously.

I actually felt like crying. How could something be this good? How could something with such a rubbish soundtrack have been this good?

"You know it, mate. You feel OK?" One said.

"Yeah, I'm really good, One. I think I get it. I genuinely think I get it."

And with that the four of us headed off to find Clarkey on the dance floor where we stayed for the next five or so hours.

The rest of them took another pill after a few hours but advised me that I shouldn't and that maybe next week or the week after I could try two.

At the end of the night, the six of us made our way out of the club and into the car park.

I wasn't "up" like I had been earlier and hadn't been for an hour or so. But I had a feeling of being somewhere else, somewhere really nice and cosy. We sat on the steps of the club, and Mick pulled out a joint. After a while it got 'round to me, I took a few drags, and suddenly the comfort I was feeling got a bit more comfortable. It was time to go home.

We bid the gang farewell and got into Gary's shit Nova, which suddenly seemed OK, and made our way home. He dropped me off close to 8.00 a.m., and I could see from the car that my parents were up and probably wondering where I had been. I didn't really know myself, so I was unlikely to be able to explain it to them. What I did know, though, was that I would be going back very soon.

"Where have you been to this time in the morning?" Mum barked at me as I made my way down the drive to the front door. I turned 'round and waved at Gary, who was in a state of muffled hysterics.

"I stayed 'round Gary's," I said, trying not to make eye contact.

"Well, you could have told us. We've been out of our minds with worry."

She continued to talk, but I drifted off, going over the events of last night in my mind. Well, as much of it as I could remember anyway. I did like the fact that she described herself as being out of her mind with worry. Very similar to myself but without the worry.

"Ok, Mum, sorry. I should have told you. I didn't get much sleep last night, so I think I'll go and have a kip upstairs."

"Well, go and say sorry to your dad first. He's been out of his mind—"

"With worry, yeah, I get it, Mum. I'm sorry." I walked into the front room where my dad sat watching television. "Sorry, Dad."

"Eh?" he asked, peering up from his paper and looking over the top of his reading glasses.

"Mum said you've been out of your mind with worry about me."

"Have I?" he said looking confused.

"Yes, David, we both have. He didn't come home last night," Mum said, still maintaining the same stressful voice.

"Oh. Right," Dad said. "So did you get lucky then?"

"Sort of yeah."

"Good lad," he said with a look of pride on his face. He then quickly looked up to see the alternative look on his wife's face and then back at me. "Yeah, er, you should have told us you were going out for the night, Tom. Don't do it again, eh?"

"No, Dad, I won't. I'm going for a kip anyway. See you a bit later."

"Yep."

As I lay in my bed, feeling like I was covered in cotton wool, I realised that something had changed in me that would probably never change back. I had stepped over a line that I hadn't even known existed, and now the line had washed away completely. Even if I did step backwards, even if I were to step further back than I ever had before, I would never be able to go back to where I was, and nor did I want to, or at least I didn't think I wanted to. Maybe I would feel different eventually.

I closed my eyes in an attempt to get the sleep that I had missed last night, but it was pointless. My eyelids twitched at an alarming speed, forcing me to open them every few seconds. It was no use; I couldn't sleep. I think I was still feeling the effects of what I ate last night but was also on a natural high from the experience. Nothing was going to stop this, but I had to try.

I sat on the side of my bed and pulled my record box over to my feet. I needed something that would relax me and at the same time, quieten this thumping in my head and ringing in my ears, something with melody and thought. There was only one choice that fitted the bill – I needed The Cure. The clue was in the name. I selected the 1981 album *Faith*. Its charming melodies and general description by non-Cure fans as "depressing" was perfect for this situation, and most other situations for that matter.

During the first track, "Holy Hour", I had another epiphany. Maybe last night wasn't for me. I bet no one else who was there was now lying on their bed listening to The Cure. Or maybe they were. The whole thing was just a series of confusions and raised questions.

I must have fallen asleep before the end of side one of *Faith*, as when I woke up about three in the afternoon, the needle was still trapped at the end in the no-music zone. The stylus arm had failed to return on its own. I concerned myself for a few moments as to how much damage this might have done to the needle. But more than anything, I was concerned about the thumping headache and general heavy feeling I now had running through my entire body.

I supposed this was the downside. Gary was very keen to warn me about all aspects of last night's events, but only as long as they were positive. He had failed to tell me that I would feel like this by 3.00 p.m. the next day.

At most points in my life so far when something good had happened, there had been always a downside eventually, so why I didn't think that something like this would have a downside was inexplicable. But now I knew. And was I bothered? Not one single bit. I couldn't wait for the next one.

Over the next week at work - I was now employed on weekdays by my Dad as opposed to Saturdays, which suited me just fine, my mind was on one thing: what was going to happen this Friday? I hadn't heard from Gary since he'd dropped me off on Saturday morning. This didn't concern me as I knew what the plans were for Friday as we'd discussed it on the way back last week. All I had to do was get through the week, which was proving to be a bit of a challenge.

"Seriously, Tom, what is up with you today?" my Dad barked at me at about 3.00 p.m. Wednesday afternoon. "I bet you're thinking about whoever it was that you pulled last Friday, eh?" Suddenly a look of panic had come over his face. "Hang on. You came back with Gary."

I wouldn't have described my dad as homophobic, not at all. He loved John Inman in *Are You Being Served?* and Chris Biggins as Lukewarm in *Porridge*, but I think he might have had a problem with coming to terms with having a gay son. Luckily for him, I was not gay, but I wanted to see how far I could take this.

"I did come home with Gary, yes. We spent the night together."

"Did you?" he replied, attempting to disguise his alarm. "He's a good lad, is Gary. W-w-was his girlfriend there?"

"No, they split up a couple of weeks back."

"Bet he's gutted. She was attractive, eh, Tom?"

"Not really my type, Dad, but, yeah, I suppose so."

Dad had then let off a few more nervous laughs as he'd tried to formulate his next question. He'd shuffled his papers on his desk and breathed out loudly as he'd looked out of the window while trying his best not to make eye contact with me.

"You'd have to be gay not to find her attractive, eh, Tom? What you reckon?"

"Yeah or another woman. Unless you're a gay woman."

"Lesbian?"

"Yeah."

"Mmm, yeah," he said, getting more and more nervous. I couldn't do it to him anymore.

"I'm not gay, Dad."

"Never said you were," he'd replied with an over-the-top look of bewilderment on his face.

"I know. I never said you said I was, did I?"

"No, no, you didn't. Well ... you sort of did."

With that, he'd put his arm 'round me and tried to hide the big breath he'd let out in painfully obvious relief. I had laughed under my breath, which he'd clearly noticed but chose not to mention. He probably wasn't sure if I was laughing at his nervous questioning or if I was laughing because I was lying and I actually was gay. Either way I think he'd decided not to find out.

The next day or so passed without incident. Clearly the whole gay question was still on my dad's mind. He knew my sense of humour pretty well, as it was the same as his, so he'd probably worked it out. Besides, many a time had we watched various TV shows together, and I had commented on the female actors. He knew. He was just having doubts because I'd turned up early morning looking dishevelled with Gary. And actually, more to the point, he probably thought Gary was gay. I know I did, despite the Beth thing.

12. Raving, Part 2

Friday night came 'round, and as usual, Gary called for me around 7.40 p.m., having left his house at 7.30 on the dot. For the first time, he didn't need to knock on the door, as I could hear the mind-numbing rave music blaring out of his car. He obviously thought that now that I was in his little gang of revellers that I preferred it to The Smiths. Very wrong.

"Mate," I said as I'd taken my position in the passenger seat of the shit Nova. "I know we've been raving together and all that ..."

"All what?" he interrupted.

"What?"

"All what? You said we've been raving and all that, so all what?"

"It's an expression, you dick. Have you been speaking to my dad?"

"No. Why would I have been speaking to your dad?"

"No, it's just he was on about ... oh nothing. It doesn't matter." That conversation was going nowhere, even more so than usual. I couldn't even remember what point I was trying to make. Oh, that was it, The Smiths.

"I'm not putting The Smiths on, Tom."

"How did you know I was going to say that?"

"Because that's what you always say when you've got that look on your face," Gary did indeed know me well.

"How about The Cure?"

"No."

"New Order?"

"*No!*" he'd said, getting quite irate.

I wouldn't normally push him this much. Well, I would really. It was just that I presumed that if I gave in to him now, then that would be it forever. Every time I sat in his shit Nova, I would also have to listen to shit music.

I know he didn't like The Smiths, and to be fair, if it had been my car, I wouldn't have one of his tapes on, so just the fact that he'd appeased me for this long was enough really. I thought I'd give in. After all, I was going to be listening to it for several hours tonight, but that would be enhanced by Ecstasy, a far cry from the current situation.

In the pub, the usual gang sat in the usual place cracking the usual jokes. We procured a drink from the bar and sat down. There was no banter with Gordon behind the bar this time. I could see his wife, Barbara, in the background, so that explained that. She was awful. Bloody junkie.

"You found out when you're likely to be famous then, lads?" Little Chris said. Nat, Phil, and Nick wet themselves laughing as usual, and Big Chris flanked by his somewhat reluctant brother, Mark, sat silent and just glared a judgemental glare.

Usually, I would defend myself or feel slightly annoyed, but this time those feelings now had pity in their place. It was odd. I actually did genuinely feel a bit sorry for them, but I wasn't really sure why.

Gary and I periodically looked at each other and grinned, which seemed to fan the fire somewhat. And so the subject matter turned to our sexuality as well as our Brosness, both of which could be quite easily be linked, even by the likes of Chris, with his limited intelligence. I thought about explaining that Bros are not gay, but then thought back to the conversation with my dad, which if I hadn't ended would probably still be going on now.

I decided, as did Gary, to take the flack and await the bell for last orders. Not that last orders were actually of any interest to us. What it would do, though, was serve as the signal for us to get on our way to the rave.

Our secret was a nice one to have, and I enjoyed it, as did Gary. I chose not to question him as to why he didn't want to discuss our raving world with them. I just presumed that, like me, he dreaded the idea that they might want to come along. He probably thought the same about me before last week. I chose not to ask him about that either. After all, it had all turned out well in the end.

We arrived at the club about 11.15 p.m. This time Mick, Dave, Clarkey, and One were all in the car park.

Although this was only my second outing into the world of raving, I was getting a strange sense from this meeting. The camaraderie of last week just wasn't there. The four of them didn't really say much as we joined them. They just sat in One's car, a green Vauxhall Astra, only just slightly less shit than Gary's Nova. The rubbish music on full blast was exactly the same, though. And the occupants rocking backwards and forwards in a vain attempt to locate the melody had a familiar look to them.

"How come you haven't gone in yet, Mick?" Gary said. Mick struggled to make eye contact with either of us and looked pretty much like our presence was a bit of a hindrance to him.

"Just listening to this. Here's your pills," was Mick's short, curt, and slightly frosty answer. He handed over the small bag to Gary, just like last week. And then wound up the window of the Astra.

"OK, well, we'll see you in there, eh," Gary replied.

"Yep."

We made our way in and took up a position near the bar. Then we purchased a bottle of water each and ate our pills.

"Mick and his mates didn't seem very chatty tonight, mate," I said to Gary.

"Well, they haven't come up yet, have they?"

"Yeah, but they're still capable of speech, aren't they?" Gary smiled a knowing smile at me. I had no idea what he meant by it really, but it looked like I was about to find out, as Mick and his mates, as bubbly and lively as they were last week, approached from the east.

"Heeeey, how's it going, Tom? You've come again. No turning back, eh, mate?" One said.

"Yeah, mate," I said, confused.

This was weird. Weren't these the same blokes we just saw in the car park or had they been replaced by imposters? I asked Gary what he thought had happened.

"Leave it, Tom," he'd said. "Just enjoy the night." Gary clearly thought this was as odd as I did. His reaction had a distinct air of familiarity about it.

As the night went on and the pills came up, things were very similar to last week. We were all getting on famously, and I forgot about the confusion between what had happened earlier in the car park and what was happening now. I've never liked fakeness, and I'd always tried to be as honest as I could be without being offensive just for the sake of it. But I did think tact was important. And at the end of the day, what made me think that I had the right to make a comment on someone else's way of thinking or acting unless it was unnecessarily offensive or tactless itself? The fact that Mick and his mates were not the most fun or friendly people in the world when they were not on drugs was not causing me any real harm.

When the time rolled 'round to about 3.00 a.m., I started to notice, very much unlike last week, that I wasn't feeling the effects of the Ecstasy anymore. I certainly hadn't expected to start building up a tolerance this quickly. Gary had already purchased himself a second and third pill and was well into the effects of his second by the time I started to come down from my first. So although he did have a spare one, I was sure he wouldn't be very keen on me eating it.

"You should have bought yourself another one," he said. I supposed I could see the rest of the night out in a sober state, but that was not going to be much fun. The music was still awful to my ears, and the revellers looked pretty stupid to a straight pair of eyes. I found myself having thoughts like "put your shirt on, mate" and "you stink of Vicks, mate" which wasn't conducive to the rave mentality of "love for all" and "we're all in this together".

"Can't you get me another one from Mick?" I asked Gary. He peered at me out of the corner of his eye and then shot off while slightly shaking his head in the process. He returned with Mick a few minutes later.

Mick didn't seem too impressed either. He didn't even look at me as he reached into his pocket to retrieve his bag of pills and provided me with one. He then walked off with Gary, onto the crowded dance floor and out of sight.

I took my new pill and sat back on my own to wait for it to take effect so I could start enjoying the night again.

Two things were fairly clear to me at this point. One, I most certainly would not enjoy being at a rave without being on drugs, which as far as I could tell was the case for pretty much everyone else as well, although I thought I was probably the only one who would have admitted it. Two, the so-called friendship between myself and Mick was based purely on the fact that we were both on drugs and that I'd bought them from him. And three, well, whatever three was I couldn't remember as my pill had just come up with a vengeance. Actually, I'd thought there were only two.

This was the first time I had done two pills and only the second time I'd done any at all. I was flying. This one seemed to have latched onto whatever was left from the first one. Maybe part of the first one had failed to dissolve, and this one had hit it on the way down and dispersed it. Maybe not. Didn't seem that likely actually.

For the next two hours or so, couldn't be totally sure, I didn't see anyone I knew. Mick and Gary were somewhere on the dance floor, I presumed. Mick's mates, including One, must have been with them, wherever that was. I hit the dance floor myself. The club wasn't particularly large, but the dance floor was always densely populated. Unlike the usual club nights, where the dance floor just had a few pissed up women on it.

At about 4.30 a.m., just as I was peaking on my second pill, a girl approached me and stood staring at me during a piano break in one of the songs. I stared back but wasn't totally sure if she could see me. There was only about a foot between us, and I was pretty sure she was actually there, but it wasn't a definite.

"You OK?" I slurred at her. She didn't respond other than to pull an even stranger face at me.

The piano break was still on. I didn't really know how you were supposed to react to these breaks in the songs which seemed to occur in most of them, although I couldn't deny that they did have an uplifting effect on me. That was the only thing that made the music acceptable to me, that it went with drug and event so well. It was a symbiotic relationship. The drug was pointless, or so it seemed, without the music and event. And the music and event were pointless without the drug.

As the piano break started to build up into a crescendo in order to drop back into the repetitive drum pattern, the girl in front of me looked like she was about to explode. I responded by involuntarily following suit. I didn't want to, but there was nothing I could do to stop it.

As the beat dropped back in, she went mental, and so did I. And then she was gone. I had no idea if she had been aware of me being in front of her, but it seemed unlikely. I thought about how much I loved my music, especially how the chorus finished and the song resolved back to the next verse and so on. This was the first time I had likened in any way the music I loved with this noise, and the first time I had been able to decipher one song from another.

A few songs later, as I now knew, having previously no idea when one finished and another one started, the girl reappeared in front of me. This time, it looked like she knew I was there.

"You OK?" I asked again.

"Yeah, I'm good. I was just saying that to you, but you didn't reply. You must be well off it," she said, gurning.

"That's weird," I said. "I saw you a few minutes ago, stood there, and you didn't respond when I asked you."

"No, I was asking you." We looked at each other, quizzically wondering what the truth might be. I thought both of us were only too aware that either version could be accurate or, alternatively, neither.

"So, what's your name?" she asked.

"I'm Tom. You?"

"Carly."

"Like Carly Simon?" I said for some reason.

"Who?"

"Carly Simon. She sang the theme to *Octopussy*."

"Oh right. 'Nobody Does It Better'?"

"Baby, you're the best," I said.

"What?"

"That's the next line in the song, isn't it?"

"Oh, I thought you were saying that about me. Yeah, it is."

Good job she knows that, or I could have looked a right dick. And to be fair, as I was standing here sweating from head to foot and pulling faces, I didn't need to be made to look any more like a dick. But then she was doing that too, as was everyone else so it didn't really matter. And with that came another epiphany. We really were all in this together. This was a movement, and I was a part of it. It felt good.

After a few minutes of dancing with Carly, a familiar group of faces came walking towards me. It was Gary, Mick, and One. They were completely off it, much like myself. We formed a circle, Carly included, pumping our fists into the air and shuffling our feet to the music that, quite disturbingly, I was starting to like a bit. The big test would be if I liked it away from drugs, the scene itself and also, now, Carly, a girl I knew nothing about but could not deny that she was most certainly having a positive effect.

We continued in the same vein for the next few hours until it was time to leave. It had been another eye-opening night in so many ways. I had seen multiple sides of Mick and his gang – from the ignorance of meeting them in the car park to the attitude of buying drugs from them and the hedonism of us all being off our heads on the dance floor. It was clear that they weren't really our friends, although Gary seemed quite convinced of the opposite.

I had also spent some time raving on my own with just my mind-bending thoughts to keep me company. And I had also met my own rave buddy in Carly.

Yep, it had been a good night, but now it was over. I'd taken the precaution this time of informing my parents that I would be out all night so they wouldn't be out of their minds with worry.

As we got into Gary's shit Nova, all light-headed and full of positivity, it became clear that the night wasn't fully over. Yes, it was

7.30 a.m., so the rave was over, but this morning was going to be my first experience another part of the rave culture.

"Were going back to Mick's for a bit, Tom," Gary said.

"OK, where does he live?"

"No idea. I said we'd follow him."

"Cool."

As we joined the long stream of cars following One's Vauxhall Astra, I got a sense that Gary was a bit nervous about this. He wasn't saying much, and when he did, his voice became tinged with apprehension, and his comments were delivered in a very snappy fashion. I decided not to talk either. I was still buzzing from my second pill, so it was hard not to at least attempt to converse with him. But he had done four pills during the last seven or so hours, the effects of which had clearly ceased, and he was entering comedown mode.

Mick's house, or rather his parents' house, was friggin' huge. It was a bungalow but had the footprint of a small town. The kitchen was roughly the size of mine and Gary's parents' houses added together. They had three ovens. What was the point of that?

Bodies of rave-weary people were littered all over the house. We took our position in the front room on the thick, shag pile carpet in front a six-foot wide central pillar that housed a roaring log fire. We sat surrounded by what could only be described as, in the large part, good, happy people. I didn't know any of them, but I was quite happy with that. Gary also didn't know any of them, and that seemed to have made him even more nervous.

"Are you OK, mate?" I asked Gary.

"I'm fine. Why? Has someone said something?" he said, and looked around as if he expected something bad to happen at any moment.

"No, course not, you just seem a bit quiet that's all."

"I think we should go soon," he said, acting really odd.

I assessed the whole situation in an attempt to come to terms with why he was acting this way. We had just spent nearly eight hours in a club, and we'd all eaten a lot of Ecstasy, some more than others, like Gary. So, really, odd was to be expected. I was still very new to this, and I was learning all the time. Gary was a relative old hand at it. Maybe this was just the way people acted after a while? But I didn't want to be like that.

After a while wondering what was wrong with Gary, Mick appeared. He sat down next to Gary and handed him a small package in exchange for cash. Mick didn't even look at me and barely even acknowledged Gary existence. He then left, and Gary opened the package.

"What's that?" I asked him.

"Cocaine," he replied. "You want some?"

"Yeah, go on," I said, not keen in the slightest but trying my hardest to sound the opposite.

I had no idea what effect it was likely to have on me. I was quite happy to leave my drug taking to the dance floor. It seemed to me like I was taking another step in the wrong direction by doing it sitting on the floor of someone's house at ten o'clock on a Saturday morning. Nevertheless, Gary set up a couple of lines, one for me and one for him. He rolled up a ten-pound note, snorted his line, and handed it to me. I did the same.

Gary's mood changed after that but not for long, and he soon lined up another one. This time, he didn't ask me if I wanted any, which was a good job, because I didn't.

It would be a bit difficult to explain my first experience with cocaine. It was, well, sort of pointless. It definitely had an effect on me, but I didn't really enjoy it, especially when you compared it to the effects of an E. It soon wore off. Plus, now my nose felt a bit weird. I thought it was pretty safe to say that I wouldn't be going in search of it again.

Gary, however, loved it. He was now on his third line and starting to get on my nerves. I was not sure what I disliked more – when he'd just had a line and thought everything was brilliant; or when the line was wearing off, generally a few minutes after he took it, and thought everything in the world depended on him having another one.

Thankfully, after a while of watching Gary's mood go up and down and so on, someone passed him a joint, which calmed him. I had a couple of drags myself, and all felt well.

I watched Gary as he folded his wrap of cocaine up and slotted it into his wallet, indicating, hopefully, that he wouldn't be having any more, but more importantly, that hopefully we would soon be leaving this so-called party.

My wish soon came true as Gary announced that it was time for us to leave. But before we did so, he was keen to locate Mick and his mates to bid them farewell. They were in the kitchen, propped up against one of the three ovens.

"Yeah, we're off, Mick," Gary said. No response. "Mick, see you next week." Mick turned his head towards Gary and nodded. No words, just a nod.

He was standing with several large-looking blokes who all stared at us and then back at Mick with a wry smile. Gary clearly didn't spot this, but I saw it clear as day. Wankers.

Outside and into the Nova we went. I was ready for my bed now but had no real idea of how far away it was. I couldn't actually remember the drive here. I knew we had been in a stream of cars, but the rest was a bit hazy.

After driving for about ten minutes, I saw a signpost that I recognized. It felt good. I still had no idea how long it would take to get home, but it couldn't be that far.

"Why didn't you say bye to Mick, Tom?" Gary asked, relatively aggressively.

"He seemed pretty busy. He didn't actually say goodbye to me, though. Or you for that matter."

"Yes, he did," Gary replied abruptly.

"He nodded at you and then looked away. How is that saying goodbye?"

Gary didn't answer. He was clearly quite angry, though, as his foot went down on the accelerator pedal like he was in the movies, which made the Nova rise from forty miles an hour to nearly fifty in a flash. I looked over to the dashboard and noticed the rev counter approaching the red. She seemed to be misfiring somewhat. Yes, Gary was indeed angry.

"They're my mates, Tom. All you have to do is be nice to them. I'm not asking you to sleep with them." That was weird, why would sleeping with them have come up?

"OK, OK. All I'm saying is that friendship is a two-way thing, isn't it?" I said, getting a bit pissed off myself.

"They're my mates." This time Gary almost shouted his response. I supposed really my best option here was to stay quiet.

"But they're not your mates, Gary, are they? They only fucking talk to you when they're off their heads, and even then it's only because you buy drugs off them. And who the fuck were those blokes they were stood with when we left? I suppose they're your mates too, are they? Are you seriously trying to tell me that you didn't notice them look at each other like me and you were a couple of pricks? I tell you what, mate; next week buy your drugs from someone else and see if they're still your mates then. When they come over to you at the start of the night, that Mick prick has already got his little bag of pills out, ready to exchange for your readies, mate. He doesn't even make an attempt at pleasantries first. And then as soon as the deal is done, he fucks off. They're not your mates, Gary. They're a bunch of fucking bellends."

The rev counter rose again as Gary's anger reached fever pitch. He knew I was right but didn't know how to deal with it. Silence had befallen the car for a few seconds as he'd digested what I had said.

"Don't you think you should change gear mate?" That was the final straw. Gary slammed on his brakes and pulled over to the side of the road nearly plunging us into a ditch.

"Get out. *Get the fuck out!*" He was not kidding. He wanted me out of the car.

"I'm not getting out, Gary," I said, calmly attempting to diffuse his anger.

Gary then opened his door, got out, and stormed 'round to my side. He was so angry that it took him several attempts to get hold of the handle to open my door. He then grabbed me by the lapels of my jacket and attempted to haul me out.

What with both of us being quite weak, but with me having the advantage of being sat down, rooted to the passenger seat, a struggle ensued.

"Get out of the car, you fucking twat!"

OK, I would get out and try and reason with him. But just as I cleared the door, he hit the lock, shut the door, and stormed back 'round to his side of the car.

"You can't leave me here, Gary. I don't even know where the fuck we are," I said. He didn't even respond, just got back in the Nova and revved the hell out of it in an attempt to screech off. Unfortunately for him, the excess pressure on the accelerator coupled with his poor clutch control made the car stall.

I peered through the passenger door window, watching as he tried to start the car up again, but it wasn't happening. After several goes at it, he gave up and started to attack the steering wheel with the palms of his hands.

"You've probably flooded it, mate," I said. He didn't react.

He sat motionless with his head on the steering wheel. I made my way 'round to his side of the car and opened the door. He slammed it shut again. I did this a few more times with the same result. I then decided to lean up against the bonnet.

I had clearly stepped over the line, but I thought what bothered him most was that he probably realised that I was right and they weren't really his mates. It was all based on certain conditions that were completely out of his control.

The sun shone quite brightly that morning, but the light of our friendship was fading fast. After a while Gary's door opened, and he got out. He stared wistfully into the distance for a few seconds, much like I was but far enough away from me so I would know that he wasn't speaking to me. I turned and looked at him. He had definitely calmed down a bit but seemed to have tears in his eyes.

"You OK, mate?" I asked.

"Yeah, I'm fine, mate." he replied, all shaky and like he was about to burst into tears. But he called me mate, so at least I knew that once we got the car started, I would most likely still be getting a lift home.

"Let's try starting it again, Gary." He didn't respond, just got back in the car and unlocked the passenger door for me. I got in, and he tried to turn the car over again. This time, it worked, and off we went.

There was no chat between us all the way back to my house. When we pulled up, Gary turned to me and smiled. I smiled back. I was not going to say anything. That would be his choice. But I decided to stay seated for a while just in case he spoke. The last thing I wanted was for this to carry on.

"Sorry, mate," he said, fighting back the tears.

"I'm sorry too, mate. I didn't mean to upset you." We held each other's gaze for a few seconds. Then Gary looked down and put his hand on my shoulder.

"I know what you're saying, mate. I did see that look between Mick and those blokes. I think they're the dealers that supply him. I've never actually met them before, and I was a bit shocked at Mick's reaction to us being there. I must admit, thinking about it, it's not really that much of a surprise. It's just, when you said what you said, it all got a bit real. Sorry, mate. Good job the car didn't start really, eh?"

"Would you really have left me there?" I asked.

"Probably. For a few seconds anyway. Pretty sure I would have come back, though."

"That's good to hear, mate," I said genuinely. "Because if you hadn't, next time I saw you, I would have fucked you up."

We both burst into laughter, as the prospect of either of us having a fight was ridiculous. But a fight with each other was an image that was just too much to take.

"I'll catch you later then, Gary, mate, yeah?"

"Yeah, mate. It's been emotional."

"It has that, mate."

And with that, I got out of the Nova and headed for my front door. I could see my parents sitting in the front room as I approached. And as expected, my mum rose up out of her chair with a grimace on her face ready to interrogate me about where I had been. I was ready for it, though.

"Where on earth have you been?" she barked at me.

"I've been out with Gary. I told you I wouldn't be back until this morning."

"Well, I don't know if you've noticed, Tom, but it's not the morning anymore. It's nearly 3 p.m." I hadn't noticed.

Blimey. How long were we stood at the side of that road? I'm pretty sure it was still mid-morning when we'd left Mick's house. But then I was not really in a state of mind to be sure about anything.

"Oh right. No, I didn't realise. Sorry." Gary, still parked at the front of the house, opened his window.

"It's OK, Mrs Joyce. It's my fault. My car broke down, and we had to wait for the AA."

"Oh, hello, Gary," my mum said with all the pleasantness she could muster.

She liked Gary and saw him as someone I should have aspired to be. If only she'd known exactly how far he had been leading her little soldier astray over the last couple of weeks, she might not have been so keen on him.

"Bye, Mrs Joyce," Gary bid Mum farewell, and she responded in kind. Me, I made my way up the stairs and into my bedroom.

It had been quite a night. My second rave and the first time I had taken two pills. I had also had my first line of cocaine, met a girl raver called Carly, realised that some people I had put my faith in were actually a bunch of dicks, convinced Gary of this, fell out with him, made up again, and also had my first encounter with drug dealers.

Given all of that happening in one night, I didn't hold out much hope of getting any sleep, especially as it was now mid-afternoon and my group of mates would be expecting me down the pub in a few hours' time. Hopefully, Gary would be as keen on this as I was, in other words, not in the slightest. Not that it really mattered. After our falling out, I did feel quite close to him in a way that I had never felt towards another man, let alone one of our group of friends who, with the exception of Gary, were pretty much the same sort of bellends that I now thought Mick and his mates were. I still had hope for One, though.

13. Raving, Part 3

Over the next few months, we attended the rave club every Friday night. Mick and his pals were still our friends when it suited them, and Gary still bought our drugs from them, which of course, as we had both now accepted, was the reason they liked us in the first place. And, to be fair, also the reason we pretended to like them.

After a while, I had to have as many as four pills per rave to keep me going, as my body had built up more and more of a resistance to them. Gary was doing six some nights, and also a gram of cocaine. I chose not to do any more of that horrible stuff, which suited Gary, as it meant more for him. I also started to notice him developing a dependency on it – a somewhat alien concept to me, as I had never felt like that myself about any drug. It was purely a recreational activity for me.

One thing that I was starting to notice about myself, however, was that my concentration levels were beginning to shorten. And my fuse was also shortening. Gary and I hadn't fallen out again during this time, but I was finding my mum's intolerance to me to be more and more unbearable. We now argued pretty much every time we clapped eyes on each other.

But the most disturbing thing about it was that I was now listening to rave music when I was not actually at one. And what was even worse was that my record collection was not only failing to increase but was actually starting to decrease.

Taking pills and going to raves was an expensive thing to have as a hobby. The pills were at least fifteen pounds each, sometimes as much as twenty, and the entry fee was also twenty pounds. So each rave I attended cost me in excess of sixty pounds. My wages didn't cover this, nowhere near, and the only thing I had in my life of any value was my record collection.

I sold numerous records that I had loved and cherished over the years since I'd started my own collection. I also had a small collection of rarities, including signed copies by the artist that could fetch, given the correct buyer, the price of a pill in one go such as several signed by Paul Weller, Jam singles. One of those, the seven-inch version of "Strange Town", was also signed by the bass player, Bruce Foxton.

I also had an original copy of *Dark Side of the Moon* by Pink Floyd, with free poster and postcards. But the one that pained me the most was my original twelve-inch of "Blue Monday" by New Order, with the grey inner sleeve as opposed to black, which was the more commonly owned rereleased version of it.

All of them went, though. The records I sold that had no real monetary value I offloaded to a local second-hand shop called Au Bon Marche where the owner would frequently rip me off with his undervaluing.

The rarer records I sold to people I knew or via adverts placed in the window of the shop Gary worked in. Despite getting more for them than the others, it still wasn't as much as it should have been. What could I say? I was desperate. My new lifestyle had clouded my judgement considerably.

After a while I had no more records to sell. At one point, I even stole some of my parents' Mantovani and James Last albums to sell to Au Bon Marche. They never noticed. They hadn't played any of them for years.

I had taken the precaution, though – which was strange, considering my current state of mind – to tape every record I sold so at least I could still have listened to them. But that had been of no use either, as the more pills I had taken, the more I'd convinced myself that I actually like rave music and, therefore, was never in the mood to listen to them.

One day, which was my lowest point, I ran out of tapes and actually taped over *Substance*, the New Order compilation album, with a tape from a rave. It should have made me wake up, but I just didn't see what I was doing.

This went on for months until one day, after a rave, we were 'round Mick's house at one of his special attitude parties when One looked at me and said, "Shall we put some proper music on?" and I had replied, "What music is that then? This is proper music." I could even see his collection; he was planning on putting a Beatles album on. I friggin' loved The Beatles. It was *Revolver* too, my favourite. But it just didn't click. I was lost and had lost so much that I held dear at the same time.

What was also quite alarming, but at times had its benefits, was that some of our group of friends had started to come to the raves with us. Big Chris, who fit in perfectly with Mick, had become a regular, and the rest of them attended on average about once a month.

The benefits of Big Chris coming along were directly attributed to his personality and way of thinking about the world. Whereas me and Gary and One saw raves as cultural events that one day we would probably look back on and say, "We were there", Big Chris saw them in the same way that he saw most things – something to exploit for his own gain. This was why he got on so well with Mick, because that was how he saw things too.

So it wasn't long before Big Chris and Mick became partners in drug dealing. This did mean that I could now get pills without having to pay for them up front and getting them "laid on". But it also meant that I had to spend more time with meatheads like them.

Of course, getting pills laid on still meant that I had to come up with the money eventually, and more often than not, I had racked up sizeable debts with the house that I couldn't afford to pay back. And that in turn meant one thing, and I didn't like it. I didn't like it at all.

"Tom, you owe me fifty quid. I'm gonna need it this week, yeah," Big Chris said to me just as we were about to leave the pub for the rave club.

"I ain't got it, mate. Can't you give me another week?"

"What's that then?" Big Chris pointed to the fifty quid sticking out of my back pocket. He was right. I did have the money, and to be fair, he had every right to take it. It wasn't like he had forced me to spend everything I had, and some that I didn't, on pills.

"I need that for tonight."

Chris now had me in his pocket. I could have paid him the money, but that would have meant not going raving tonight, something that I was not prepared to do.

"That's not my problem, mate. You owe me," he said with a look on his face like he was about to punch me quite hard.

I handed him the money and sat back down. I supposed I would just have to give it a miss this week. I didn't like the idea of that at all. I was not addicted to drugs, not at all, but I did feel addicted to the lifestyle. It felt like if I didn't go I would in some way be missing out on something that I couldn't afford to miss out on. And also that I would risk losing my ranking in this pseudo-hierarchy that I imagined I had some sort of place within.

"Let's go, mate," Gary said excitedly as the clock approached 11.00 p.m.

"I can't, mate. I'm skint."

"You had fifty sheets earlier. Where the fuck has that gone? You've only had one Pepsi."

"I owed Big Chris it, didn't I?"

Gary reacted with sympathy, not for me, but for him. He clearly didn't relish the idea of going without me, not enough to lend me any money, though. Big Chris had been listening in and had an idea.

"Tell you what; if you sell ten pills for me tonight, I'll give you a free one." Gary looked at me and nodded like he thought it was a good idea.

"You want me to sell pills? I don't think so, mate," I said, almost laughing.

"Well, fuck you then. I'm trying to do you a favour."

Well, that was a reasonable response. Besides, he was not doing me a favour at all, quite the opposite. He seemed to forget that I knew how much he paid for them. He still stood to make a good two hundred percent profit even if he gave me a free one.

But, despite knowing this, if I was going to go tonight, this was my only option. I quickly weighed up the pros and cons of doing this. If I did, I could go to the rave, and that was it for the pros. If I didn't,

I could still go, as I did have enough money for the entry fee, but I wouldn't be able to have any drugs, which was an unbearable thought. But also if I did, I would only have one pill unless I managed to sell twenty or even thirty. And judging by my recent pill taking, I would need to sell forty just to have a good night.

Also, if I did, how long would it take for me to sell enough to have one myself, and more to the point, how the fuck was I even go about approaching people to sell them in the first place. But if I didn't go, I was convinced that my life would in some way take a wrong turn and I would become irrelevant. Every piece of reasoning I had was screaming at me not to take him up on his offer.

"OK, I'll do it." The paranoia in me trumped all the reasoning.

Gary put his arms around me and assured me that I would be OK. I doubted that very much, but I could hardly have backed down now. It would have been bad enough if I had said no to start with, but to reverse my decision after saying yes was social suicide.

In the car on the way up and my mind was on one thing only: *How the fuck am I going to carry this off? I'm not the kind of bloke who does this sort of thing.* By now, I was well and truly the kind of bloke who took drugs but did not sell them. This was madness.

"You don't want me to take them in, do you, Chris?" I asked, knowing full well that only one answer would stop me getting out of the car right now.

"No, they're already strapped to my leg. Just leave it, will you, Tom? I'll give them to you when we get in there."

Big Chris was quite angry, but what hadn't been apparent until now was that he was quite nervous too. It was not his first time taking drugs into a rave, and it wouldn't be his last. But clearly even with that much experience, he still had doubts that it would go well. Now I really was panicking.

As we approached the door, a small queue of revellers were trying to get in. A lot of them knew that Chris was a dealer and approached him to supply them before they got in. He, unsurprisingly, wasn't happy about it, as it was drawing attention to him.

Mick suddenly appeared behind us and made a beeline for Chris. As they began to engage with each other, he turned and nodded at Gary, and then, as usual, gave me a look like I was a bit stupid, which, let's be honest, tonight I most certainly was. *What the hell am I doing?*

Once we were in, Chris and Mick called me over.

"Are you sure you can do this, Tom?" Mick asked. "If you lose any, it ain't gonna work out well for you."

"In what way?" I enquired. Mick then sidled up to me and placed his face about an inch from mine. *God, his breath stunk.*

"What I mean is that if you fuck this up, I will personally fuck you up."

"Right, yeah, that's what I thought you meant."

I really didn't like this prick, but he was right. This had to go well, not only so I could have a good night by earning myself a few pills, but also so I didn't get my head kicked in by this moron – something that if he decided to do, I would most certainly not be able to stop. And I most certainly would not be able to rely on Big Chris backing me up either.

"Just sell to one person, and they will let others know that you have pills to sell," Chris said.

"And what if that doesn't happen?"

"Then just keep doing it until it does." *Well, that's helpful.*

He handed me a clear bag containing thirty pills. That would equate to three for me as long as I got rid of the lot. I looked at the bag for a while. It definitely looked like there were more than thirty in there. It barely fit in my pocket.

I wandered the dance floor for a while, trying to find someone to sell to. I spotted a group of lads blowing on whistles and horns, standing about three centimetres from the speakers and smothering each other in Vicks VapoRub. They seemed like prime candidates to me. I sidled up to them and started to dance.

In a normal clubbing situation, this would have been seen as an aggressive move, but as with most things, at a rave, it was quite the opposite.

"You guys sorted?" I asked.

"Yeah, man, well sorted. You sorted?" came the reply. I didn't think he'd gotten what I was saying. I decided to try again.

"I mean, do you want to buy some pills?"

"Yeah, yeah, yeah … yeah, yeah, yeah, yeah, we'll have some, yeah." Success at the first try. Maybe this wouldn't be as difficult as I'd thought.

"How many you want?"

"Er, er, yeah, yeah, we'll have four, yeah."

These lads were already completely off their heads. I quickly calculated that they would probably have about an hour left on their current pill, plus maybe two to three hours on the one they were about to buy from me, which would leave a few hours at the end of the night when they would be fairly straight. So I decided to try and sell them eight instead. They thought it was a good idea.

Just as Big Chris had said, they then went off and told others that I had pills to sell. Plus, a lot of other people saw me sell them and now wanted some themselves.

Within about thirty minutes of being a drug dealer, I had sold twenty pills. If this had been a legitimate business, that would have been a reason to expand. But for me, I just wanted them gone from my pocket so I could get on with being just like the people I was selling to, which, after all, was the only reason I was doing this.

I thought the difference between Big Chris and me was that I didn't see dollar signs before my eyes. It was just a means to an end. I contemplated for a moment that someone might have a bad reaction to one of these pills or that they might not be very good. This highlighted another difference between the dealers and me: I had a conscience. You simply cannot have a conscience if you were going to sell drugs.

My problem now was the big bulge of cash in my pocket. I need to offload it as soon as possible, so I went in search of Chris and Mick. I found them in the same place we'd started the night, looking miserable and handing out attitude to anyone unfortunate enough to look at them.

I found that really strange as the recipients of their wrath were generally their customers. I couldn't imagine someone walking into a local shop intent on making purchases and the shopkeeper looking at them like they were in some way inferior because they didn't sell the same wares as him.

"'Ere, take this," I said to Chris, removing the large wad of cash from my pocket.

"Christ. Nice one, Tom." Chris was impressed and for a brief moment attempted to treat me like an equal.

"I've sold twenty, yeah. So I get two, right?" I said. At that point, Mick piped up.

"You ain't having two, mate. You can have one for selling twenty."

The cheeky bastard. The deal had been to sell ten and get one, ergo, sell twenty, get two. I stared at him for a second and then looked to Chris. Surely he would come down on my side, and I would get two. Wrong.

"I said one for twenty," he said, glancing back and forth from me to Mick. He knew full well what the fucking deal had been. The bastard.

"So why the fuck did you give me a bag of thirty then? What, were you gonna give me one and half if I sold the lot?" Mick grabbed hold of me and pulled me towards him.

"You get fucking one, alright."

It wasn't like I had a choice, I suppose. Chris was level pegging with Mick on the hardness and perceived-coolness front, and so my only hope was his intervention. But it never came. I took my one pill, knowing full well that it wouldn't see me through the night.

So now I had a choice. It was clear that selling pills wasn't a problem for me, so I could always sell another twenty. The question was, did I do this one now and then sell some more when I started to come down, or did I sell more now and then relax for the rest of the night? Two still wasn't going to be enough, but if I was to have four like I had been recently, then I would have to sell eighty, and that would take all night. I decided my best bet was to take this one now and then see how much of the night was left once it had worn off.

About twenty minutes after dropping it, I was up. They were good pills. I hit the dance floor, surrounded by the people I had sold to. They were just as fucked as me, and I was now their hero.

I revelled in the glory, people constantly coming up to me, thrusting Vicks inhalers and bottles of poppers at me. As I looked around, I kept catching sight of people pointing in my direction as they told their friends that I was the bloke who had gotten them their pills. I couldn't lie. I was loving it. I was completely off my box, and everyone was my friend. This was a massive high point.

After an hour or so – it could have been any length of time, to be honest – the group of dancers surrounding me started to diminish. I was still going strong on my pill, but as they took theirs before me, i.e., when I'd sold them to them, our E clocks were out of sync. While their focus on me remained, it was now for different reasons.

"Mate, you gotta get us some more of those pills. They're fucking amazing," came a voice from over my left shoulder.

"Mate, this is fucking fucked up, man. I am friggin' wasted," I said.

The last thing on my mind was carrying out his wishes. I turned away from him and carried on dancing.

"Mate, mate. Can you get some then?" came a different voice from the first one. I was now surrounded again, this time not by E'd up ravers but by bored people with headaches. Maybe that was why rave music sounds the way it did, so people had to keep taking more pills in order to make it bearable, like in some way the producers of the music were in cahoots with the dealers to line each other's pockets.

More requests were coming in, almost constantly, so much now that my own buzz started to diminish. It was like when someone on a long car journey wanted to go for a piss, but the driver refused to stop, so they started talking about flowing water until they both needed to go.

I was now virtually completely straight, and paranoia was setting in. One bloke surrounded by lots of others who all wanted to have a word with him must be a very suspicious-looking sight. I had no choice. I could just have walked away, but I was missing the attention I had been getting earlier.

"Chris, give me another twenty; I reckon I could get rid of them easily." He didn't hesitate in giving me a freshly filled bag. "I get another one, though, yeah?"

Mick wasn't around, so Chris put his arm 'round me and confirmed I would be getting another. I should have fucking well thought so too after he'd ripped me off earlier. He knew what he'd done. I could see it in his eyes.

I returned to the dance floor with my new bag, ready to deal them out and get everyone's buzzes going again, including mine. But none of them were there. Not one of them. I looked around for a while, trying to catch sight of them, but they were gone. I had no choice again. I had to find some new punters.

"You wanna buy some pills?" I said, sidling up to a new group of ravers.

"You selling, are you, mate?" came the reply. This guy didn't look like he wanted any, so I stepped away, but his hand soon landed on my shoulder, pulling me back. Then another hand landed on my other shoulder. I was now flanked by two massive blokes who didn't look like they were that keen on me.

"What the fuck's up with you?" I asked, trying not to sound weak.

"We fucking sell up here, mate. Not fucking you. You get that?"

I didn't know what to say. I wanted to run off and get Big Chris and Mick to deal with this, but I couldn't see them, and the two hands on my shoulder didn't seem like they were about to let me leave. I had no idea what was going to happen now, but every scenario I played out in my head didn't work out well for me.

"Alright, alright, mate. Just let me go, and I'll let you get on with it." I wanted out.

"You ain't fucking going anywhere until you give us what you've got in your pocket."

Now I was in it. I could have just handed them over and gotten away, but it was unlikely that Chris and Mick would have believed me when I'd told them what had happened. The only thing I could do was somehow try and get away from them.

Luckily, I didn't need to, as suddenly their grasps of my shoulders released as Mick waded into the biggest one.

"What the fuck are you doing? That's my fucking seller," Mick said through gritted teeth.

A standoff ensued, which gave me just enough time to slip away. I looked around and noticed that the skirmish between Mick and the other dealer had attracted the attention of the bouncers. They quickly released their grips on each other and moved in opposite directions. Then the hole in the dance floor crowd that had been made by the aggro filled back in, and it all seemed to be over. The bouncers turned 'round and returned to their positions.

I quickly decided that this was not for me and went to find Chris to give him the bag back. I now didn't care how stupid I looked; I just wanted to see the rest of the night out, whether I was E'd up or not. *God, this music was awful. What the hell was I doing here?*

I spotted Chris sitting in a corner with several other mean-looking revellers. I approached him as quickly as I could and went to retrieve the bag from my pocket ready to hand it over and get the hell away, but I didn't manage it in time.

Two more hands grabbed my arms, both attached to bouncers. They violently pushed me up against the table and kicked both of my legs at the inside heel as if about to search me.

The pills were still in my pocket. If they found them, I didn't know what would happen, but once again, every possible scenario was not looking very favourable to me. I might either have ended up being given a good kick in, or even worse, they might have fucking arrested me. Or both.

Pressed up firmly against that table, I knew one thing: I had to get this bag out of my pocket without being seen. There was no way that could happen, but I had to try. I reached inside with my one free arm while the two bouncers stood just behind me.

The table was in a small corner of the room, surrounded by people sitting in seats, all looking at me, horrified and wondering, just as I was, what my fate would be. As I glanced around at them, I noticed one of them not looking horrified at all. He was smiling. It was one of the blokes that I had earlier tried to sell the pills to. I held his gaze for a while and knew full well that he had grassed me up.

I didn't know why, but for some reason it had never entered my mind that the bouncers might have been selling drugs themselves and it was actually they who saw me as their competition.

If this guy was selling drugs and if he was able to go to the bouncers and grass me up, then he must have been in it with them. If that was actually the case, I really didn't know. I grabbed the bag of pills and slowly took them out of my pocket, dropping them on the floor under the table.

For a few seconds, there was no reaction from the bouncers. They just stood behind me. But then they spotted the bag on the floor. They must have seen me take it out. Everyone must have seen it.

Two huge hands clasped firmly around my neck, and my left arm was pushed up behind my back. The bouncers violently propelled me towards the fire exit just a few feet away from where I was standing and used my head to open it.

The door slammed shut behind me, and I found myself stood outside, flanked by two of the biggest blokes I had ever seen in my life, dressed all in black and wearing headsets.

They began to push me back and forth to each other like they were playing catch with me. I thought about running, but where the fuck was I going to run to? We were effectively in the middle of nowhere. The nearest town was a good mile away. The only manmade object in sight was a petrol station across the road, hardly a place to have sought refuge. And even if I had chosen to run, I had no doubt that they would have been able to run faster. I decided to stand it out.

"You're fucked now, mate," one of them said aggressively but at the same time with an unnerving calmness.

"What the fuck do you think you're doing, eh? Call the cops, Dave," the other one said.

I didn't know what to do. My next move may well have decided my fate. I got the feeling that I was definitely going to get a kick in now. But my head was pretty clear. I had to think quickly.

"What the fuck are you going to tell the cops? I've got fuck all on me. You think they'll trust you over me? I fucking doubt that very much."

The two bouncers smiled at each other as they watched this bloke half their size talk to them as if he weren't scared.

I'd rolled the dice; what else could I do? I'd thought back to the gangster films I'd seen and what I knew about dealing with people like these guys. It seemed that standing up for myself may well have been the right choice to make. I started to wish that I had employed the same tactic at many other times in my life.

"You little prick," Dave the bouncer said, pushing me to his mate for the last time. This time, his mate grabbed hold of me but didn't push me back. And then they both walked away, laughing, leaving me standing motionless and fucking clueless.

Clearly standing up to them, coupled with knowing full well that they didn't want the police up here any more than I did, had worked. Many times in my life I had come up against what might have been described as strong, silent types like these guys, and I had always reacted exactly how they'd wanted me to, by giving them exactly what they'd wanted and succumbing to their physical presence by showing fear, thus giving them a weakness to concentrate on. These people fed off fear, and if they didn't get it, well, they didn't really have anything else in their armour, did they? Life would get them back in the end.

I was now alone. I sat down on the steps outside the fire exit, trying to work out what to do. Maybe the ordeal wasn't over yet. I was pretty sure Mick and Big Chris would have something to say about all this. I didn't even know if they were aware of what had happened.

After a while I realised that no one was going to come to my rescue and it was highly likely that I would be sitting here for the rest of the night. I couldn't exactly expect Chris to come and help me, or anyone else for that matter as then they would be under suspicion themselves. If all of a sudden a couple of big blokes had come out to help me, it would be obvious that they were the dealers and little old me was just one of their sellers.

Then I made one of the strangest decisions I have ever made. I decided to put myself back in the lion's den and go sit on the door with the bouncers, who just a few moments ago had made me fear for my life.

"Come and sit down, mate," one of them said. I obliged and sat down on the bench near the front door of the club, surrounded by huge blokes.

They all started to talk about me like I wasn't there.

"Not much of a drug dealer, is he? Looks like he's just left school."

"Looks like he's decided to put long trousers on tonight, lads. Suit him, don't they?"

"Where the fuck did he get those shoes from?" One of them then picked up my leg by the ankle to give his mates a closer look at my shoes. They all laughed heartily.

"What the fuck is wrong with desert boots?" I said.

"Oh my god, it's got a voice. Maybe we should shut it for fucking good."

"What, you gonna fucking kill me, are you? That'll look good. Few too many witnesses, mate."

With that the entire group of bouncers let off a high pitched "ooh" as they mocked my confidence. I couldn't help but laugh.

"So who you with tonight mate?" Dave the bouncer asked.

"Yeah, right, mate, like I'm gonna tell you that. Yeah, I'm with Tony and Colin. They're in there dressed in tin foil. Fuck's sake." Now they began to laugh with me rather than at me. This was weird.

"You can go back in if you want, mate," one of them said, putting his hand on my shoulder like we were old mates.

"I don't think so, mate. You'll be following me around all night," I said.

"We've got better things to do, mate."

"Like what?" I asked sarcastically. They all laughed again.

"He's got a point. What's your name, mate?"

"You really think I'm a fucking idiot, don't you? Just get on with your bouncing or whatever it is you're doing and leave me the fuck alone. I'm quite happy sat here. A cushion would be nice, though."

"Oh, I am sorry, sir. Have we not made you comfortable enough? Get him a cushion, would you?" Dave disappeared for a few moments and reappeared with a cushion for me, bringing with him someone I recognised.

Carly, who I had met a while ago off her head, now stood in front of me. I wondered why I hadn't seen her in ages. She'd clearly got herself a job on the door.

"Hello, Carly. Blimey, you a bouncer now? You don't look the type."

"Hello, Tom." I was a bit surprised she remembered my name. "No, I look after the cloakroom. Are these boys treating you nicely?" she asked.

I wasn't really sure how to answer that because, well, they sort of were. We were having a bit of a laugh. And they'd gotten me a cushion which I was now sitting quite comfortably on.

"You can go back in, mate, if you help Carly clean the doorway a bit."

"You said I could go back in anyway. Why have I now got to clean the fucking doorway? Yeah, alright, get the Jif, Carly. Jesus." We're like old mates now. I was actually starting to like these blokes, and I thought they might have liked me too.

"So you're not going back in then?"

"No, I am not," I said with as much contempt as I could muster while being conscious not to step over the line. I thought I had done enough damage to these guys pride for one evening.

Two things had clearly stopped me from getting a kick in tonight. One was my sudden ability to stand up to people physically larger than me, which was pretty much everyone. And the other was that even they must have thought it would have been a bit out of order to kick the crap out of a bloke half their size in height and width. Plus, of course, they now had procured a free bag of pills from me that I presumed they would be selling.

A couple of hours later, the sun came up, and the music stopped. The night was over. I would have said that my ordeal was over too, but it hadn't been that much of an ordeal really. I'd enjoyed sitting with the bouncers more than I'd enjoyed being in there.

As the revellers began to pour past us, their faces gaunt, with sweat pouring from them, I began to wonder if I would ever come to a rave again. They all looked really stupid. Mick, Big Chris, and Gary were some of the last to leave. They nodded at me as they went past with a look of shock at the banter that was flying back and forth between the bouncers and me.

"You coming up next week, mate?" Dave the bouncer asked.

"Doubt it, David," I said.

They all surrounded me and gave me a group hug. Then they started to jump up and down, and as I was so tightly squeezed between them all, I was propelled along with them. I loved it. Absolutely hilarious.

"See ya, mate. Behave yourself."

"Yeah, you too," I said.

I slowly wandered over to Gary's Nova, periodically looking back over my shoulder to see if the bouncers were watching me, which of course they were. They might like me a bit now, but they obviously still wanted to see who I was selling for. I wondered what the reaction from Big Chris would be when I got there. I presumed he would blame me for losing him money. I supposed on some level it was my fault, but surely even he would be able to show some sympathy for me.

They were already sat in the car when I got there. Strangely though, Chris sat in the back. As I approached, he opened his window.

"Alright, mate. I've saved you the front seat," he said, sounding for all the world like a genuine person.

As I took up my position in the much desired front seat of the Nova, I thought about the scene in the Martin Scorsese film *Goodfellas*, which I had recently seen. Maury thought he was going for a quick chat with Robert De Niro about getting his share of the cash made from their heist, only to be stabbed in the neck from behind by

Joe Pesci. It seemed a bit extreme that that might happen to me, but I couldn't completely rule it out.

"Alright," I said.

"Is that all you've got to say?" Gary said.

"What else am I going to say Gary?" I replied, still not fully gauging the situation.

Big Chris's hand landed on my shoulder, and he leaned through the middle of the two front seats with a look on his face like he wasn't planning on stabbing me, which was a relief, but I was still not ruling it out.

"Are you sure you're alright, mate? What happened?" he asked.

"It wasn't that bad, mate. Bit of pushing and shoving. They played human tennis with me for a while, and then, well, like I say, it wasn't that bad."

"We thought you were gonna get fucking killed, mate," Gary added.

"Not enough to come out and help, though, eh?" I said jovially.

"Yeah, sorry, Tom. Carly told us you were OK, so we thought it better that we stayed put until the end of the night," Chris said.

"What did your mate Mick say?"

"Fuck him," Chris said. "The bloke's a dick."

"Why? What did he do?"

Chris leant back in his seat and took a deep breath, not looking happy at all. Chris had this thing he did when he was getting angry where he flicked his two front teeth with his thumbnail. He did it about four times before responding.

"I think it might have been him who grassed you up," he said.

"Why would he do that? They were partly his pills, weren't they?" I asked.

"Well, you know who the biggest dealers in there are, don't you?"

"I've always presumed the bouncers are," I said, trying to sound like I had already worked that out before tonight's events.

"Exactly. Well, apparently Mick's been working with them for ages. He wasn't really grassing you up; he was trying to grass me up.

He suggested to me a few weeks ago that I ask you to sell some pills for us. He was planning this result all along."

"I don't get it. Why would he do that? He still stood to lose out, surely."

"They've probably promised him an increased share in what they make together if he points out all the other dealers to them."

"I still don't get it, though. Why didn't he just grass you up then? Why create this charade?"

"I probably would've been next, Tom," Chris added.

"But why?"

Chris sat back in the seat again and flicked his teeth. "Well, basically, mate, he didn't think I would find out. Then, him and his bouncer mates could just keep ripping me off week after week until I just gave up. He wouldn't lose a penny. He keeps his share, I get nothing, and he gets a much more lucrative partnership."

"The sneaky fucker," I said. "Is this definitely true?"

"Well, him and One fell out a few weeks ago, and he told me then that he'd done it before. Got to be honest with you: I didn't really believe him. But just after your head hit the fire exit, he cleared off. Didn't see him for the rest of the night. Then I did see One, and all he said was, 'I told you so.'"

Big Chris was fuming but thankfully not at me – quite the opposite. He was adorning me with the same hero worship I had been getting earlier in the night from the people I had been selling the pills to.

Suddenly the car door opened. One stood there. He got in the back with Chris and adopted the same aggravated position but without manically flicking his teeth.

"Is this true, One? That Mick is a fucking grass?"

"'Fraid so, mate. I suspected he was lining you up a few weeks back. I wanted to warn you, but by the time I found out you were selling for him tonight, it was too late," he said.

I still didn't think One was completely blameless in this. Chris seemed like he wasn't bothered, though. I supposed really he wouldn't tell Chris all this if he was not trying to protect him from Mick's double-crossing in some way.

"Look, I've gotta go, mate. Sorry it worked out like this," One said, opening the door to leave.

"How are you getting home?" Chris asked. One hesitated for a moment, almost stuttering as he attempted to answer the question.

"I'm … I'm getting a lift with a mate. See you later, yeah."

Chris clearly picked up on One's nervousness; I could tell by the look on his face. We watched intently, all of us brimming with mistrust as he walked away.

"Just pull 'round there a bit, Gary," Chris said.

As we pulled towards the entrance, we spotted what just a few seconds earlier we had all suspected. Sitting in a black BMW were three of the bouncers, including Dave, and in the back with him was One. They were exchanging money. It looked like we'd been double double-crossed. But where was Mick?

The three of us looked at each other as the full story became clear. One was in with the bouncers, not Mick. It did seem a bit strange that if someone was going to rip us off that they would, to an extent, rip themselves off too.

We peered through the Nova's windows and into the BMW, apparently unnoticed, until all of a sudden One looked up and stared straight at us like a rabbit caught in headlights. The cheeky fucker smiled and waved while nudging Dave next to him, who then also did the same. Then they all burst into laughter and pulled off at speed, spraying Gary's shitty Nova with car park gravel, making it an even shittier Nova.

We all sat silently as we realised what had happened. That fucker had just sat right next to us, feeding us stories about Mick, acting like butter wouldn't melt in his mouth, when all along it had been him doing the double-crossing. He'd clearly thought he was going to get away with it but hadn't planned on us seeing him with Dave and boys in the BMW.

"Fuck me," Chris said, flicking his two front teeth. "Well, there you go." He was fuming but strangely resigned to what had happened.

I mean, what could he do? Nothing. He was not exactly going to take on the bouncers. He would happily take on One, as would I at this point, but not now that we knew who his backers were.

Strange thing was, though, I was more concerned about the fact that my new friendships with Dave and the bouncers must have been completely fake. I really thought I had been getting on with those guys, but all along I was just a stool in their plan to rip Chris off. I was gutted, but like Chris said, there you go.

Life was all about learning lessons, and I had learned several big ones tonight, mainly not to trust anyone unless you really knew them. And even then, should you really trust them?

I felt uncomfortable at this revelation but also knew it was a valuable lesson to learn. But the lesson that was far more important to learn was that this scene really wasn't for me.

In a relatively short amount of time, the scene had gone from being a movement that I felt a part of, something that I felt was beginning to identify me as a person, to something that was full of deceit and at the root of it all was, of course, making money. I must have been blind not to see it before.

14. Raving, Part 4 - Realisation

We chose not to go to the club for a while. For Chris, the reason was obvious. If he did go there, the likelihood was that he would end up getting hurt. Even he knew that he wouldn't stand a chance against his newfound foes. It must have been eating him up inside. Just about every situation that he had managed to come out on top in during his entire life had been because he was far more physically capable than the person on the other end, but this time it was just not the case.

Gary wouldn't go because he was just happy to follow whatever Big Chris decided upon, and me, well, I just didn't want to. Admittedly, I did fear for my safety in the same way Chris did, but mainly I was just going off the whole idea.

We did however visit one rave club during the couple of months following that night on a few occasions. One particular night, Gary, Chris, and I were joined by one of our group called Wayne. I had never really liked Wayne. We hadn't actually met him until a few years after we'd left school when Gary had gone to college with him. He told people that we'd all gone to school together. It was really weird. Things that we'd all got up to before we took up raving, like riding around on Vespas when we were fifteen, he did several years later just so he could speak about them in a retrospective way. I didn't think anyone else noticed. Maybe they had, but just chose to ignore it. Would make sense.

I did a pill that night, as did Gary, but Big Chris and Wayne just stood propping up the bar all night. The pills weren't very good, but even if they had been, my heart just wasn't in it anymore.

At one point during the night, I stood and watched Wayne and Chris for a while. Wayne was wearing the most ridiculously tight, striped trousers and frilly shirt. Chris was wearing something not far from that. But what really hit me was that they were both drinking heavily all night and were quite pissed.

It was the first time I had been at a rave and seen people drinking. And they weren't the only ones. The bar was full of pissheads, and they spent all night staring at the pillheads on the dance floor with contempt.

"This is over, mate," I said to Gary.

"What do you mean?" he replied.

"This scene, mate. No one seems to be enjoying it anymore. The place is full of pissheads. I mean, look at those two idiots. Look what they're fucking wearing, Gary."

Gary turned and watched with me for a while. He had the same look of resignation on his face that I did.

"You might be right, mate. These pills are shit."

"Just another reason it's all over, mate. How much did you pay for that?" I asked

"A fiver," he replied.

"There you go, mate. That's why they're shit. I've not had one person offer me anything else other than those for a fiver all night. It's over, mate. There's even fucking rave songs in the charts now. It's lost its edge."

For the rest of that night, Gary and I sat moaning about how everything had just become bit too popular.

It used to be that there were ravers, and then there were clubbers. But now the two were beginning to mix. The attitude of the clubbers had infiltrated the rave scene and was winning the battle, hands down. And also, there now seemed to be more dealers than were punters, which had created angst where there was once love. It had destroyed the atmosphere beyond recognition.

That night laying in my bed, I started to think about my record collection, or rather, the lack of it, since this whole sorry affair began. I sat bolt upright, turned on my bedside light and looked over to where my records used to sit. A tear formed in my eye as I realised what I had done. I'd completely lost sight of what I loved in life – thought-provoking music by artists who played instruments and wrote songs to explain themselves, not drugged-up idiots who pressed buttons in sequence to make repetitive sounds that could only be properly enjoyed by someone on narcotics.

I had to get my life back, but more importantly, I had to get my records back.

15. Raving Part 5 - Illegality

The phone rang early one Wednesday morning. It was Gary, and he was excited. I didn't like it.

"Guess what," he said.

"You're finally coming out as gay," I replied.

"No. No, I'm not doing that."

"It's only a matter of time."

"I'm not gay, Tom."

"Why, who said you are?"

"Look, shut up. There's an illegal rave this Friday and we're going." Then he went silent.

I can quite clearly remember telling him that I was out of the rave scene and my main intention now was to get my records back. I told him again.

"I don't see what that's got to do with it," was his reaction.

"It's got everything to do with it, Gary. I need all my money to get the records back now. I can't be spending money on bloody drugs and raves anymore," I informed him for the third time.

"Apart from weed?" he said.

"Yes, apart from weed."

I didn't really see weed as a drug as such. Well, I did, but only in the same way that someone who drank a lot saw alcohol as a drug. I'd never really been a drinker, so I'd always thought that it was only fair that I had something a bit mind-bending to escape the monotony of life. I justified this to myself by thinking that it was the only illegal drug that was ever talked about in terms of being legalised. So it couldn't really be that bad. You wouldn't hear someone say that about heroin.

"Where is it then?" I asked.

"That's the whole thing about it, though, Tom. You don't know where it is," he replied in an almost mystical manner.

"So how do you know it's local?"

"I didn't say it was local." That's true; he hadn't.

I most certainly did not want to go, but it might be worth having a look and see what illegal do's were like. I quickly reversed my decision from not going in a million years to going this week. But I would be there purely in an observatory capacity. I was not going to do any pills. Definitely not.

"OK, let's do it. I'm not doing any pills, though."

"Yeah, OK," Gary responded, heavily tinged with sarcasm. He clearly didn't believe me. I didn't care.

I hung up the phone and got back to calculating tax returns for my dad. I really didn't enjoy seeing the sorts of figures these people were earning. Some of the invoices alone were six figures. I had no idea what profit they were making from each one, but I really couldn't ever imagine myself having that sort of cash.

"Who was that on the phone?" Dad asked, peering up from his newspaper over the top of his reading glasses.

"Gary," I said.

"The gay one?" he asked.

"Yes, Dad, the gay one."

He held my gaze for a while. I could see the panic in his eyes. He was not homophobic and didn't hold any sort of prejudice against anyone, but I knew full well that he wouldn't react in the same way if it were his son.

"Is ... is he really gay?" he asked. His voice went up a few octaves. "Not that I care. Each to their own, eh?" Maybe it was time I put his mind at rest.

"No, Dad, he's not gay," I said while letting off an involuntary wink, thus throwing him in and out of a panic at record speed. He must have enjoyed that second or so of thinking he knew the truth.

Gary rang me again later that day to give me the details for Friday. He informed me that we would be leaving at 10.00 p.m. and then meeting in a town centre car park about twenty miles from where we lived.

I was fairly convinced that this rave would be completely out of our range. What if he asked me for petrol money? That had never happened before, but it was feasible now, which would mean even more money coming out of the record collection restoration fund, or RCRF, as I was now calling it. Plus, I had already spent most of the money I had on weed.

Bang on time, Gary arrived on my doorstep at 10.00 p.m.

Everything I had learned about tonight so far made me not want to go, but now that I could see who was resident in the passenger seat of Gary's Nova, I wanted to turn back 'round immediately.

So, it was Big Chris in the front and bloody Wayne wearing a frilly shirt in the back. Bollocks.

"Alright" I said as I took my place next to Wayne in the back. Big Chris didn't even turn 'round. Oh joy, this was going to be fun.

"Tom. You good, mate?" Wayne asked.

"Yes, mate."

"Did you get some weed?" Gary asked.

"Yep." Now Big Chris did turn 'round. Common courtesy wasn't enough to make him acknowledge my presence, but now that he knew that I had something he wanted, he was able to muster some up.

I produced the bag of weed from my pocket and handed it to Gary. He opened it and took a sniff.

"Fucking hell, Tom. That stinks lovely. Where did you get it from?"

Now I had a bit of problem. I bought it from a guy called Donny who was mates with my sister, but who was also notoriously not mates with Chris.

"Got it from Donny's brother," I decided to lie but not effectively enough to completely keep the name Donny out of my answer.

"Donny hasn't got a brother," Chris said.

"Yeah, OK, it was Donny," I cracked.

Chris grabbed the bag from Gary and took a sniff. He passed it back to me with a look on his face like he wanted to say it was shit but actually couldn't because it wasn't. Well, at least he'd be quiet for a while.

"Let's have a sniff," the colourfully dressed Wayne asked.

I know full well that he hadn't smoked any weed before, but I was also aware that he knew we all had. This meant that in order to talk about it, he would have to smoke some.

The smell of weed was hardly a beautiful smell like a nice bubble bath or a butterscotch Angel Delight. But if you liked weed and were used to smoking it, it smelled like a little bit of heaven. I think that must have been the first time Wayne had smelt any at all, as his genuine reaction was quite clear to see under his thinly veiled actual look.

It took forty-five minutes for Gary's shitty Nova to get to the car park in question, all along country roads. I was fairly convinced, and had been throughout the entire journey, that Gary didn't really know where he was going. I would have asked him but could hardly even hear myself think, let alone speak, over the top of the sound of his awful Nova stereo playing rubbish rave music.

Thankfully, as we arrived, he turned it down. But now we were sitting in a car park full of about fifty cars, all playing the same rubbish. So it hadn't really made much difference.

We'd clearly arrived just in time, as not long after, the lead car drove out beckoning the rest to follow. As we set off, Gary turned the volume back up. However, just in front of us was a BMW with a much better stereo. The sound of both of them together, thumping out drivel, just made them sound equally shit.

"How much further is this, Gary?" I asked as we passed a signpost for our home town that read fifty-seven miles.

"I don't know, Tom. I thought we had this conversation."

"Yeah, we don't know, Tom. That's the whole point," Wayne added. *Shut up, you idiot. What the fuck do you know?* I chose not to say.

Big Chris still sat silent in the front, but if he thought I hadn't seen him give that derisory look to Gary, then he must have been even more ridiculous than I thought he was. I wondered if it was because of my question or Wayne's answer. Who was I kidding? Of course it was me. I mean, Wayne might have been a complete twat, but let's not forget he was physically bigger than me, which even to someone with Chris's attitude to life must have thrown some doubt as to whether he could beat him in a physical confrontation or not. It would be foolish of me to imagine that any of this was based on anything other than that.

A little while later and just after driving through a small village, which in a convoy of cars, probably a hundred or so long, all pumping out shit music, must have looked to the locals like war was about to break out, we arrived on an industrial estate. In front of us stood a very large warehouse with lights and music emanating from it.

The first thing I noticed as we entered was that although a lot of people had turned up, the warehouse was far too big.

"'Ere you are," Gary said, handing me a pill.

"I said I wasn't doing one. Didn't I say that?" I replied. Nevertheless, I took it.

A few minutes later and all I could think was, *This pill is incredible.* I was buzzing more than I ever had before. The sights and sounds were amazing. Had I made the wrong decision regarding not doing pills anymore? Was this still the thing for me? I felt defined again. I was a raver.

Gary looked equally off his head. We informed each other several times how much we are off it. Big Chris disappeared somewhere, presumably followed by Wayne in his silly trousers. But their absence only added to the buzz.

After a while, I also realised that I didn't know where Gary had gone. Not that it mattered. There were plenty more people for me to tell and be told by how much we were off our heads.

A group of people approached me, giving me a group hug like I was their long lost brother. I hugged them back with equal fervour. We danced together for a few moments, and then they were gone.

Several more groups came and went with the same result. This was brilliant. I felt so alive.

About an hour or so later, the effects of the pill started to diminish. I wanted another, so I headed off in search of Gary. I found him in exactly the same state as me, wanting his buzz back as soon as possible.

"I need another pill, Gary. Starting to come down. They were fucking amazing."

"I'm trying to find Chris. He's got them."

We both headed off to find him, which was going to be quite a difficult job given the size of this place. The only thing that was on our side was that each group of people dancing had several feet of space around them, so at least it wouldn't be like searching through a crowd but more like searching through lots of little crowds.

When we found him, we couldn't quite believe what we saw – completely off his head, gurning and sweating like a maniac. Big Chris wouldn't normally allow himself to be seen in such a weakened state. Maybe that was why he'd disappeared.

"You got any more?" Gary asked him.

"Hang on," he replied.

Then we got our second surprise in quick succession. Out of the dry ice, like in a really bad pop video, appeared Mick. He did not look good.

"What the fuck happened to you?" I asked him, seeing that he was bleeding quite badly from the nose and lip. Chris seemed equally surprised.

"The bouncers are here with One. I just went up to him to give him a slap, and they jumped me. They're over there."

He pointed to his left at the group of burly bouncers looking in our direction. I didn't know what to do. The last time I saw them we were on good terms, but I still had no idea if that was genuine or not. I suspected not, though. And besides, then they were there in professional capacity. Now they were just like us – punters. But punters in a land where there were no rules.

"We should move," I said, beckoning the rest of them to follow me. They did so. I looked back again and saw One satirically waving at us, flanked by the bouncers. They beckoned me over. I waved at them but chose to continue on our path and out of their sight.

We found a nice area to converse, something not too difficult to do given the size of this fucking warehouse. I handed a tissue from my pocket to Mick. He was grateful, not at all like the Mick I'd known a while ago. He seemed humbled by what had happened to him, and my simple touch of generosity seemed to have gotten to him. Then he handed me back the tissue covered in his blood and snot without even attempting to make eye contact. Now I was back to wanting to punch him again.

"Yeah, I don't want that, thanks," I said.

Mick then handed out the pills, and we were off again. This one was just as good as the first. Maybe even better.

For a while the four of us acted like best mates, periodically stopping dancing to engage in a group hug. It was strange. Mick and Big Chris seemed almost human. They obviously felt safer with us than not. I knew it wasn't a genuine feeling that we were having towards each other. It was, as usual, one based on the effects of the drugs but this time coupled with Mick and Chris's panic at not wanting to be alone. Not that either me or Gary would have been any use should it have gotten violent again. I suppose it was like hiding under the covers of your bed when you thought someone might be in the house. It was not going to protect you but only give you a strange feeling of safety.

Then, all of a sudden, a huge hand landed on my shoulder. I looked up at Chris and Mick. Panic set into their faces, and so I knew it had to be one of the bouncers. I turned 'round.

"How's it going, mate?" I said.

"Yeah, good, man. You good, yeah?"

"Yeah, I'm fucking off it, mate. These pills are amazing."

I had no idea what was going to happen now. Mick and Chris were rooted to the spot, and all the colour had drained from their faces. Gary looked equally perplexed.

"I need to speak to your mate. The one with the red nose," he said and chuckled. I couldn't help but join in. I tried to turn my face away from Mick so he couldn't see me laughing.

"Mick, he wants to talk to you."

Bit strange that he had asked me if he could speak to Mick. Earlier he'd punched him on the nose without asking, but now he thought it appropriate to do so just for a chat.

"Look, I'm sorry, mate," he said to Mick. "Is that geezer really your mate?" he asked pointing to his left.

We all looked over and saw One, barely conscious, being held up by another one of the bouncers. Only now his face was leaking the red stuff and considerably more than Mick's had earlier. *Oh dear*, I thought, *what has One done?*

I started to wonder why I hadn't ended up leaking blood during my encounter the other week with these guys. Maybe they really did like me. Or maybe they thought, as I had already assumed, that the idea of a bloke like me being a drug dealer and effectively a threat to them was so laughable that violence towards me just wasn't an option. But here they were now using me as a go between to talk to other drug dealers. I was confused.

"So what's he done to end up looking like that then?" I asked.

"Who? Him?" he said.

"Yes, him." *Who else could I be talking about? Idiot,* I obviously did not say.

"That fucker just tried it on with me."

Now that I was not expecting. I looked over at One and felt sorry for him. What on earth would have made him do that? If he was looking for a male sexual partner, I would have thought his first port of call would have been Gary, given his natural demeanour.

I struggled to fight back the laughter. The whole idea was just hilarious. How had he gone about it? Did I ask? I mean, did he just grope the bloke in the middle of this huge warehouse, or did he just give him the impression that he fancied him? The state he was in, I imagined he must have tried to get up him, right there and then. Surely just a sexual approach didn't warrant the beating that he had clearly been given. I really didn't know what to say.

"Oh dear," I said. The bouncer just stared at me.

"Is that all you can say?"

"Well, yeah. It's difficult to know what to say to that, mate."

"What I want to know, though, mate," he said, "is are you all fucking gay then?"

"Well, no. I don't really know him, mate. Didn't know he's gay. He's Mick's mate," I said, pointing to an extremely sheepish-looking Mick. Maybe Mick had tried it on with him too. But if that was the case then why would he apologise to him?

The bouncer holding One up then propelled him in our direction at speed. And then as quickly as they had appeared, they were gone.

"What the fuck are you doing trying it on with a bloke like that?" I said. "I would have thought that Gary is more your type."

"That guy is gay," One said. "I've been sleeping him for the last few months."

We all stood silently as One made his revelation.

That couldn't be true, could it? As open minded as I was, I didn't actually know any gay people. Well, not until now anyway. I had always imagined, rather ignorantly, that if I'd ever met a gay person that they would be like John Inman in *Are You Being Served?* or Christopher Biggins. Or Gary. I certainly didn't think that they could come in the shape of a huge bouncer. Not sure why, but that was how I'd always seen it from my small-town-in-the-middle-of-England vantage point.

Chris decided it was time for him to say his piece. "Look, mate. I don't give two fucks where you like to put yer dick. What I don't fucking like is that you ripped me off the other week."

Charming. He'd lost him money. He wasn't upset with him because he'd risked one of his mates' lives, i.e., me. Just the money. What a dick. Why in the name of everything that was right and true in the world was I friends with this bloke?

"I … I had no choice mate," One pleaded. He looked genuinely frightened. But then I thought back to when we'd seen him in the bouncers' car the other week after I had been caught with Chris's pills and, in particular, how he'd waved at us. That wasn't the face of a bloke who felt like he didn't have a choice. That was the face of a bloke who was revelling in putting one over on us. He was lying. He had to be. It was just now he'd lost his back up, and so he was desperate.

"Everyone has a choice, One," Mick said. "I've been your fucking mate for years, and you didn't just rip me off; you fucking enjoyed it. You're a wanker, mate. I think you should just fuck off."

"No, hang on a minute," Big Chris interjected. "Why the fuck does he get to walk away from this. You owe me money, One, and I want it now."

"Chris, mate, please, I ain't got it. I sold those pills, but they just took it all off me."

"You're fucking lying. Give me the money, or I'll do yer now."

Big Chris puffed his chest out and began flicking his two front teeth, clearly revelling in One's diminished social standing. I didn't really blame him, but I also didn't like the way he was talking to him. One was clearly distressed and probably had never felt this low in his life before. I was not about to give him any sympathy, as I was a victim of his actions too, but Chris needed to give him a break.

"Leave him alone, yeah, Chris. Look, One, I think you better go, yeah. But we do need to meet up and sort this out. At the end of the day, you ripped us off, and you could have got me fucked up, and you did seem to be enjoying it," I said.

Chris seethed in my direction, but then Mick agreed and so he backed down.

One wandered off into the distance with his head held low. I couldn't help but feel sad for him. I knew what it was like to be ostracised. But then I was only treated like that because of my physical appearance, or at least that was what I had always presumed. One had actually done something to deserve it. I was confused. I was torn between being a good guy, wanting justice, and just not giving a rat's arse.

At the end of the day, things hadn't exactly worked out badly for me. You could say that One's actions had actually done me a favour on all levels. Apart from the fear I felt from the point when I was first pushed up against that table to the point when the bouncers stopped pushing me around outside the club, everything had actually improved. I had made some friends, the bouncers, who I actually quite liked. Mick had dropped the arrogance over me, and even Big

JON REEVES

Chris seemed to have developed a bit of respect for me for surviving the whole ordeal.

"Who the fuck are you to let him go, Tom?" Chris said aggressively. *Maybe I'm wrong about the respect. It does seem unlikely on reflection.*

"Don't you think he's had enough for tonight? I mean, the bloke doesn't even have a means to get home now. And let's face it; none of us actually know where the fuck we are anyway. Just give him a fucking break, will you?"

Gary looked at me, smiling. He hadn't said anything for quite a while. Maybe he was a bit upset that One didn't try it on with him first. I really should have stopped that. I knew he wasn't gay, but he did come across like he wanted people to think he was.

Big Chris said nothing. He looked at Mick and raised his eyebrows, but even Mick didn't respond in kind. It seemed even he thought that One had had enough for one night, and clearly Gary did too.

It was strange, but at that point I started to like Mick more than I did Chris. It felt like Gary, Mick, and I had found some common ground. But what was most strange was that the common ground was a disdain for Chris. I couldn't lie; it felt good. A few minutes ago, I wanted justice from One, but this piece of justice felt like it was genuinely warranted. Chris deserved to be taken down a peg or two.

Over the next hour or so, we went back to normal. Mick handed us all a free pill each, much to Chris's obvious displeasure, not that he said anything. And then we all got down to some dancing and being ravers. It was a nice feeling. The pills weren't as good as they had been earlier. They were the same pills, but we'd all had three each now.

It seemed very much like the drama was over for the night, but given what had already happened, that was never really likely to be the case.

Gary leant in to me and pointed towards the warehouse door. There seemed to be a bit of a situation occurring. My eyes were struggling to see a few feet in front of them due to the effects of the pills, but what I could make out, I had serious doubts as to whether it was really happening.

The entrance to the warehouse was at least a hundred feet away from us. All I could see was a bright light and bodies moving in all directions.

"What's going on?" I asked Gary. By now we were all looking in the same direction, as was just about everybody else.

"No idea. Probably some dealers fighting. Best we stay here," Gary replied.

We maintained our position but became more and more aware that something wasn't right. Now everyone standing in their respective little groups started to point towards the warehouse doors.

After a while, the groups began to disperse, and we decided that it might be time for us to leave. None of us could focus on what was happening. The lights were getting brighter, and the noise level was becoming audible even from our position. Then the music stopped. Now the noise became clearly audible, and it had a distinctively aggressive tone to it.

We made our way towards the exit, the crowd of people trying to get out growing all the time, maybe as many as fifty people thick and spanning a good hundred feet in width. There was still quite a big gap between us and the back of the crowd when suddenly a wall of fluorescent yellow burst through the confusion and made its way at pace towards us. Clearly emblazoned across the front of the yellow was the equally fluorescent word: "Police".

We spotted it too late and the collision course between us and them became unavoidable. Gary and I had nothing to hide other than being at an illegal party, but Mick and Big Chris had gone into panic stations.

"Jesus fucking Christ," I said loudly, as I was pushed clean off my feet, landing heavily on the concrete floor. Gary suffered the same indignity.

We both lay there as several more police surrounded us and started to shout at the tops of their voices. One of them took a swipe at me with his right foot but missed. Gary didn't have the same luck. He took a kick to the top of the head and screamed out in pain. I looked over and saw a trickle of blood go down his temple. This was serious. We had to get back on our feet, or we might not be getting up again.

"Grab my arm, Gary," I shouted as I managed to get a footing. Then we were both up.

The line of blood flowing from Gary's temple reached his chin and started to drip down.

"Awww, man," he cried out as if kicked again in the same location.

"What's up?" I asked concerned. "Gary, what's up?" I asked again with increasing fervour.

"This fucking top cost eighty fucking quid, man. Now look at it."

He was right; it was ruined. I think there might have been a chance of saving it if we had had access to running water, but we just didn't.

"That cost eighty quid?" I said, even more alarmed than before I knew.

Gary looked up and stared with a look of demonic intention at the group of police who had just a few moments ago trapped us on the floor. I couldn't help but laugh.

"Seriously, mate, you're not gonna attack the cops, are you?" I said sniggering. He was angry indeed, but he wasn't stupid.

"Well … no … but they should know what they've done … shouldn't they?" His question lost credence with every word, and his grin became wider, as did mine.

"I'm not really sure they'll care, mate."

"It's Hugo bloody Boss, though," he said. "Didn't they used to design the cops outfits or something?" he added as if to add weight to his argument.

"Outfits?" I said.

"Well, uniforms then … Look, I don't friggin' know, do I?" He certainly didn't know.

"No, I think that was the Nazis, mate," I said.

"Same fucking thing. They're bloody Nazis if ever I saw any," he said a too bit loud, prompting one of the coppers to turn round and look straight at us. Definitely time to go.

Mick and Chris were nowhere to be seen, and we didn't have time to locate them. This was an emergency situation. There was no time for sentiment.

"Come on. This way," I said.

By now, huge surges towards the door were coming from all over the warehouse. We decided that the safest place for us would be in the middle of the crowd trying to get out. But that had its own problems.

We were now trapped amongst sweating bodies, being carried with the flow of the crowd. I was lifted from my feet several times as the crowd moved back and forth. I couldn't see this diminishing in any way. We were going backwards as often as we were going forwards. Then Gary managed to get sight of why.

"There's a line of coppers pushing us back Tom. We need to get the fuck out of this as soon as we can," I agreed. It seemed that the police were not as keen for us to leave as we had previously imagined.

"There's a hole in the wall over there, Gary."

The warehouse was very old, and in places the walls were patched up with wood. I could see a small amount of light coming through one of them. We attempted to break free from the crowd and make our way towards it. Gary managed it easily, but I became stuck. He grabbed my arm and pulled as hard as he could, but it was no use, and I began to sink back into the mire.

The grasp Gary had on me was more painful than being in the crowd and being pushed over by the coppers added together. But the adrenaline and the Ecstasy in me were making it seem bearable. And besides, it was my only way out.

His grip tightened momentarily, and he gave one last almighty tug. I left my feet again. This time Gary's pull lifted me on top of the crowd, and for a moment, I felt as if I were surfing at a gig. A broad smile briefly came across my face as I began to think of the times I had been in just that position, crowd surfing at a gig. I couldn't wait to get back there again, away from all this drugs crap and bullshit music. I allowed my body to go limp, and Gary pulled me free.

"Christ, that was frightening, man. Head for that hole."

Both of us ran like we never had before towards the small light beaming through the wall of the warehouse. I kicked at it as hard as I could, and we were through.

There was still no sight of Mick or Big Chris. We could only presume that they were somewhere in the middle of the crowd, trying to get out. We stood and watched the line of coppers, arms tightly linked together, pushing the crowd in the opposite direction of which they themselves were pushing. The ones at the front caught onto the fact that they needed to go back but had no chance of getting the ones at the back to work with them. The crowd was so thick and the noise so intense that they were almost out of sight of each other.

"Someone's gonna get fucking killed if they don't let go soon enough," I said, adrenalin still pumping through my veins.

"There's nothing we can do, Tom. We need to get out soon as." Gary was right, but I just couldn't stand by and let this happen.

Then with all the anger I could muster and with Gary screaming at me not to, I approached the line of coppers at speed, ramming into the middle of two of them as hard as I could, breaking the link between their arms.

This sent two lines of fluorescent yellow in opposite directions and literally hundreds of ravers in my direction. I hit the deck again and was stood on by several of them. But then in the last act of raver-to-raver camaraderie I was ever likely to see, two of them bent down, risking their own footing, to pull me to my feet.

"Christ, mate. You ok?" one of them said.

"Yeah, I'm OK," I confirmed. "Let's get the fuck out, though."

Gary, now behind me, grabbed hold of me as tightly as he had before. Only this time, he didn't need to pull as I was free to go in his chosen direction.

"That was mental, Tom, mate. You're a fucking hero, man." He was right, I supposed, but I was in no mood to stop and receive the adulation that I richly deserved. I wanted out, out for good. This was over.

Back in the car, we sat and watched out for Big Chris or Mick to appear. I contemplated everything that had gone on in the last few years with this whole rave scene. It was dead. The drugs didn't have the same effect anymore; the people had gone from being a gang I wanted to belong to, to being a bunch of idiots I wanted nothing to do with. Gary didn't feel the same way, I could tell. But I could also tell that one day he probably would. The first signs of disdain were already clearly on his face.

After about ten minutes waiting for Chris to appear, he did so. I imagined him lost in the crowd and in pain. I had genuinely felt sorry for him. But when I did catch sight of him for the first time since we were put on our arses by the coppers, all of that drained away.

The coppers had dispersed and, luckily for me, seemed to have no idea who it was who had broken their literal grip on proceedings. But for Chris and Mick, as always, it was about one thing – selling drugs. And that was exactly what they were doing as they made their way back to the car.

When they got in, both me and Gary turned to them to see how they were, but they didn't even acknowledge our presence. They just sat congratulating each other on how many pills they had sold. Gary and I looked at each other, and once again I saw that look of disdain on his face, only this time even more pronounced than before. He knew it was over. It was just going to take him a bit longer to realise it.

When we arrived back home, Gary dropped Big Chris off first, and Mick got out with him. They had spent the entire journey discussing their dealing. Not once had they even talked to either of us in the front. Neither of us cared. Well, I didn't anyway. As they got out, they said thanks for the lift but no goodbye or arrangement for the next meeting.

I hoped that was it now, and I didn't have to see either of them again, but Gary was clearly a bit hurt. I also knew full well that I would still have to deal with Chris, but it was good to know that Mick was now out of my life for good, I hoped. Who knew, really? He and Chris were obviously close now, drawn together by their shared experiences of dealing in drugs, much like me and Gary were, but with us, it was a genuine kinship related to shared experiences of life. Once the effects of the drugs ceased, mine and Gary's friendship was even stronger, but for the other two, their relationship depended on drugs and the selling of them. I think it was safe to say that this was the most content I had felt in a long time.

We watched the two of them make their way up Chris's driveway and into his house, and then we looked at each other and smiled.

"Do you reckon they're doing it?" I said to Gary.

"Probably," he replied, laughing. "Not sure who goes at the goal end and who is taking the penalty, though."

"Probably take it in turns," I said. We both agreed and set off on the road to my parents' house to drop me off.

I did something when I got into my parents' house that I hadn't done for a while. It was early morning; they had both just got up and were eating their breakfast. The mood was happy. They no longer questioned where I had been all night, as they were used to it by now. And so I sat down to have a chat with them for the first time in what seemed like years.

"Where you been this time, Tom?" my dad asked.

"Nowhere interesting. Just to a party"

"With Gary?"

"Yep."

"Wh-what sort of party?"

"Gary isn't gay, Dad. We haven't been to a gay club."

"No, no, I know. I wasn't saying that." He went silent but kept looking at me like he wanted to say something else.

"I'm not gay either, Dad," I told him. "If I was or if I decided to be, you will be the first to know."

"If you decide to be?" he said with his eyebrows raised as far as they could go. "I didn't think it was a decision, thought it was something you're born with … like … I mean …"

I planted a reassuring hand on his shoulder, told him not to worry and that he should just get on with his Bran Flakes. He smiled and took another spoonful into his mouth.

"Anyway, if I am gay, you wouldn't think any less of me would you?"

"Course not, Tom, eh, Cynthia? You're still our son, no matter what you do," Mum nodded, smiled at me, and looked awkwardly at Dad.

I wondered if they knew exactly what I'd been up to recently whether they would feel the same way about my life choices. Well, it didn't matter now. It was over, and they didn't need to find out.

I left the table and, within seconds of lying on my bed, fell fast asleep, dreaming about how I was going to get my record collection back to its former glory. Tomorrow would be another day and another life. But this time, it had a purpose – to get those records back.

16. Records, Part 1 – The Job

The most important thing to start off with is that I had to accept what I had done, and take full responsibility for the ramifications of it.

I had taken the one thing that meant more to me than anything, my record collection, and I'd sold it all to buy drugs. That was bad enough on its own, and sounded like a plot line in a rubbish soap opera. But what was more important than that was that I had to accept that I did, in fact, disown those records. Yes, I sold them, but I had also forgotten about them in favour of a repetitive noise that had given me nosebleeds.

It was not easy to look at myself anymore. I had committed crimes against music. All of my records were gone, sold for a few measly pounds that I then spent on drugs which had given me a few hours of fake pleasure compared to the unconditional pleasure that the records had given me. I never had to go anywhere special to listen to them. They were always there for me and expected nothing more of me than to play and enjoy them.

First off, I needed to make a list. It would comprise of as many as I could remember, categorised according to emotional and chronological relevance.

During my time raving, I had only been listening to tapes of raves, and I was frighteningly out of touch with musical formats. The CD was now the main choice of the music purchaser. The last time I added to my collection in earnest, vinyl had been my only choice, but now I had to accept that the CD was not only the better format but also gave me the opportunity to make a clear and clean start on a new collection.

The seven- and twelve-inch singles I owned, and certain albums, would need to be obtained on vinyl, but all new albums, and some old, would be on compact disc, despite the fact that they were soulless-looking bits of plastic.

Also during this time, guitar music had returned. The emergence of The Stone Roses a few years back had created a scene, and new bands were sprouting up all the time.

The rave scene was, when in its infancy but most certainly not now, something extremely original, and this new music seemed to be linked to it in some ways, but was also heavily influenced by the sort of artists that I loved from the 1960s, '70s and early '80s.

New albums by bands like Blur, The Charlatans, Suede, Super Furry Animals, The Inspiral Carpets, and, of course, The Stone Roses would be my first targets to obtain. They would be easy. I could just go to the record shop and buy them. But that opened up another problem. I couldn't afford them. I had to get a proper job.

For quite a while now I had been helping my dad out with his accounting business, but it paid peanuts. I had spent pretty much every penny I'd earned, plus the money I'd made from selling my records on drugs for years now. I had no decent clothes, not that I'd ever had them anyway. In fact, I had no decent belongings whatsoever.

"Dad?"

"Yep."

"Can I have a pay rise?"

"In what way?"

"In the way that you pay me more for helping you do accounts and stuff." I thought that was pretty obvious.

"Tom. You do ... now how can I put this ... er ... fuck all." Can't really argue with that. I did do pretty much nothing, but there was no need to swear.

"Good job Mum didn't hear you say that."

"I'm not scared of your mother," he said confidently. I looked over his shoulder, and his face changed.

"She's behind me, isn't she?" He turned 'round quickly and then turned back just as swiftly. "Don't do that."

"So you're not scared of her then?"

"Shut up. Look, if you want to earn more money, you need to do something. I can't afford to pay you much, and more to the point, I haven't really got that much for you to do, and even more to the point, I don't want to. Maybe it's time you got a proper job, full-time like."

"Yeah, suppose. What do I do though?" I had no idea.

I left school with nothing, qualification-wise, and with no chance of going to university or anything like that. And besides, even if I did do that, it would mean two more years of earning nothing. How was that going to help me get my records back? It wouldn't.

"I can put you in touch with people who you could possibly work for. You'd have to impress them, though. They won't just give you a job because I ask them to."

"Doing what, though?" I asked.

"Accounts, you idiot. It's the only thing you've got any experience of. You enjoy it, don't you?"

"No. Course I don't. It's bloody boring. Why, do you enjoy it?"

"Work isn't supposed to be fun, Tom. Get used to it. Eventually you're going to want to move out of home and make a life for yourself." He was right. I wanted to do that now, but I hadn't even got one foot on any ladders whatsoever.

Over the next few weeks, my dad set up various interviews for me with people he knew from the exciting world of accountancy.

He bought me a suit and made me have my hair cut, which I hadn't done for quite some time. I still had my standard raving haircut, messy and in a curtain formation. I quite liked it really, as it took the attention away from my shit clothes. It was the only thing that had actually made me look like a raver. But I was not one anymore, so it had to go. From now on, it was going to be short back and sides, with minimal fringe.

My first interview was with a local footwear manufacturer. They were looking for someone to work in their accounts department on the purchase ledger, whatever that was.

I put my suit on and made my way out of the door to my dad's car, who, of course, I needed to give me lift there.

"Good luck," he said as he dropped me off. "And remember: don't act like you normally do. You need to impress this bloke."

"Well, that's hardly helpful, is it?" I said. If I wasn't lacking in confidence before, I certainly was after that bloody comment. I'd always been under the impression that being myself was important, but now I was being told that I had to be someone else.

"I mean, just don't be an idiot. They need to know they can trust you." OK, that did make it a bit clearer, but I still had no idea how I was going to carry it off.

"OK. I'll see you in a bit."

I quickly spotted the sign indicating the location of reception and headed towards it. Inside I approached the front desk. Sitting behind it was a very large lady eating cake.

"I'm here to see Mr Tovey. My name is Tom Joyce."

She looked at me over her big, colourful Deirdre Barlow–style glasses. Without any sort of response or expression whatsoever, she carefully placed her cake on a napkin and slowly picked up the phone, still looking at me over the glasses, which was no mean feat, as they nearly reach the middle of her forehead. I smiled at her. Didn't really know what else to do.

"Take a seat, Mr Joyce. Mr Tovey will be out in a few minutes."

I sat down awkwardly and feigned interest in the pictures adorning the walls of the reception area. I picked up a magazine about shoes and flicked through it but without actually focusing on any of the pages.

After what seemed like an eternity, the door behind reception opened and in walked a weasely looking man wearing a dark-brown suit and thick, black-rimmed glasses. He reminded me of the line in "The Headmaster Ritual" by the Smiths, *Same old suit since 1962*. He looked at me briefly but gave no indication as to his identity.

"Can you get this in the post tonight, please, Sandra?" he said to the receptionist.

"So you're Tom Joyce then?" he sort of asked but really just said as if telling me.

"Yes," I said, my voice involuntarily going up two octaves.

He beckoned me to follow him with his forefinger. I got up and did just that.

Mr Tovey's office was quite a walk away. I had to pass several people sitting at their desks. Most of them looked up at me. Some smiled and some frowned. I smiled at all of them, though. Seemed like the right thing to do.

One particular smile I gave was a bit over the top. Just before the door to his office sat a gorgeous brunette who looked about my age. She was on the phone but still managed to give me a lovely smile back.

Inside, he told me to sit down and took his position opposite me, with only his desk separating us. He didn't say anything for ages, just shuffled a few papers on his desk. *Should I say something? That's what I would normally do.* But Dad had told me not to be myself. I would stay quiet.

"So, Tom," he said. I smiled. "What makes you think you could come and work for me then?"

How the hell should I know? I supposed I could have just been honest and told him about my record collection, or that Dad had suggested it and it beat getting cold outside. I got the feeling that he wanted me to come up with some reason why I would be good at it, though. As far as I knew, there wasn't one.

"Well ..." I paused. "I've been helping my dad for a while now with his accounting business." That seemed like as good a reason as any.

"Yes, yes, your father, David. The accountant."

Mr Tovey fell silent and began to rifle nervously through the papers on his desk. I peered over and could see him concentrating on one piece of paper with my name near the top of it and my dad's signature at the bottom.

"OK, I'll give you a go, Tom." Well that had been easy. "You can start in a couple of weeks. I'll get the job offer in the post to you over the next couple of days."

And with that, it was over. He stood up and reached out to shake my hand. I reciprocated and turned to walk out the door.

"Make sure you tell your dad that I gave you the job," he said with an uneasy smile. This was weird. I hadn't really put any effort into that at all. Just the mere mention of my dad seemed to get me the job.

My dad often jokes when we're watching the news and a politician gives in too easily that he probably "had the Polaroids" of whoever he is giving in to. I wonder if my dad had the Polaroids on Mr Tovey. He was no oil painting, was Mr Tovey. I dreaded to think what those photos might have had in them. Didn't bear thinking about.

"I will. He's outside waiting for me," I said.

"Is he?" Mr Tovey went quite red in the face. "I'll come out with you and tell him myself."

As we approached the car, my dad got out to greet us. He patted me on the shoulder and shook Mr Tovey's hand. He then told me to wait for him in the car, as he wanted to have a quick chat with my new employer.

As I sat there watching them talk, my dad with his back to me, I noticed two things. One, my dad was doing all the talking, and two, Mr Tovey kept looking over his shoulder at me in the car. There was clearly history between the two of them, but I had absolutely no desire to know anything about it.

"Well done, Tom. Tovey said you did really well."

"I did fuck all. He just gave me the job when your name came up."

"Don't swear, Tom, especially in front of your mum. She'll kick the shit out of you." He was right; she would do that.

Dad drove off with a slightly remonstrative look on his face. It was definitely the look of someone who had just managed to put one over on someone else. Once again, I had no desire to know what, but I was pretty sure that I was going to find out at some point.

17. Records, Part 2 – The Plan & the List

A few weeks into my new job, my first pay cheque arrived. I now had more money in my possession than I had ever had at any one single point in my life so far. It was still not that much but was definitely enough to get to work on my plan to recoup the collection.

The new artists I had discovered my love for would have to wait for a while, most of them anyway. I did intend to get the Stone Roses album as soon as possible, but the likes of Blur, etc., would come after I had regained the records I'd sold.

During the time I'd been waiting to be paid, I had spent a great deal of time preparing the list of records and drawing up my plan. I would at first concentrate on the artists that meant the most to me, and then, once I had their full catalogues back in my possession, I would go in search of the individual records that I loved but that I was not necessarily obsessed with the artist.

The ultimate goal, once both of these were achieved, would be to regain the rarer records. The ones that I was going to struggle to replace and would therefore require more of my time and ingenuity.

I identified these records while preparing the list. I still couldn't believe that I had sold them in the first place and was still highly ashamed of my actions. It was a short section of the list. I had highlighted it in red. Those records were:

Dark Side of the Moon by Pink Floyd – limited edition gatefold sleeve that included poster and postcards

'Blue Monday by' New Order – original twelve-inch single with grey inner sleeve

Still by Joy Division – double live album and unreleased studio recordings with access to inner sleeves via the top edge rather than the right edge. I had no idea if this was rare or not, but ever since I'd sold it, I had only ever seen the latter version and I wanted mine back.

Magical Mystery Tour by The Beatles – original double EP six-track film soundtrack.

'Funeral Pyre' by The Jam – seven-inch single signed by Paul Weller.

'Absolute Beginners' – seven-inch single signed by Paul Weller.

'Strange Town' – seven-inch single signed by Paul Weller and Bruce Foxton.

But all of these would come later. First up would be the back catalogues of The Smiths, The Cure, The Jam, Joy Division, and New Order, but this time on compact disc.

18. Records, Part 3 – CD Back Catalogues/Sold Items

"Where … the fuck … have you been?" record shop Bob said to me as I turned up at his counter one Saturday morning. "You look a mess."

"Charming," I said. "I come with money, Bob. And I have a list."

"Give me the list then." Bob clearly wasn't very happy with me, but I was hoping he could put his personal feelings aside in order to concentrate on getting the money out of my pocket and into his till.

"Well, I haven't actually got the list with me."

"So why tell me about it then?" He had a point.

He handed me a pen and paper so I could write down the names of the bands I had predetermined would be replenished first.

"What do you mean I look a mess?" I'd missed that to start with, cheeky bugger.

"You look gaunt, mate, like you've been on heroin or something." That was very astute of him. Obviously not the heroin part, but he wasn't far off the mark. "I know you and your mates have been going raves."

"How did you know that?" I asked.

"I still see Trevor, you know. He's been wondering where you've been too."

My god, I'd forgot all about Trevor. He had been going out with my sister and had become my record-buying buddy before the raving days.

"Blimey. How is he? I ain't seen him for ages."

I presumed he and my sister were no longer an item. It would be strange if they were, considering what a dick she was. Surely I would have noticed him in my parents' house if they were still together? My sisters' bedroom wasn't that far away from mine.

"He's alright," Bob replied. "When I said he's been wondering where you've been, he knows full well where you've been physically, but mentally neither of us have a clue."

This was alarming news. Not only had I not seen Trevor, my sisters' boyfriend and cohabitant of the bedroom less than ten feet from my own for god knows how long, but he must have known where I was all the time. Admittedly, the times he would have been visiting would pretty much always have been when I was coming down from the Ecstasy, but I thought I would have noticed him surely.

"Yeah, things have been a bit weird, Bob."

"You're telling me. Trevor said you look like a fucking ghost most of the time, and I can see he's right. What do you think you're doing?"

I wasn't expecting this from Bob, but it was giving me a warm sense of happiness, like Bob really cared about me. And Trevor for that matter. I felt a bit emotional.

"Well it's over now, Bob. Problem is, I sold all my records to pay for it. I need to get them back."

"Well, you're in the right place, Tom; I've got friggin' loads of them here. I take it you'll be buying CDs now?"

"Yeah. I want all the singles and twelve-inches back too, though, so I need them on vinyl."

Bob came from behind the counter and put his arm around me. He looked really concerned for me. I didn't look that much of a mess, did I? I supposed really Bob hadn't seen me since before drugs, so if I did look different, it would stand out more to him than anyone else.

"Is that it? You not after anything else?" Bob asked.

"Yeah, I've got a load of new bands I want, but more than anything, I've got a list of rarities I need to get back. That ain't gonna be easy."

Bob could see how much this meant to me. I was still feeling a bit emotional after his impromptu show of affection earlier and was struggling to fight back the tears.

It was weird. To me, I had just been doing something else for a while, but to the people I'd left behind, they were seeing a different Tom coming back from it, almost like I'd been off fighting a war or something and had seen lots of terrible things happen. Admittedly, I had seen some pretty horrible situations and had been right in the middle of a few of them too, but I didn't really feel any different. It was like I was Robert De Niro in *The Deer Hunter*, returning home after being in Vietnam, wondering what had happened to Christopher Walken.

"Look, Bob, I need to go up to Bon Marche. He got a lot of my records. I might as well see if I can get them back from there before I start buying new ones." Bob agreed. He wished me good luck on my quest and promised to collate a pile of CDs for me based on what I'd told him I was after. Bless him.

As I left the shop I turned 'round to see Bob closely watching me walk out. He really did give a shit about me. A broad smile found its way to my face. I was genuinely happy, not like the happiness I had experienced over the last few years, which was completely false and due to my drug intake, but a real happiness. I felt like no one could touch me. This was good. And so off I went to get what I could retrieve of my records from Bon Marche.

It was only brief walk from Bob's shop to Bon Marche, and I was soon there. As I entered, the owner looked at me knowingly and prepared to see what I had to sell him today.

"I'm not selling today, mate. I'm buying. I want everything back that I've sold you." He didn't seem too hopeful.

"Well, good luck. Thing is, until you came along, all I was selling record-wise was things that no one really wants, then you started selling stuff that was only a few years old, if that. Like I say, good luck."

Just as I passed the front counter of Bon Marche, an aroma met with my nostrils. It was one of the most beautiful smells I had ever experienced. I looked to my right where it seemed to be coming from and headed in that direction.

I found myself in a room full of marbles and oddly shaped soap bars. A young girl stood picking them up one by one, taking a deep breath while closing her eyes and smiling. She looked so content and happy. I picked one up to see if it would have the same effect on me.

She looked at me and smiled innocently. She was a few years younger than me and clearly hadn't had the opportunity yet to sample how horrible life could be. I thought back to when I was her age and briefly wished I were again.

"Smell this one," she said, holding a small, pink seahorse-shaped bar of soap to my nose. It smelt of summer.

"That's lovely," I said. "What's in your bag?" I asked her.

She opened the bag she was so tightly grasping and showed me the contents. It was full of marbles.

"I love marbles," she said with the sweetest of smiles. "The colours and the sound they make when they hit each other." I smiled back and tried to imagine what it would be like to get such pleasure from something so small and insignificant.

Life, specifically over the last few years of drug taking, had made me quite cynical, and I just couldn't picture genuine and unconditional happiness anymore.

The girl turned and headed for the exit to pay for her wares. I watched as she left and felt happy for her. She turned and gave me a wave as she disappeared out of site. I stood motionless for a few moments, taking it all in – the smell, the happiness of the girl, and how simple life can be when you were content to just let it happen.

As I walked up the stairs to the record room, still smiling at my encounter with the soap and marble girl, I mulled over what the shop keeper had said to me a few minutes earlier, and soon enough I was back down to earth.

As far as the records problem was concerned, I had no one else to blame. It was all completely my fault, and as I had already ascertained, I had to take full responsibility for it. If the records weren't there, then I would have to find them somewhere else, but I would get them all back. Well, the ones I could remember anyway.

The first familiar things I spotted were the Mantovani and James Last records I'd stolen from my parents. I pondered getting them back as a nice surprise for them but quickly decided against it. After all, they hadn't even noticed they were gone, and I am pretty sure that my dad had only bought them in the first place because of the half-naked women on the front covers.

But then I did start to find some, only seven-inch singles, though. All the twelves had gone, apart from "Big Apple" by Kajagoogoo, which I didn't really want, then or now.

I was up there for a good hour, and when I returned to the front desk to pay for my findings, I now had the following seven-inch singles back in my possession:

- The Cure – "The Lovecats"
- Tears For Fears – "Change"
- Siouxsie and the Banshees – "Dear Prudence"
- Howard Jones – "New Song"
- U2 – "New Years Day"
- REM – "Radio Free Europe"
- Duran Duran – "Rio"
- The Thompson Twins – "We Are Detective"
- Tears For Fears – "Pale Shelter"
- Echo and the Bunnymen – "Never Stop"
- Depeche Mode – "Everything Counts"
- Dexy's Midnight Runners – "The Celtic Soul Brothers"
- The Style Council – "Speak Like A Child"

It was a good haul. Now to find out how much he was going to charge me for them, but I was prepared to pay whatever he asked as long as I had enough, of course. I also had to bear in mind that Bob was back in the record shop collating a pile of CDs that would more than likely cost a lot more than I was about to pay Mr Bon Marche, although I was pretty sure that wasn't his actual name.

What made me most happy, though, was that one of the singles I had found was "Speak Like A Child" by The Style Council with the brilliant "Party Chambers" on the B-side. It had been my first-ever purchase. I didn't know for sure if it was the one I'd sold in the first place, but that didn't really matter.

I found fourteen singles, and he charged me ten pounds for the lot. I was extremely happy with that. I'd expected him to at least make me pay a pound for each one.

So with bag in hand, quite a heavy bag, I began my journey back to see Bob. As I entered the shop, Bob immediately saw me and beckoned me over. To my surprise, Trevor stood at the counter.

"Trev, how's it going, mate?" I said as if greeting a long lost brother. He reciprocated in kind.

"I'm good, mate," he said putting his arm around me. "You look a mess."

"Yeah, yeah, I know. Bob already told me. Anyways, that's all over now."

Trevor looked pleased and exchanged a look of satisfaction with Bob that made me go a bit glassy eyed again. I turned away so they couldn't see me in this weakened state, but they both knew.

It was strange, as were most things nowadays. I had to remind myself regularly that these guys weren't Big Chris. They were not Mick or One or any of the bouncers. They were my mates and didn't expect anything from me but to be theirs in return. I went glassy eyed again. This time they both saw it.

"Come here, you," they said.

I now had Bob on one side of me and Trevor on the other, both with their arms around me. "Don't cry, little Tom. We're just glad to have you back."

Well, that was a bit much. I was in full-on crying mode now. Bob told me to come behind the counter and have a sit down to compose myself. I did so, and within a few minutes, I was ready to converse again without bursting into tears.

"You ready, mate?" Bob said.

"Yeah, ready. What you got for me, mate?"

Bob reached below the counter and produced a pile of CDs taller than I was. It certainly reached above my head when you took into account the height of the counter.

"Blimey," I said. "That's a big pile of CDs. Are you sure this is the format, Bob? It ain't gonna be replaced by something else in a couple of weeks, is it?"

"No, mate, this is it," he assured me.

One thing was for sure, there was no way that I was going to be able to afford all of those in one go. My god, I wanted to, but there was no chance.

"So how much for the lot then, mate?" I took a deep breath and swallowed heavily awaiting the result.

"Well, mate, more than you can afford, that's for bloody sure." Bob laughed, as did I and Trevor. The mere idea of me having that sort of cash was bewildering to say the least.

"So go on, how much?" Trevor said.

"Two hundred quid."

"*Two hundred quid*!" I said a bit too loudly. "I've never seen that sort of money in my life."

"Well, Tom, you know I like you. So I've drawn up a little repayment plan for you. You can take all of these today and pay me twenty quid for the next ten weeks. How does that sound?"

A few quick calculations in my head later, all of which were probably wrong, and I'd decided, not that I hadn't already, that we were in a "go" situation.

"That sounds bloody marvellous, Bob."

I couldn't thank him enough. This was a big enough task as it was, and here was Bob taking a huge chunk out of it without me even having to try. What a damn decent fellow. Trevor also seemed pleased. Not only because he could see that I was extremely happy, but also because he could tape the lot of them. I knew this was on his mind. He was almost salivating looking at the pile. I decided to strike up a deal.

"Trev, mate."

"Yes, Tom."

"You're gonna want a copy of these, I presume?"

"You presume correct," he confirmed.

"So how do you fancy making a little contribution?" He nodded his head furiously. But Bob looked a bit perturbed.

"What's up, Bob?" I asked.

"Well, I'm doing you a favour here, and now rather than Trevor buy them too, you're gonna copy them. I've a good mind to withdraw the offer." Bob was clearly not serious, but he had a point. I had to try to appease him.

"That is true, Bob," I said looking at the still-nodding Trevor. "But Trevor will have to buy some tapes from you, and also, with Trev's input, you get your money back quicker."

"Suppose so, Tom. I'm only kidding, ain't I?" he said.

"Yeah, yeah, but I'm a business man, ain't I, Bob, doing deals and that?" I said attempting to look shifty.

"No, you're not, Tom. You're an idiot." That was true; I am a bit.

"Fair point." It was a fair point.

I now had a huge amount to transfer back home. The stack of vinyl from Bon Marche was going to be easy to carry compared to the huge stack of CDs supplied by the wonderful Bob.

Luckily, Bob produced a box from under his counter. No reason to think he wouldn't have a box really. After all, he was in the buying and selling business, and boxes were abundant in both directions. We filled the box, and I lifted it proudly from the counter on which it was placed, and then put it straight back down again.

"Jesus, that's heavy," I said out of breath. "Think I might have to make two trips."

"No need, Tom, mate," Trevor said. "I've got a motor now. I'll bring it 'round and we can take them back to your gaff."

"Splendid, Trevor."

I stood at the counter, chatting with Bob while Trevor went to get his car. We discussed the new music scene, now in full flow, led by The Stone Roses. We decided I should make another list of artists. Upon completion I gave it to Bob along with instructions to let me know whenever something arrived in his shop by any of them. And then, money permitting, of course, I would be purchasing the lot.

Once I had paid off my current debt, that was. Bob was my mate, but he was not stupid.

We also had a small discussion about what I had been up to since I last saw him. I was just beginning to explain why I'd become embroiled in the rave scene when Trevor reappeared, ready to load up his new car. Both Bob and Trevor said they wanted to hear the full story. I said I would tell them definitely, but for now, Trevor was parked on double yellows, and we had to go.

I gave Bob the first of many twenty pounds notes that I would be giving him over the next few weeks and months, and bid him farewell, as did Trevor.

19. Records, Part 3 – List Completion and New Music

I managed to pay Bob off, with Trevor's help, in just a few weeks. It had only been a relatively short while ago that I'd been selling my records in order to take drugs and dance to rubbish music until eight in the morning. But now I had a collection that I would have been envious of before all that happened. Not only had I recouped a good portion of the vinyl I had sold to Bon Marche, but I also had all the albums that I'd owned before, and a few more, only now on CD.

My CD collection, albeit non-existent before the raving period, was now in full flow. I had all studio albums by The Smiths, Joy Division, New Order, The Jam, and The Cure. During this time I had also discovered, on Bob's recommendation, a love for Iggy Pop and the Stooges, in particular, The Stooges first three albums, released between 1969 and 1973. I played *The Stooges*, *Fun House*, and *Raw Power* over and over again from the first moment I owned them. Brilliant.

Although replenishing the collection had been my main aim in life since my self-imposed removal from the rave scene, I also accepted that having a full-time job had enabled me to do this and, therefore, was almost as important, but not in such a pure way. It was a means to an end, the end being the ability to listen to whatever music I wanted to. Plus, it got me out of the house for eight hours a day, which in turn made for less frequent arguments with my mum. But then she was actually quite pleased with me that I managed to get a job, and so even the evenings were less testy nowadays.

I was not paid particularly well in my job, but it was enough. I still didn't quite understand how I managed to get it. The relationship between my dad and my boss, Mr Tovey, continued to baffle me, especially when after just a few months in the job, and for no apparent reason whatsoever – definitely not because I was working hard, because I wasn't, at all – Mr Tovey deemed that I should have a pay rise. This put an extra thirty pounds in my pocket each month. Not that much I know, but enough to buy a few more records per month.

I also started to visit Bon Marche on a regular basis just in case some of my old records were being sold back to him, maybe by someone now looking for drug money themselves, or maybe I might find some that I'd missed during my many inspections of his wares. It was quite a big room where he kept the records, and it was very badly organised. The records weren't even in a recognisable order.

One morning, as I was standing at the counter waiting to pay for the twelve-inch single of "Bizarre Love Triangle" by New Order that I had previously sold to him, a bloke in front of me was selling.

I peered over to see what he was trying to offload. A lot of it wasn't my taste, but he had several Kraftwerk albums. I was not a huge fan, but I was very aware of the influence of the German techno kings, especially on the work of Joy Division and New Order. I wanted them.

As he turned to leave with his meagre few quid in his hand, our eyes met. He did not look good. His eyes were gaunt, his face was pale, and he was sweating profusely. He did not look happy at all. It felt like looking into a mirror from just a few months earlier. This guy was me. Now I know what I must have looked like to Trevor and Bob that first morning in the record shop after the end of the rave period. Blimey. Not a good look.

He smiled at me but failed to look me in the eye for any length of time. I wondered if he knew that I was him, only a few months later. I looked up at the owner of Bon Marche. He looked very happy. I wondered if he knew what was going on here. Maybe this had been his plan all along, to capitalise on weak-minded fools who spent a lifetime trying to put together a record collection that they could nurture and love, only to eventually take to drugs and sell them all to him for an extortionately low price, so he could then sell them on for a hefty profit. What a bastard. Mind you, that might not have been the case, I supposed. But he definitely looked the type.

I wanted those Kraftwerk albums. Something inside me screamed that it would be wrong of me to buy them. I presumed that eventually the bloke selling them would want them back, just like I'd wanted all of mine back. The rave scene was already a commercial nightmare, so surely it wouldn't be long before he worked it out like I had. Or maybe he was new to it and therefore would have no frame of reference from the good days. Oh well, he would have to learn the same way I did.

I thought back to my many visits when I was selling and wondered if there were a fellow just like me waiting in the wings to snap up whatever I was offloading.

I made my peace with it pretty quickly to be honest, maybe a bit too quickly, but hey ho, that was life. There was no time for sentiment when it came to the cut-throat world of record ownership.

"How much you want for those Kraftwerk albums?" I said to the shopkeep. He peered up at me, giving a full frontal, almost pornographic view of his moustache, and then looked straight back down again.

"I need to price them up," he said.

"OK, well, once you've priced them up, how much do you want for them?" I would have thought that was pretty obvious.

"Come back in an hour, and you can have them. I'll keep them down here for you."

Now, I knew how much he had just paid for them and therefore had a pretty good idea of how much he was going to charge me. But this guy was so shifty, and he knew full well that he could rip me off as he had done so many times before.

I left the shop and made my way to Bob's.

"Bob," I said.

"Tom," he said. "I've put you a pile of CDs together."

On my last visit I gave Bob a list of new artists that I was interested in. This time the pile wasn't quite the size of the last one, and I was just about able to see over the top of it. However, it was still quite large and far too much for me to buy all in one go. I wondered if Bob was up for implementing the same hire purchase scheme as last time.

"As before, Tom, you can take these and pay them off." Bless him, I loved Bob.

"Excellent, Bob. Twenty pounds a week, yeah?" He agreed.

"Trevor's already bought all of these, though, so you're on your own this time."

"So I could tape them off Trev then?" I was joking. Bob knew that.

"You could, Tom, but how is that going to make the collection look? All those lovely CDs and then a load of tapes making it look all messy." He was right. I couldn't do that to the collection. I took the lot.

They were:
- *The Stone Roses* by The Stone Roses
- *Some Friendly* by The Charlatans
- *Leisure* by Blur
- *Modern Life Is Rubbish* by Blur
- *Suede* by Suede
- *Dog Man Star* by Suede
- *Definitely Maybe* by Oasis
- *Bummed* by The Happy Mondays
- *Pills, Thrills and Bellyaches* by The Happy Mondays
- *His and Hers* by Pulp
- *The Beat Inside* by The Inspiral Carpets
- *Revenge of the Goldfish* by The Inspiral Carpets

I took them all home and prepared myself for a day of musical discovery. I had only heard certain singles by all of these bands and really couldn't wait to hear their albums.

I had always been of the opinion that if you really wanted to know what a band were about, then you must listen to the music that was only supposed to be heard as part of an album of work. That was the real band. The singles they released, as brilliant as they often were, I think were basically the vehicle to get people to buy the albums. The album tracks might not have been as commercially viable as the singles, but that in no way meant that they were not any better. Well, sometimes it did.

I fell in love with all of them immediately. The one that I had heard the most of before owning the album was *Definitely Maybe* by Oasis. Although a few of the bands released work before Oasis, it was they who had captured the general publics' interest more than any other with the singles they had released, and also the characters of the brothers Gallagher. Noel and Liam seemed to have enlightened the music scene for young people and crapped the life out of the establishment equally with their lewd and perceived socially unacceptable behaviour.

Although having said that, and being a music purist, I had to say that there was nothing particularly original about it. I didn't know. Maybe this was the end of originality in music. Maybe that godawful racket known as rave music would be seen as something so revolutionary when I'm older that I would spend half my days telling people it was shit. Who knew?

Oasis were nowhere near my favourite of the new bands. That honour was reserved for Suede and Blur. But I had to accept that they were the leaders of the new school, as it were. It didn't in any way detract from the brilliance of the other bands, but it was a factor of great importance in the success of this new scene. And I loved a scene, me.

It was hard to believe that in just a few months since I'd stopped going to raves and subsequently put my plan together to regain my record collection, I'd managed to get as far as I had.

I had also rekindled my relationship with Bob and Trevor, got myself into full-time employment with the remote possibility of a career, and also built a collection of new music that I love. It all seemed to be going too well. Something had to go wrong surely. Maybe not. I just didn't know.

So now all I had to do to complete the list was to go in search of the records I knew would take the most effort to find – the ones highlighted in red. The ones that I'd sold to other collectors. It wasn't going to be easy, but my success so far was spurring me on to greater things. I was ready.

First off, I needed to put them in the order that I would search for them. They were my Holy Grail, and I was determined to sip from their goodness again and maybe even find eternal happiness and stay young forever. But that was unlikely.

First off was *Dark Side of the Moon* by Pink Floyd, with postcards and poster.

20. The Ones in Red – Dark Side of the Moon

Early one Monday morning, I arrived at work and took my place at my desk. Just as I removed my apple from my bag, Mr Tovey's secretary, Jane, appeared in front of me. I had made advances towards her a few times now, and she clearly knew full well that I fancied her. But I also knew that she had a boyfriend. There was a picture of the two of them on her desk. Horrible-looking thing, it was.

He was a big-looking fellow and certainly not one I wanted to tangle with. However, at times it was difficult to care, as Jane was a stunning brunette and flirted with me every time I saw her, just my sort of girl, apart from the having-a-boyfriend part.

"Jane," I said. I'd now got past the whole uncomfortable nervousness I'd previously displayed towards her and was now able to converse with her properly.

"You good, Tom? Nice weekend?" Oh god, I loved her. I may have gotten over being uncomfortable around her, but I still felt it inside.

"Lovely, thanks, Jane. You enjoy yourself?" I asked.

"Yeah, me and Justin went away Saturday night. Was lovely."

God, that hurt. It hurt more every time. Why did she always bring him up? Of course, I knew full well why she always did that, to hurt me. Bitch. I didn't mean that.

I knew she wouldn't seriously want to hurt me. She was a really lovely girl, but like lots of other pseudo-relationships in the workplace, she enjoyed the attention, and it gave her an ego boost, which it also did for me when she paid me attention.

I knew the flirting was just flirting. But deep down I believed that one day it might become more. And I was pretty sure that she knew I thought that too. In fact, I thought she was relying on it. Otherwise, she would have had to rely on bloody Justin for compliments, and I got the feeling that they were few and far between. *Surely, she would leave him and be with me*, I thought nearly all of the time I was in her company, while knowing full well that she wouldn't, and also that I would undoubtedly be better off if she didn't. It was confusing.

"Mr Tovey wants to see you," she said, leaning towards me, clearly not wanting anyone else to know what she was saying, but at the same time inadvertently giving me a look at the top bit of her bra.

"What now?" I said swiftly moving my gaze from bra to face.

If there was one thing I knew about Jane, it was what she looked like when she was walking away. I had watched her so very many times before. Sometimes when she knew I was watching and sometimes when she didn't, and they are very different indeed.

When she knew I was watching, like now, she moved like she knew I was watching. And when she didn't, well, she didn't. Maybe I was overanalysing this a bit.

"Sit down, Tom," Mr Tovey instructed pleasantly as I walked into his office "You're doing a good job, Tom, but I think I'm going to move you to a different section." Didn't like the sound of this but instructed him to go on. "Seems to me that you would be better off doing credit control rather than purchase ledger." This meant that rather than being moaned at on the phone, I would now be the one doing the moaning.

It was a moral dilemma. I had, since I'd begun the job, put up with some quite hostile credit controllers attempting to get payments out of the company, and now I was to become one of them. It felt like I'd be betraying the world of purchase ledgery, and that didn't sit right with me. But I knew it was all a game. Every company had an accounts department set up in the same way, and everybody wanted to get paid and, at the same time, not pay anyone else. It was a game, simple as that, but a game that held lots of people's livelihoods in the balance.

There were two factors that meant I would have to make this change. One was that Mr Tovey, the bloke who after all was paying me, had said that I had to. And two, I genuinely had absolutely no interest in either role, so it didn't really matter which one I did. He thought he was doing me a favour by giving me all this experience, but all I thought was give me the money, so I could get some records.

"Fine. When do you want me to start?" I asked.

"Um, well, now, Tom. You don't need any training, just reverse your thought process, and you're there, mate." *Mate?* He'd never called me that before. Strange. I knew what was coming next.

"How is your father?"

"He's fine, thanks."

"Make sure you tell him about this promotion." It was not a promotion. I knew that and so would my dad. "Did you tell him about the pay rise?" Oops, I hadn't.

"Yes, he was really pleased."

"That's good, Tom. We go back a long way, me and your father."

"Yeah, he said."

Mr Tovey's face changed to alarm. "What's he said?"

"Oh, nothing really, just that you go back a long way ... like you said."

"Oh. OK. Well, we do. Known him a long time."

"Yeah, he said."

"Said what?" he snapped back nervously.

"That you've ... you've known him a long time."

"Yes ... good. OK. Well, off you go then, Tom."

I left the room, feeling just as confused as I did every time I spoke to him. I stopped off at Jane's desk on the way back to mine. She gave me the smile she always gives me, and I gave her the one I always give her. Difference was that I'm pretty sure mine didn't look how I thought it looked.

Jane and I had recently taken to spending our lunch hours together. We went for walks up the dual carriageway and talked about her boyfriend. I loved those walks. Friday dinner times, we often discussed the weekend. She'd tell me what her and Justin were getting up to but always without ever actually saying anything affectionate about him. She periodically said something obviously negative to keep me interested. I knew what she was doing. I didn't care.

"So what you up to, Tom. Seeing one your girlfriends?" *What girlfriends?* Oh yeah, the ones I'd made up.

I had earmarked this weekend to begin my search for the copy of *Dark Side of the Moon* with poster and postcards. I decided to tell her. She seemed genuinely interested.

"I sold it a couple of years ago from an advert I put in a shop window," I said.

"So why did you sell it?" I couldn't tell her that. Maybe I could. She was pretty cool. She might have been into drugs once, or even now. Not that I now thought there was anything cool about the rave scene or taking drugs. It seemed a bit that way at time. I supposed it still did a bit, now that I was looking back on it in a sort of romantic way, but I knew it wasn't really. It was all pretty stupid.

"I just needed some money, and all I had that I could sell were my records."

I had detailed my love of music to Jane a number of times. She didn't like the same music as me but was always so interested in what I had to tell her, which was one of the reasons that I loved her so much. *Damn it.* I needed to stop thinking that or it was going to leak out of my mouth one day.

We sat down on the bench we frequented most dinner times. I'd carved my name in it a few weeks previous while I was trying not to listen to her tell me stories about her and Justin.

"So why does this record mean so much to you then, Tom?" she said adorably. Fuck's sake.

"I wouldn't necessarily say it means a lot to me, but it's one of the first albums I ever owned. It was actually my music teacher at school who gave it to me. He brought it in one day when he got us all to do a project about our favourite band. Pink Floyd were his favourite, so he played us the album and said whoever makes the best project would get to keep the record. I didn't even know until I got it home that it had the poster and two postcards with it."

"Did he know?" she asked.

"I told him the next day. He said he had no idea. He definitely wanted it back, though. But that was never going to happen, and he knew it. That baby was mine."

"So what was your project about?"

Jane turned and put one leg folded at the knee up on the bench, looking straight at me. I did the same. She was great. *Stop it.*

"It was about The Smiths. But more specifically about the album *Hatful of Hollow.*"

"It must have been really good," she said, her voice getting softer as she bought into the premise.

"No, it was shit. All I did really was photocopy the cover and write the lyrics out. It was just a bit less shit than everyone else's. Plus, he liked The Smiths."

"So how are you going to get it back? Can you remember who you sold it to?"

"Never actually met him. I put an advert in my mate's shop window. I think he lived round here somewhere, though."

Maybe Gary would know the bloke's name. I hadn't even thought about that until now. I had to see Gary tonight and find out what he knew.

That might have been difficult. Gary was still well into the pills, and I hadn't seen him for a while. We did speak briefly on the phone a few weeks back, but we didn't really say anything to each other. He'd said he was going to a rave, and I'd said I wasn't. He'd asked me if I had any money he could borrow, and I'd said I hadn't.

That night when I got home from work, I rang him and arranged to go 'round to his house. I didn't tell him why. It was just on the premise that we hadn't seen each other for a while.

When I got there, he took a while to answer the door.

"What ... the fuck ... has happened to you?" I said.

Gary stood there, like a ghost, holding a bowl of cornflakes and wearing jogging bottoms that were way too big for him and quite dirty, not a good look, even on Gary.

"Don't know what do you mean. I'm fine. You look weird. Where you been?" *I look weird? Christ, how is that possible?*

"What, healthy?"

"No, sort of …"

"Clean?" I said finishing his sentence.

"No, like …"

"Awake?" I said, doing it again.

"Nah, nah, I was going to say … er … boring. Yeah, you look boring."

I looked down at myself, still wearing my work clothes, a cheap shirt and tie, cheap trousers, and cheap shoes. Yeah, I supposed I could see why that might look boring.

"You gonna let me in then?"

He stood aside, and I squeezed myself past him. The house smelt of weed, stale weed. But it didn't really manage to cover up the main smell wafting up my nostrils, which was B.O.

I walked in the front room to find several bongs pumping out weed smoke with several hoody wearing, screwed-up-looking people attached to those bongs. They all looked up briefly and nodded at me. I took a step back out of the room and grabbed hold of Gary's arm.

"Who are they, mate?" I said.

"What, are you mental? Wayne's in there. And Little Chris. It ain't been that long, mate." He was right; it hadn't been that long. But obviously long enough to screw all three of them up. They were virtually unrecognisable with their hoodies on. They looked dirty and their faces older.

I took a seat. Gary sat next to me. No one spoke for a good few minutes – me because I was just incredulous at how they all looked, and them because they all had their faces stuffed in bongs.

I looked down at the table in front of them to see something else that helped explain the way they looked. Several freshly used crack pipes littered its surface and various pieces of discarded tin foil surrounded them. Clearly the Ecstasy wasn't enough for them anymore. There were also some of those on the table too. But they looked like kids' sweets compared to the hard-drug paraphernalia accompanying them.

"Seriously, mate. You're doing shit like this now? Why?"

"Why not?" Little Chris replied.

"Chris, the last time I saw you, you didn't even smoke weed. Now you're doing crack, yeah. That's fucking mental, mate."

"Yeah, I know, man."

Chris responded like a typical drug user. He thought I was complimenting him on his ability to take hard drugs. That was one of the problems when you did a lot of drugs. You spent all of your time with other drug users, either doing drugs or talking about doing drugs. It became normal and then, much in the same way that a drinker will think, you believe you are better than someone else because you can take more of it without passing out or dying. It was a strange thing to be proud of, but you had to be there to understand it. And then you had to come out of it, like I had and they hadn't, to understand how ridiculous it was.

"You want some gear, Tom?" Gary passed me a bong. Couldn't see any reason not to have a quick go. At least I might have been able to converse with him if I was a bit stoned "It's got coke in it too," he added. "Oh right, second thoughts, no, thanks."

"Listen, mate. Do you remember the bloke who bought that Pink Floyd album off me?" He stared at me for a moment.

"What the fuck are you on about. What Pink Floyd album?"

I could tell that he really didn't know what I was on about. On reflection, this wasn't a surprise, not just because he was so out of it, but also, well, why would he? It was important to me, but that didn't make it so for him.

"I put an advert in the shop window, and that dude came and bought the album." Gary went pure white all of a sudden. "You remember him then, yeah?"

I couldn't work out what was going on here. Maybe I was passively smoking the weed, and this wasn't really happening like I thought it was. But no weed was that strong. This was weird. I had never seen Gary act like that before. He was strange at the best of times, but this was different.

"Um ... yeah, I remember him," he said, slowly sitting forwards.

"Well, I want to get that record back. How do I contact him?"

Gary sat bolt upright, his face still white and with the sweat on his forehead beginning to freeze over. Wayne and Little Chris weren't moved at all. Whatever it was that was freaking Gary out, they definitely didn't know anything about it.

"Um, I don't think he picked it up, mate. It might still be in the shop."

But surely he'd paid me for it? Then I remembered: he hadn't paid me for it. He'd just given me a pill that night. Maybe it was still in the shop then.

"Can you have a look on Monday then, mate?" No answer. "Mate?" He looked up. "I said can you have a look on Monday, yeah?"

"Yeah, no problem. Leave it with me. Hang on; it might be here you know."

Gary's record collection sat in the corner of his front room. If it was there it would be pretty easy to find as Gary mainly only owned white-label rave records. His actual record collection from before even he started taking Ecstasy was crammed to the back of the pile as if completely irrelevant. Actually it was totally irrelevant. As awful as rave music is, it was still an improvement on what he'd used to like.

I leafed through them, and he was right. There it sat in between two faceless rave white labels in all its glory. I inspected it for flaws. There were none. And then I opened the non-record-carrying part of the gatefold sleeve. Inside, I could see what I was looking for and removed them carefully, still in pristine condition – the poster and two postcards.

I placed them back in as carefully as I'd taken them out and sat back down in my seat next to Gary.

"So how much do you want for this, mate? Don't tell me you want to keep it, because I know you don't." It would be typical of Gary to do that. But Gary, on this particular evening, was being anything but typical. I felt like I didn't even know him anymore.

"Take it, mate. It's yours anyway," he said. "And you might as well take this one too."

I couldn't believe it. He had my "Still" by Joy Division double album with access to the inner sleeves via the top rather than the side as well. The cheeky fucker.

"How did you get hold of that?" I said accusingly. Well, I was accusing him.

"I don't know, do I?" He clearly didn't know, and I didn't care. I now had them both back. So that was two regained with little or no effort whatsoever.

I would happily have paid him however much the pill cost him that he'd effectively paid for *Dark Side of the Moon* with, but he didn't want it, so fuck him.

What I did want, though, was to leave as soon as possible. It felt like I was in a crack den. Then it hit me. I was in a crack den. It was just a crack den with nice curtains. What was the difference really? All it took to make a crack den was crack and crack users. Just because they all looked like toilets in the movies and on the news didn't mean that was the reality of it.

I bid my farewells and made my way out. Gary didn't see me out, as he was still sitting bolt upright and staring at the wall above the fireplace. He didn't even say goodbye, just let off a grunt. Wayne and Little Chris didn't make a sound. I'm not sure they even knew I was there. Worked for me.

So I had the first of the records back that were highlighted in red on the list. A good feeling came over me, like I had really achieved something. I didn't really have to put any effort in at all. The thing was 'round Gary's house all the time. What I did have to endure, though, was seeing that Gary had, in a relatively short period of time, fallen into a hole and was getting deeper into it. He wasn't even trying to get out. I didn't like it one bit, but there was nothing I could do about it.

I got my list out and crossed off *Dark Side of the Moon* and *Still,* two down. Then I placed the records back in their rightful places. I chose not to play either of them, as I now had them on CD. I just looked at them comfortably leaning up against the twelve-inch of "See You" by Depeche Mode.

21. The Ones in Red - Blue Monday, Part 2

A couple of days later at work, Jane hadn't turned up; she was off ill. That meant I would have to spend my dinner hour on my own. I didn't mind.

I'd recently purchased a Walkman and was happy to sit at my desk for the duration, listening to the tapes that Trevor had copied from my new CDs. We had a deal going. I gave him full access to my collection in return for borrowing whatever tape I wanted whenever I wanted it. It was a good deal. Whatever tape I wanted that day, Trevor could listen to the CD. We were both very happy with the deal. He didn't have a Walkman.

That night in my bedroom I sat listening to *Leisure* by Blur when my mum shouted up to me that I had a phone call.

"Who is it?" I shouted back down.

"Well, if you come down you'll find out," she bellowed back. "It's a girl."

"A girl!" My dad suddenly appeared at the foot of the stairs, looking excited. "Hurry up, Tom. Don't make the lady wait," he said.

"I'm not gay, Dad. And stop grinning like that; you look mental." I said as I walked past him on my way to the phone which was kept under the stairs.

It was Jane. I couldn't make out what she was saying. She was crying. I knew she was ill, but she must have been really ill if it was upsetting her this much.

"What's up, Jane?" I asked her comfortingly.

Both of my parents stood peering through door to the hallway, my dad with a manic grin on his face like he had just found out that his son, who he'd always thought was gay, was, in fact, not gay.

Of course, in his head, that was probably the case. I supposed I had never really done anything to dissuade him from thinking that I was gay. In fact, I had gone quite far out of my way to make him think it was the case. It was fun for me to do this, and I liked fun.

"Can I meet you?" Jane said, managing to sound coherent for a second.

"Of course. When?"

"Now," she said.

Jane didn't live that far away from me, and although it was a bit cold outside, my hopefulness that she would fall in love with me overtook my sense of logic. And so I agreed to walk to the location she specified, approximately fifty yards from her house and about half mile from mine. I didn't want the poor girl out in the cold for too long, especially considering how upset she was. Plus, she might fall in love with me. Had to stop thinking that.

When I got there, she was already waiting. I sat down next to her on the bench. She said nothing and just flung her arms around me and held on tight. I did the same.

My chin rested on her shoulder for at least two minutes. I wondered all sorts of things. What had happened? What had that bastard Justin done to her?

She pulled back from the embrace and looked me squarely in the eyes. Well, the one that she could open properly anyway.

"What's happened to your eye, Jane?" As if I needed to ask.

"Justin went mad. I … I don't really know what I did. He just went mad." She put her head down as if in shame.

"Hey, hey, look at me, Jane." I was now extremely concerned for her. Justin had obviously punched her. "Look, where are you going to sleep tonight? You can't go back in there."

I concerned myself for a moment that she might think I was trying to crack onto her, but she was so emotional I didn't think she would notice if I were, which I wasn't, much.

"Can I come with you?" she said, still holding on tightly to my arm.

I stood her up and put my arm around her like I was trying to keep a long-distance runner from passing out at the end of a marathon and then pointed her in the direction of my parents' house.

As we approached, I could see my dad peering out of the window. He caught sight of me with my arms around Jane, and that stupid excited look appeared on his stupid face again. Then he swiftly disappeared behind the curtain. I did wish he would fuck off. Idiot.

The door opened before we got within ten feet of it. My dad stood there with his grin on until he saw how upset Jane was, and then his face changed.

"Are you alright, love?" he asked her.

"Course she's not alright, you idiot," I said without thinking.

"Thomas," my mum shouted from the room. "Don't call your dad an idiot."

"OK, you're not an idiot, Dad."

"I know I'm not. What, you think because you said it, it's true? That's not the way it works, Thomas, me old son."

"Old? I'm not old. You're bloody old."

"It's a figure of speech, ain't it?" he said.

"What is?"

"Saying, you know, me old son."

"Shut up, man."

"Don't tell your father to shut up, Tom."

"Ok, sorry, Mum. Christ's sakes," I said.

"And no blaspheming."

"Yeah," Dad whispered "No fucking blaspheming, eh, Tom."

"I do wish you would fuck off," I said.

"Charming. I brought you into this world, and you tell me to fuck off."

"How did you bring me into this world? I'm adopted. All you did was sign a bloody form."

The argument made me forget momentarily about the crying Jane under my left arm, although she'd stopped crying now. Well, she was still a bit, but now it was because she was crying with laughter at the sight and sound of me and my dad going 'round in circles.

I put her to bed in the room next to mine. At about 3.00 a.m., I heard her moving about a bit. She was obviously getting ready to go back to him. I left her to it. Surely she must know that when a bloke gives you a black eye, that he's a wrong'un, although I had no way of guaranteeing that. I had seen on only too many occasions, mainly in soap operas, where the same thing had happened and the girl not only stayed with the perpetrator but seemed to love him even more.

Women. All I could do was wait and find out. But I had to admit, all this did give me hope that she would leave him for me.

I heard her open the front door and leave but chose not to see her out. It was so early that she clearly didn't want anyone to know she was going. And besides, she had a violent idiot to dump. Hopefully.

Me? Well I had another record to find. The original copy of "Blue Monday" by New Order with the grey inner sleeve. Black would not do, as that was the rerelease, or so I thought anyway. It was a Peter Saville design, as are nearly all of Joy Division's and New Order's record sleeves. It was well documented that the band had actually lost money from it due to the costs of producing the sleeve. It was designed to look like a computer floppy disc and did so admirably.

I had no idea who'd purchased it, but alarmingly, as was the case with *Dark Side of the Moon*, I'd sold it via an advert in Gary's shop window. I was going to mention it when I was 'round his house searching for the Pink Floyd album, but the whole situation had thrown me off track. And besides, I hadn't actually thought I would get the Floyd album back that easily.

At about 10.30 a.m., Saturday morning, I made my way 'round to Gary's house. And then turned back 'round again as I realised that although I was extremely keen to get going on my quest, Gary would still be recovering from the previous night, and so I would have to wait until at least early afternoon before I could safely approach him.

When I got there about 2.30 p.m., he opened the door looking like a ghost, much in the same way he had last time I'd seen him but ever so slightly worse.

"Alright, mate?" I said cheerfully.

"Yeah … what's up, Tom?"

Looked like I was not particularly welcome. I peered over his shoulder to see the usual reprobates sitting in his front room looking as ghost-like as him.

"Can I come in?" I asked, bemused as to why I hadn't already been invited to do so.

"It's not a good time, Tom."

"Well, I can see that Gary. No time seems to be a good time nowadays. What the fuck's up with you, mate? You're going bad."

He really was. I was concerned for him, but I needed that record so I persisted to get an invite in. He was not giving in. Fair enough. We'd have the conversation on the doorstep then.

"Will you shut the door, Gary? It's fucking cold enough in here," came a voice from the sofa.

Gary stepped out onto the front step, pushing me slightly backwards at the same time and shutting the door behind him.

"What do you want, Tom?" he said, getting a bit angry.

"Have you got my twelve-inch of 'Blue Monday'?"

"What?" Fair question. I supposed a bloke in his situation might have thought I was being a bit weird.

He disappeared back into his house, closing the door behind him, presumably to keep me out. I had no idea if he was going to have a look for the record or if that was it. A few seconds later he reappeared with a record in his hand, just the record, though, no sleeve.

"Here you are." He handed me the naked record. I looked at him confused.

"Where's the cover?" He would have been better off not giving me anything, to be honest.

"I don't know," he said.

"Why would you have the record and not the cover, mate? That's mental. I need the cover."

"OK, OK, I know where it is. You're gonna have to give me some time to get it back."

What the ...? How the hell did he know where the cover was if it had become detached from the record itself? That must mean they had been separated on purpose.

"Well, when you gonna get it?"

He sighed and looked to the sky. "I'll get it tonight. It … it's with a bloke I know."

He couldn't even look me in the eye now. He had the same expression on his face as when I'd asked him about the Pink Floyd album, like there was something he didn't want to tell me.

"I'll come with you then, mate," I said.

"*No.* No, I'll get it. Don't worry about it, mate. I'll get it for you, but you don't need to come," he said nervously.

Fine by me. I didn't want to go anywhere with him. He looked a mess and smelled quite bad. It concerned me greatly, as Gary was someone who always took such a pride in his appearance, but now that he had a new friend called Mr Crack, looking smart didn't seem to be very high on his list of priorities.

My suspicions coupled with my concern for Gary were starting to get the better of me. I'd recently purchased myself a cheap Vespa scooter and decided that when he left to get my record sleeve, I was going to follow him.

Gary was very much a creature of habit. Even taking into account his newfound love of harder drugs, he would undoubtedly still keep to his schedule. In fact, I would imagine, even more so now.

His routine was based on his paranoia, and now that was at such an increased level due to the harder drugs he was taking, I had absolutely no doubt whatsoever that he would be leaving his house at 7.30 p.m. Don't ask me why; it was just the way it was. If I could have explained it, then I suppose I would have been just as bad.

I parked up the Vespa just 'round the corner from his house but with a clear view of his front door. Bang on time, he emerged and got into his shit Nova. I knew I would struggle to keep up with the Nova as my scooter was painfully slow. But then so was his Nova. And even if it had been a bit more powerful, the way he drove meant that I shouldn't have had too much trouble keeping him within sight.

A couple of miles away on the edge of our hometown, he pulled into an industrial estate. I couldn't really have followed him in without been seen. My scooter rarely got over thirty miles an hour, and it constantly sounded like a kraken being released. I think there might have been a hole in the exhaust. So he might not have seen me, but he would most definitely have heard my transport. I was gambling on him not realising it was actually me, though.

The estate wasn't very big, so when I reached the entrance, I parked up the Vespa and made my way on foot. I knew the general direction in which he was heading but lost sight of him quite quickly. However, it wasn't long before I found him.

He'd parked at the front of a small warehouse. The lights were on inside, despite it being a weekend and well after working hours. I held back, standing at the gate about fifty feet from the entrance.

Gary banged on the door, and within seconds, it opened. I couldn't see who opened it, so I waited for it to shut again before making another move. Once I was sure it was safe, I moved in closer.

There was a window on the side of the warehouse, and as it was dark outside and the lights were on, I could easily see inside.

Sitting 'round a table covered in bags of pills and powders were some familiar faces.

One was there, so was Mick, and so was the bouncer who'd given One a slapping at the illegal rave for supposedly trying to shag him.

One of the other faces looked familiar, but I couldn't quite put my finger on it. I definitely hadn't met him before. He just looked familiar.

The window wasn't exactly thick, and the surrounding area was quiet enough for me to be able to hear what was going on inside.

"You take these, and I don't want to see you again until they're fucking sold. You get me," the bouncer said aggressively to Gary as he flung two bags towards him, one full of pills and the other full of wraps of what I presumed was cocaine.

"Yeah, yeah, OK," Gary replied.

"Is that all then? Cuz if it is, you can fuck off now."

These guys clearly had issues with Gary. I was shocked to see him with them and even more shocked to hear the conversation between them.

Gary wouldn't normally have had anything to do with people like that. Or at least that was what I had always thought. I supposed now things were different. Gary had gotten himself a proper drug habit now, not one that could be described as "recreational", but one that was far more dependent. I felt bad for him and really wanted to burst in and defend him, but that would have been suicide.

I watched Gary take a few drags on a crack pipe that was handed to him by One. How was he there? Both Mick and the bouncer were hardly friends with him the last time I'd seen them all.

My concern for Gary was growing all the time. He had clearly gotten himself mixed up in something quite unsavoury and with some horrible characters. But what concerned me most was when was he going bring up the subject of the "Blue Monday" record sleeve? After all, that was the only reason I was here. Well, apart from trying to find out what was making Gary freak out all the time. OK, so there were two reasons I was here, but the record sleeve came in a clear first.

"And take that will you," One pointed to a sideboard just behind Gary. He picked up what he had been told to take and put it under his arm. I didn't believe it. It was my "Blue Monday" sleeve. He hadn't even asked for it.

"We're gonna have to use another one from now on. Tom wants this back," Gary said.

"Tom?" Asked Mick. "What the fuck has he got to do with this?"

"It's his, ain't it?" Gary replied.

Just as he said that, the bloke that I didn't know but who looked familiar stood up at speed and pinned Gary up against the wall. I couldn't hear what he was saying, but Gary looked terrified. Mick stood up and restrained him.

"Leave it, yeah," he said. "Just give that back to him and get another one. But make sure you fucking tell us what to look for."

That was strange. How did my record sleeve have anything to do with whatever was going on in there? Oh well, at least I was getting it back, and that meant another one in red crossed of the list. Happy days.

Once Gary was released by the oaf, he turned at speed and began to make his way out of the warehouse, which was my cue to leave.

I ran towards where I parked up the Vespa, got on it, and headed in the opposite direction from Gary's house. I stopped not far up the road and watched as his shit Nova made its way out of the industrial estate.

I was very much looking forward to being reunited with my record cover. The record itself had survived the ordeal quite well. It was a bit dusty, but there were no scratches on it despite it being separated from its protective cover.

Gary was a good guy, although recent events were starting to make me doubt this. He knew how much that record meant to me and had kept it in good condition.

The next morning the phone rang.

"I've got your sleeve, mate. You wanna come round and get it?" I agreed and set off on my way to his house.

He handed it over but, as was the case yesterday, didn't invite me in. I once again looked over his shoulder and saw the same scene that had met me the day before. Pipes and knobheads sat 'round a table. I didn't care. I had my record back.

Back in my bedroom I slotted the record into its sleeve and placed it back in its rightful place in my collection. I then took out the list and crossed it off.

I was doing well, the collection was looking good, and I could see the end in sight. I had only a few more to get. Hopefully the rest wouldn't be as hideously revealing as the first two had.

The three singed Jam singles would be next, mainly because this time it wouldn't have anything to do with Gary. I knew it was going to be difficult to get them due to the identity of the person I sold them to. He was more of a geek than me. I was fairly sure that he wouldn't want to relinquish control of them, but we'd see.

22. The Ones in Red – Signed Jam Singles

A few weeks later there was a bit of shock. Gary rang me and informed me that he would be coming to pick me up that Friday night to go to the pub. This hadn't happened in ages, and I had intentionally made no effort whatsoever to try and make it happen. I initially thought he must have wanted to talk to me about the events that surrounded our last two meetings. Not the case, though, as he informed he would be picking Big Chris up first, and then we would be meeting the rest of them in the pub.

I was not keen. I was enjoying life without Big Chris. The rest of them I could take or leave. Nevertheless, I agreed. And after a while thinking about it, I decided that it might actually be a bit of a laugh. Gary did sound quite coherent on the phone, and so I had high hopes that we might be able to rekindle our friendship, which had gone completely off the boil since I'd stopped taking drugs with him.

The next day at work, Jane was back. Her eye had gone back its natural colour, and she seemed quite happy. Obviously, Justin hadn't launched another attack on her since. I supposed really I should have been a bit pissed off with her. I went well out of my way to help her that night, and this was the first time I had heard from her since. Not even a thank-you. My dad did mention this to me a few days ago, but I had lied to him and said she was very grateful. I didn't want him to think badly of her.

"You're back then?" I said as I sat on the side of her desk with my concerned face on. She looked up at me but struggled to make eye contact. I knew what was coming next.

"Yeah. Look. Thanks for the other night, but I shouldn't have rang you. It wasn't fair of me." She was right, of course.

"I just want to make sure you're OK, Jane. What's happened to Justin?"

"He's … he's at home."

She was still with him. Of course she was still with him. Why wouldn't she be? I mean, he'd only punched her in the face. That was all. Jesus. Bloody women and their love for a bastard. Defied sense.

"So he's not done it again then?" I asked. She then became very defensive, but her true feelings about it were obvious.

"He wouldn't do that, Tom. He wouldn't."

"Yeah, but he did do it, though, didn't he? If he's got it in him to do it once, likelihood is that he's going to do it again."

She knew I was right, I could tell. But she couldn't let on. I felt bad for her. I knew that love could be the strongest of emotions and made people commit to strange decisions in life. I'd been there. But surely getting punched by your other half, especially when it came from the man in the relationship, should only have led to one conclusion: dump him.

I supposed really we were all animals, and our job was to reproduce. It was love and lust that made us commit to each other. If it weren't for those two emotions, the human race would have died out years ago.

"Leave it, Tom. He won't do it again. I promise you."

"Well, if he does, you ring me, OK?"

I leant in to her so she could clearly see the whites of my eyes and me hers. She knew I meant it and was a bit grateful, I was sure. She didn't have to say it; I knew.

As I dismounted from her desk, I noticed her looking intently at the picture of Justin. It was a very different look she had now, compared to the way I had seen her look at it before. I took a look myself at the monster. How could he have done that to her lovely sweet face? Then I did a double take at the picture.

The last time I'd seen that face had not been the last time I'd looked at the picture. The last time I'd seen that face, it had been attached to two massive arms that were in turn pinning Gary up against a warehouse wall. I knew I'd seen him before.

I looked back at Jane. She was still staring at the picture. I couldn't possibly tell her what I had just realised. My sense of concern for her suddenly increased tenfold. Justin was obviously mixed up in whatever Gary was in on and clearly had very little control, if any, over his aggression.

I wanted to grab hold of her and tell her that she had to leave him as soon as she could. Surely if I didn't tell her what I knew, then I was responsible if it happened again. But if I did tell, she might not believe me, and that would have been awful. Also, if I did tell her and she told him, well, then I thought we all knew what was going to happen. I just had to be there for her.

Maybe I could get some info from Gary tonight that might help me prove his involvement. But then if she was so in love with him that she was prepared to let him get away with punching her, what was the point? It was a dilemma alright.

"Just let me know if you need me, Jane. I mean that. Anytime."

What a stupid thing to say. Not only did she now have an escape plan should it happen again, but it also made me look like a complete pushover, not that I didn't already. But what if she did get hit again and then decided I was the man she wanted to be with? My god, I was so very pathetic.

On my way home from work that night, I knew I'd done the right thing regarding Jane and Justin. I would have preferred to tell her, but there were several possible resulting scenarios, and all of them could only have worked out badly for me. Only one could have worked out well, and that one was highly unlikely. *Maybe I should become a bastard? The worst that could happen was that she might get punched again. Christ, what had I done? I should have told her.*

Gary, being the creature of habit that he was, tooted the horn of his Nova outside of my house at exactly 7.40 p.m., having, of course, left his house at 7.30 p.m. on the dot to pick up Big Chris.

He couldn't even be bothered to get out and knock on my door anymore. That was how much our friendship had suffered in recent times. I, in turn, albeit slightly immaturely, decided to keep him waiting for a couple of minutes, thus throwing his schedule out and his mind into turmoil.

"How's it going?" I said as I got into the back seat.

Gary responded with a nod and a quick peer over his shoulder. No such reaction from Big Chris. To be fair, the rubbish music was pumping out of his little two-watt speakers to the point that it just sounded like distortion, so he might not have heard me.

In the corner of the pub waiting for us were Wayne, Nat, Little Chris, Phil, Nick, and Weezel. I hadn't seen most for them for a while, and so it was all a bit uncomfortable initially. The mood always changed whenever Big Chris was present, but there was something else to this. I couldn't quite put my finger on it. It was like there was an air of resentment, and the battle lines had been drawn firmly between Wayne, Little and Big Chris, Gary, me, and then the rest of them.

There was an obvious reason for the battle lines having been drawn. The difference between the two camps was drug taking. We all had, and in the case of everyone but me, still were. And they all hadn't. They looked down on us because they thought we are stupid to get involved, and we looked down on them because we thought they didn't have the guts to do it themselves.

To be fair, I was slightly in both camps. I had done the drugs but now saw that it wasn't for me. They all knew that, but only one side had any resentment towards me about it. That side was the users, of course.

I felt strangely like I was in a privileged position to be able to see it from both perspectives, but it also had its downside. I had become the mediator in all discussions on the subject. I was Switzerland.

"You look a mess, Gary," Nat said to him. He wouldn't have said it if Big Chris were still in the room, but he'd just gone to the toilet.

"I've told him that already," I said.

"You look like Bros," Nat then said to me.

"How can I look like Bros? I can only look like one of them at a time. Anyways, that was fucking ages ago. Get over it."

Why was I trying to reason with him? He had discovered a way to get to me, and he was using it to the best of his ability. Fair play to him, I would have done the same, but with more class.

"Well ... you look like ... a knob." OK, so that hadn't been classier, but it seemed to have done the trick.

Gary failed to react to being called a mess again, as he knew he needed Chris to be there for him to defend himself. Gary wasn't stupid, just weak. He knew that the drugs were taking their toll on him, but he couldn't admit it. All he could hope for was that Big Chris would defend him, because he looked a mess too, and for the same reason.

There wasn't a great deal of chat that night. The differences between us all were beginning to take hold, and we were drifting apart down two clearly defined paths. This was the first time we had all been out together in a very long time, but individuals from each group had seen each other regularly.

There were the drinkers, and then there were the drug takers. The drinkers were in the pub and then went home drunk at 11.00 p.m. and argued with their other halves, whereas the druggies were off their heads until 7.00 a.m. in a rave, and then spent the next five days arguing with everyone. Each group thought the other was ridiculous, and that wasn't going to change.

Me, I didn't really care either way. I thought they were all stupid. I just wanted my records back and to get with Jane. The record retrieval was likely, but the Jane thing wasn't. And that reminded me, I had to try and get some info out of Gary about that Justin idiot. How I was going to go about it, I did not know. I couldn't let him know that I'd followed him to the warehouse the other night, and that had been the only time I had seen him with Justin, so I had to be clever about it.

"So are you going to tell me who had my records then, mate?" I said to Gary. Big Chris, now back in the room, gave Gary a knowing look as soon as I mentioned the records.

"Does it matter who had them?" Chris said. That was strange. Chris hadn't been in the warehouse. I hadn't even told him I was looking for the records, so why was he answering for Gary?

I didn't really want to find out. Thinking about it, why wouldn't he have been involved? And more to the point, what exactly was it that he was possibly involved in. I still had no idea what was going on. All I knew was that Gary, Mick, One, the bouncer, and that Justin dickhead were up to something that centred around drugs and that warehouse. The only thing that didn't add up at all, and the only thing that I gave a rat's arse about, was what it had to do with my records.

Thankfully, the three Jam singles had nothing to do with whatever this debacle was all about. I decided it was time for me to forget about it and go in search of them. I did still want to find out information about Justin's inclusion in it all, mainly so I could be ready for whatever problems it brought upon Jane but also to put my mind at rest. Jane was hardly being fair to me. She was taking my good nature for granted and probably enjoying the attention at the same time. But I couldn't help who I was, and I would not become a wanker, no matter how much easier life might have been for me with the ladies if I were to do so. I was really worried about her.

At the end of one of the most pointless nights I had ever spent with my so-called mates, which was really saying something, I set off to walk home. The drinkers were extremely pissed and the druggies about to make their way to the club. It did seem strange to me, considering what had happened on my last visit there, that Big Chris actually still went. Actually, it seemed strange that any of them still went. They all kept away for a few weeks after that night but soon had become regulars again.

Gary's happy-go-lucky nature had gone for good, it seemed. He now acted like going to the club was like going to a business meeting. He was overly nervous and clung to Big Chris like his life depended on it. He pretty much always had done that, but before it was because he'd wanted to be seen with the bloke that everyone was scared of; now it was more of a dependency. Big Chris's attitude towards him had changed too. He was much more dictatorial now and acted like he had something on Gary, like Gary owed him something.

About halfway home I realised that I had achieved nothing tonight. I'd found out nothing about Justin or anything else surrounding what I'd seen at the warehouse. But more importantly, I had made no strides whatsoever in the recovery of the Jam singles. I would need to start early tomorrow morning if I were to get anywhere.

Before I got into my bed that night, I located the name and phone number of the chap I'd sold the singles to. I'd written it on a piece of paper that I'd then slotted into the front of my seven-inch singles box. Luckily, I remembered. Of course the box had been empty for a while and had stood gathering dust. When I'd refilled it with the regained singles from Bon Marche, I'd seen it in there and known that I would need it quite soon, not enough to have gotten it out ready, though.

I made the call the next morning. His name was John, and he lived in the adjoining town to mine.

"Is that John?" I said as the male voice answered the phone.

"It is indeedy do. Can I ask as to whom this is calling please?"

Oh yeah, I remembered now. This bloke was a twat, but a harmless one. I knew there was something about him I had been forgetting.

"This is Tom. I sold you three Jam singles a couple of years ago. Signed by Weller and Foxton. You remember?" I asked.

"Indeed I do, good Sir Tom of Selling the Records-shire. And what may I verily do for you?"

Christ on a bike. I knew he didn't mean to be, or even know he was being, a twat, but he really was. I decided to be on his level; maybe that way there would be more chance of him selling them back to me.

"Well, Sir John, I am in search of reconciliation between myself and said records."

No, that was not going to work. Now I was a twat. This bloke was fairly thick-skinned, but he could probably work out that I was taking the piss.

"Ah, forsooth, young Friar Tom." I was wrong; he didn't realise. "I would love to be of assistance to your good self but cannot, can I not?"

How was this bloke a fan of The Jam? He should have been listening to, I don't know, The Wombles or something. The way he talked you'd think all his music was played on a lute by groups of minstrels.

"Oh dear. Have you sold them on then?" I was now talking normally. Hopefully he would follow suit.

"No, my noble friend. I cannot sell them to thee as they are verily sitting comfortably as part of my collection, are they not?" Again, was he asking me a question?

OK, this was a problem. I had accepted this as a possible outcome in all cases of getting my records back. I supposed really I was doing well to have gotten to my third quest before it had become an issue. Maybe that was it; I should tell him it was a quest. I bet he liked a quest, did John.

"You see, good Sir John of Owning the Records-shire." Yeah, I'd gone back to it. "I am on a noble quest to regain what I had sold for yonder pieces of silver and now must complete the quest in order to gain the hand of a fair maiden, so I must." The phone went quiet for a moment.

"Are you taking the piss?" Of course I was taking the piss. I just hadn't thought you would realise mate.

"No, no, I just thought you might like to help me on this quest."

"So what's all that bullshit about a fair maiden?"

In a way there was a fair maiden involved – Jane – not that it would make any difference to her if I owned the records or not. At least I didn't think it would. Maybe it would. No, it definitely wouldn't.

"Was just joking with you, John. Like you are with me, yeah?"

"Joking?" he said enquiringly. OK, so he wasn't joking. So what the fuck was he doing then?

I was losing him. My only hope was for him to sell me the records. Failing that I would have to buy them again and then try and find Paul Weller and Bruce Foxton to get them signed, which was never going to happen. I mean, Weller was now a successful solo artist and Foxton was in Stiff Little Fingers, who were playing venues smaller than my bedroom.

Yep, that was the reason I wouldn't be able to get them signed. Because the two of them didn't mix anymore. Nothing to do with the fact that we didn't really move in the same circles, me and those two. It was their fault.

I had one more option. It could work out expensive, but it might just work.

"So do you really need the signed copies, John?" I asked. "I could get you some new copies and then still pay you for the signed ones? What you reckon?"

I could hear him mulling over the idea. I couldn't actually hear his mind ticking, that was obviously not possible, but he made a sort of purring noise. I didn't like it one bit, but at least it meant that he hadn't completely dismissed the idea.

The longer it went on, the more likely I thought it would be that he might succumb to my whim. Really should have stopped talking like that.

"Well, I could do with the money," he said. "How much are you thinking of?" Not a fucking lot really, mate.

"I could get the singles and then pay you an extra five quid for yours?"

That seemed fair enough to me. Obviously I was prepared to go a bit higher, but that was my starting point.

"I think it should be a least a tenner," he said. Fair enough, I would go to a tenner.

We settled on eight after visiting seven, nine and eight fifty along the way. Standard procedure. Not a bad result, really. The whole deal was going to cost me more than a tenner, as I had to buy the new singles, but it was going to be worth it. As soon as the phone call ended, I headed out the front door and made my way to see Bob in the record shop. Trevor was in my sister's bedroom as I left. He'd stayed the night, so I presumed that he must be pretty fed up of her company by now. I knocked on the door to see if he wanted to accompany me.

"Who is it?" came the muffled and agitated response.

"Is Trev in there with you?"

"Fuck off, Tom."

This time the response was slightly less muffled and accompanied by a faint snigger that sounded like Trevor. Trevor was such a great bloke, but my sister really was a knob. She didn't have to be that rude. I meant, if she was eating something, which was what it sounded like, she could just say that. Depended on what she was eating, I supposed. I decided to tell her that.

"Seriously, Tom, you need to fuck off." This time Trevor responded, and although he was trying hard not to laugh, he failed badly.

"You want me to go, yeah?" No response. "Trev?" Still nothing. "OK, I'm going. Last chance, yeah. I'm going to see Bob."

"OK, hang on, mate."

"*What!*" my sister screamed, obviously not too happy about it. Trevor then appeared at the door to her bedroom, all dishevelled.

"Jesus Christ, mate, do your fucking flies up, Trev," I said.

Trevor grinned and did as he was instructed. My sister, sitting on the bed, looked daggers in our direction and then removed her shoe and threw it at us. But it was too late and only hit the door. There was a chance that if she had had a more accurate throwing arm, she might have got us, but we were already halfway down the stairs by the time she'd cocked the trigger. Amateur.

Trevor drove. We parked up outside despite a traffic warden clocking us from the other side of the road. It was worth the risk. We both know what we wanted, so it would more than likely be a short visit. Trevor made that point to the fluorescent-jacketed warden. She accepted it and walked off in the other direction.

I, however, didn't trust her promise, and as we disappeared into the shop, I quickly peered back out. Sure enough, there she was, back with ticket book in hand, writing Trevor's number plate on it at speed.

"Trev, told you, mate. You better get moving before she manages to stick it."

"Bloody civil servants these days, Tom, can't fucking trust them." He was right. You couldn't. But I wasn't sure you ever could really.

"I bet you're on commission, eh, love?" he said. "I said I bet you're on com—"

"Yes, I heard you the first time, sir," she replied.

"OK … well … that's ok then, isn't it?"

There followed a bit of face pulling from both sides but nothing too serious. Trevor moved his car to a legal parking space just a few feet away. He might as well have gone there first, really. I respected his choice not to, though.

By the time he returned, I had already procured the singles I was after from Bob. He was in a bit of a bad mood. I told him about the deal I'd struck up with John, but he wasn't interested. Normally he would at least try and sell me something other than what I came in for, but not today. Miserable git.

I turned and headed out. Trevor was just coming back in. I told him about Bob's mood. It didn't deter him from visiting the counter. I chose to hang back and watched from the front of the shop as he made his purchase. I couldn't hear their conversation. And then a few seconds later, bag in hand, Trevor made his way towards me.

"Miserable bastard. Fuck's up with him today?" Trev said so very eloquently.

I didn't know what was up with him. Given that Bob had accommodated the two of us for so long now, we were prepared to let him off. Nice of us really.

We returned home. I went straight for the phone in the hallway to arrange for the single exchange, and Trevor went back to Tracey's bedroom to finish off whatever he had been doing before he left.

Once the phone call was over, during which I arranged to meet John on the edge of town that night, I could once again hear a great deal of commotion coming from my sister's room. She was shouting, and Trevor was attempting to appease whatever it was that was making her so very angry. As I walked past to get to my room, the door was open, and I glanced in.

Trevor sat on the bed with his hands in the air like he was trying to be Switzerland. Tracey stood in front of him, finger pointing and shouting. She saw me, rushed towards the door, and slammed it shut. I managed to catch sight of Trevor just before it closed. He sat giving the Vs to her turned back and sticking his tongue out at me at the same time. I really liked that bloke. I supposed really I should have done everything I could to keep him and Tracey together. But then if they'd split up, I would have had him all to myself. It would have made for a few potentially awkward situations, I'm sure, but I think we would both have been very happy together.

I had a little sleep that afternoon. Periodically I was woken up by raised voices from across the hallway. I was expecting Trevor to come and find refuge in my room eventually, but after a while, the noise dissipated. I dreaded to think what was happening in there now.

That night I set off on my Vespa to meet John the harmless twat and complete the record exchange. It was still a bit warm, and the sun hadn't completely disappeared as I set off.

The Jam singles I purchased to replace his signed copies, along with the ten pounds we arranged as compensation for the signatures, sat comfortably in a bag that I'd wedged inside my coat.

By the time I reached John, it was dark. He was already there in his Ford Fiesta XR2. Bit of a cool car for someone who was essentially as cool as a fire on the equator.

We made the exchange in virtual silence. I think he was still a bit upset with me for taking the piss out of him for talking like an Amish villager. Didn't bother me. I was hardly likely to see him again. What it was good to see again, though, were my signed Jam Singles. I couldn't wait to get them home and cross them off the list.

As I made my way back from the deal, the exhaust of my Vespa sounding like Barrie White with laryngitis, I passed the industrial estate where I'd followed Gary while looking for the twelve-inch of Blue Monday.

I chuckled to myself as I regaled what I'd seen that night at the warehouse and the fact that I now only had one more record to get back. Things were going better than I could had ever hoped for on my quest, and in a way, I was not looking forward to it being over. What would be my quest then? Probably wouldn't have one. Shame.

As I began to descend the hill just past the industrial estate and potentially reach speeds of nearly thirty three miles an hour, I spotted a familiar sight. Gary in his shit Nova coming in the opposite direction. I flashed my lights and put my hand up. He'd definitely seen me, as I could see the whites of his eyes as he did so, but he quickly turned and looked in the opposite direction.

I was becoming increasingly confused by his reactions to me lately, and so I decided to wait a while and follow him. After all, I was fairly sure I knew where he was going.

23. The Ones in Red - Magical Mystery Tour

As per my last visit to the industrial estate, I parked up the Vespa and headed in on foot. Gary's Nova had disappeared out of sight by the time I had turned 'round and headed back, so I just presumed he would be parked up at the warehouse. When I finally got there, I wasn't disappointed. This time, several other cars were present: a BMW, two Land Rovers, and a bright-blue, shitty Vauxhall Nova.

I could see light coming from the same window as before, so I approached carefully.

I peered in to the well-lit room from the darkness of the outside. Gary, Mick, and One sat 'round the table. The table this time was covered in many more bags of pills and powder than before. Clearly whatever operation was going on here was growing quickly. It hadn't been that long since I had last looked through this window, so I could only presume that the job was going well.

After a few minutes watching the three of them sitting in silence, another person entered the room – the bouncer. He had several more bags with him and placed them next to the others. He sat down and stared at the three of them, still in silence.

By this time there was still no sight of Justin. What concerned me was that the amount of bodies in the warehouse was disproportionate to the amount of vehicles in the car park. Surely Mick and One hadn't made enough money from these deals to buy themselves a Land Rover each? If so, Gary was most certainly not getting as good a result as them, as he was still driving the same hunk of crap. One of the Land Rovers must have been the bouncer's; that was a given. The BMW was maybe Mick and One's transport for the evening, but whose was the other Land Rover?

I didn't have to wait long to find out.

Suddenly, a firm hand clasped itself over my left shoulder and spun me 'round violently. I hit the side of the warehouse just inches from the window. I couldn't make out who it was. He grabbed me by the throat and spun me 'round once more, this time facing the window, now adorned with agitated-looking faces staring back at me.

The bouncer, Mick, and One all smirked at me as they realised what had happened. Gary's look was very different. He was shaking his head, and his eyes were as wide as they were when I'd seen him in his car just a few minutes earlier.

My face, by now being pushed up against the window by the unknown aggressor behind me, was starting to hurt. He then swung me 'round once more, and I realised it was Justin. And he wasn't alone. Standing just behind him, and slightly to the left, was a face that I would normally be happy to see, but this time it filled me with dread – Jane.

For a moment, I imagined that she would scream at Justin to leave me alone, but it didn't happen. She looked just as aggressive as he did. I wasn't sure what to do now.

"What are you doing here, Tom?" she asked coldly. I had no choice. Honesty was my only option.

"That's my mate Gary in there. I saw him coming up the road and followed him in here. What are you doing here?" She didn't answer.

Justin seemed to be taking a back seat in the negotiations and was happy for Jane to quiz me. Surely she couldn't be involved in this, could she? It was only a while ago that I'd saved her from getting a proper kick in from this bloke, and now she was acting like she was the main aggressor of the two.

"Get him inside," she said to Justin.

Justin grabbed me, almost lifting me off my feet, and dragged me towards the door of the warehouse. At this point I had far more pressing issues on my mind, like not getting killed by this twat, but my only real concern was that I still had the three Jam signed singles tucked inside my coat. Whatever was going to happen now, I had to protect them. I thought I'd had to protect Jane from Justin, but I appeared to be very wrong. What I did know, though, was that the Jam singles would not let me down in the same way. Shame on her.

Justin then violently propelled me into the room containing Gary and his cohorts. They all immediately surrounded me. Gary looked, as he had from the other side of the window, incredibly scared. The rest were revelling in their catch.

"Tom, Tom, Tom," Mick said as he pushed me down onto a chair.

As he did so, I could feel the corner of one of the Jam covers poke into my chest. I attempted to manoeuvre myself in order to release it and avoid creasing the cover. It worked, and I could once again feel them flat against my chest. Sweet relief.

"What are you doing here, Tom?" One said as he leant in close.

I was not sure how to deal with this. In the past I'd had moderate success dealing with aggression by just returning it, but I got the feeling that this time it wouldn't go well for me. After all, I was on a side of one. Not One, but one, i.e., just me. The look on Gary's face suggested that he was undecided as to which side he was on, but it was also clear that he wasn't about to let them know that. I still had no idea what his involvement in this was, but it was fairly clear that he had no influence on the situation. I decided my approach would be a dismissive one. I would see how that went.

"Tom" – this time Mick addressed me – "he asked you a question. What the fuck are you doing here?"

I looked around at the faces now staring down at me. I had to say something. I didn't really want to mention Gary's name again; he looked worried enough as it was.

"Was just passing. Why, what are you doing here?" I said nonchalantly.

All of them then stood up straight and looked at each other. I slumped back in the chair, inserting my hands in my coat pockets to attempt to check the bag of singles. They seemed safe.

Gary stood opposite me, looking fearful. More than I was to be honest. Mick, One, and the bouncer leant into each other and started to whisper. I couldn't hear them. I was not actually sure they were saying anything. They then called Justin and Jane over to them and carried on the conversation.

I looked straight at Gary and tried to converse with him silently. He just shook his head again and again and then looked away from me. What was he so frightened of? Surely he was in this as much as the rest of them. I really couldn't work this out.

The group then broke free from each other, and Justin launched himself at me. He grabbed me violently and pulled me to my feet. The Jam singles started to feel uncomfortable again. He then pushed me against the wall.

"Tell me why you're here you little shit. *Now!*" He was very angry. I had already told him why I was here. How much more detail could I go into?

"I told you. I saw Gary as I was passing and wondered where he was going. Look, mate, I don't get this. Why are you being so aggressive with me?"

Jane then pushed him out the way and without any warning whatsoever, kicked me squarely in the groin. I doubled over and fell off the chair.

"What the fuck did you do that for?"

My god, I was in so much pain, mentally and physically. She was wearing some fairly sturdy boots and had just made contact with my nuts at point-blank range. But that was nothing compared to the gut-wrenching pain my heart was going through, thanks to her.

My concern for the Jam singles was paramount, but the pain now emanating from my groin was too much for me. There was nothing I could do, not only did I need to bend over to alleviate the pain, but also to protect myself and the Jam singles from another attack. It was clear to me that if I ever managed to get them back to my house and cross them off the list that they would no longer be in mint condition.

"Tie him up," Jane instructed her band of followers.

"What's the point of tying me up? It's not like I'm going anywhere."

My pleas fell on deaf ears. One then disappeared into the warehouse and returned a few seconds later with some rope.

"You do it," Jane barked out, pointing at Gary.

As he tied me to the chair, I tried my hardest to make eye contact with him, and he tried his hardest to do exactly the opposite. He had tears in his eyes. I didn't know if this was because he could tell the Jam singles were getting all bent out of shape or because he didn't want to do it. Or both. Or neither.

"Gary, what are you doing?" I said as quietly as I could.

"Don't fucking speak to him," the bouncer barked at me as Gary's head shook in apparent disbelief.

His whole body was shaking. I felt that I may have been underestimating this situation slightly. So far I was not taking it that seriously. I knew I was in a tight spot – that much was obvious – but they could have just given me a slap and told me to fuck off. There was no need for all this gangster-like behaviour.

Jane handed Gary a roll of duct tape. "Put that over his big gob," she said.

"Whoa, whoa, hang on, what's the point of that?" I said. OK, now I was scared.

"Because, Tom, we're having a meeting here tonight, and we don't want you making any stupid comments."

"Comments about what? I don't have a fucking clue what's happening. You might as well just let me go."

"Yeah, you'd like that, wouldn't you?" One said.

"Well, obviously. Dumb ass." One came at me aggressively, but Mick stopped him.

"Leave it, One," he said. "Just get him out of here and out fucking there, would you?"

Once I was fully tied and gagged, the bouncer dragged the chair, with me on board, out of the office and into the warehouse, placing me behind a large wooden container about twenty feet away. But I was still just able to see through the door to the office. Not very clever of him.

Mick and One then began to pile up the bags of pills and powder in an orderly fashion on the table. Whoever it was that was coming to meet them was clearly a stickler for tidiness.

After a few minutes, I heard a car pull up. This must have been who they had been waiting for. The door to the warehouse opened, and the bouncer went to greet their guest.

I couldn't work out why they had decided to put me somewhere where I could see all this going on. Maybe it was by accident, maybe not. Either way, it was where I was. And so whatever was about to happen was going to be well within my sight.

Two burly looking men walked in first and embraced the bouncer. I recognised them from the door of the club when I had been kicked out. They shook hands with the rest of them and gave Jane a peck on the cheek.

Then something really strange happened. She looked over to me and smiled. She could clearly see me watching as all of this happened. Surely her best bet was to move me somewhere that I couldn't see. Maybe she wanted me to see. The rest seemed completely oblivious to my whereabouts.

The last person to walk in was much smaller than the bouncers. He must have been the lynchpin of this operation, I thought. I tried to get sight of him, but it was impossible. He was so small and was easily obscured by his huge protection. They disappeared into the office but not before Jane gave one last look in my direction. This time, she winked. What … the fuck … was going on?

As the door to the office closed, I became bathed in silence. For the first time since I'd arrived here tonight, I was on my own. I had been manhandled several times, including getting kicked firmly in the groin by a girl who I'd thought was my friend, and then tied up and gagged. My only option was to try and break free, but the more I moved, the more I could feel the Jam singles losing value. The rope that Gary had tied round my chest was to an extent, holding them in place, but that was causing its own damage. I had to forget about them. They were lost. My main aim had to be to get out of this in one piece.

After about ten minutes, the door to the office opened slightly. I got ready for whatever was going to happen next. But the door didn't fully open. There was just enough of a gap for me to see in. Jane had definitely opened it as I could see her hand in the gap. She had lovely hands … I should shut up.

She sat with her back to the door, so she must have been doing it on purpose. Surely. And she was clearly trying to ensure that no one else in the room could see what she was doing as well. Crafty. God I loved her. She was like Barbara Bach in *The Spy Who Loved Me*.

Through the gap, I could see Gary looking as nervous as he had before. Mick, One, and the bouncer were looking intently at their guest who was doing all of the talking. I couldn't actually hear him, but he must have been, or they wouldn't be sitting in complete silence.

Jane's hand then appeared in the gap once again, and the door opened a bit more. Now I could see the legs of their guest. Why was she doing this? She obviously wanted me to see in, but what possible use would that be? I didn't really have a clue what was going on apart from the obvious drug deal. What was the benefit in me seeing any of this? Would it be the same if it had been someone else and not me? Or was it specifically me that she wanted to see in?

It was no use. I couldn't get my hands free, even considering that I had given up all hope of not damaging the records any more. All I could do was sit and wait for whatever was about to come my way.

After about half an hour, there was some movement from the office. I could see the bags of pills and powder being gathered up, placed in a larger bag, and the occupants getting to their feet. Now, surely I would get a chance to see who was in charge of this operation. Who was this poison dwarf who needed two bouncers to protect him?

The guests clearly didn't know where I was, as the group stood outside the office door for one last chat before setting off. The main man was still obscured from my view. Jane continually glanced in my direction. Then she moved towards the guests and went to give them each a goodbye peck on the cheek. As she leant in to kiss the main man, I still couldn't see his face, but as she backed away, he just about came into view.

I did not believe it. As she moved away from him, she looked at me once more. She clearly wanted me to see who it was. The rest of them were oblivious. Gary stood in the doorway, somewhat surplus to requirements. The guests didn't even seem to know he was there.

As they walked towards the warehouse door, I got one last look at them. I could now see why she was so keen for me to see who it was. And also the fact that she wanted me to see surely meant that she couldn't possibly be involved in the way I had previously presumed, despite the rather convincing kick in the nuts. If I had got this right now, which I think I had, that was a classic move on her part.

I was in shock, so much that I lost concentration momentarily, and as I took a deep breath, the bag of singles under my coat dropped to the floor.

"What was that?" he said.

"Oh nothing. Probably just a rat. It's a very unclean warehouse." She was right. It was disgusting. But he wasn't convinced.

"Go and see what that was," he said to his bouncer. "You better not be hiding anything from me, Jane. You don't want to make an enemy of me, do you?" Jane shook her head.

I really tried my hardest to remain unseen, but being tied and gagged in a fairly empty warehouse while simultaneously attempting to protect a bag of signed records was making it impossible. It didn't take long, despite his Neanderthal looks, for the bouncer to spot me.

"Who the fuck is this?" He ripped the tape from my mouth. "Who are you?" he slapped me. "I said who the fuck are you?"

He was by now shouting quite loudly. Then suddenly I was surrounded by everyone else. It was only then that I could see a distinct difference in the looks on each of their faces.

Gary, Jane, and surprisingly, Justin, all seemed to be signalling something to me. Whereas Mick, One, and all the bouncers shared an increasingly aggressive look.

Then the crowd parted and the so-called main villain of the peace showed himself clearly to me for the first time. He stood in front of me and leaned forward to make full eye contact.

"Well, hello, Tom. And what might you be doing here?" He said.

"Like I said to the rest of them, I was just passing. I might ask you the same question."

"I don't think that's any of your business what I'm doing here."

He stood back up, turned to the rest of the group, and then quickly turned back using his momentum to slap me as hard as he could with the back of his hand.

"Fucking hell, Bob, that really fucking hurt."

24. The Ones in Red – Magical Mystery Tour, Part 2

It really did hurt and produced a trickle of blood from my forehead. But it didn't hurt anywhere near as much as knowing that Bob was in charge of this operation. Bob. I bloody loved Bob. *Bloody hell, Bob. You were my fucking hero.* Why would he be mixed up in this? He was disgusted with me when he'd found out that I had been taking drugs while I wasn't visiting his record shop. I actually felt that I had let him down. I wanted to apologise to him, and now I found out he was in this crap up to his eyeballs.

"Get him in the office," Bob said. "I want to see the whites of his eyes."

His two bouncers then took a side of the chair each and dragged me into the office.

So here I was again, but this time with a few more people. Bob sat down and faced me.

"So what are you going to do now, Tom? You can't leave here. You do know that, don't you?"

"You don't need to worry about me, Bob. Why would I say anything about all this?"

"All what?" he replied loudly, giving me another backhander.

"I can't believe this, Bob. You're my mate. I buy my records off you. That makes you closer to me than family." Bob leant back in his chair and took a deep breath.

"OK, you better get him on the phone. He'll need to decide what to do about this."

"Get who on the phone?" I asked.

"None of your business, Tom. I don't think you quite realise how serious this is. One, get him on the phone now, yeah."

One picked up the phone and dialled.

"We need you to come down to the warehouse. We've got a bit of a problem," he said. And that was the end of the conversation.

Now the rest of them sat down, all looking at me. No one said a word, apart from me, that was.

"I need a wee."

"Well, you can't," Bob replied.

"It's coming out whether you like it or not Bob. You either let me go or this room is about to get a new fragrance," I said.

Jane stood up. "I'll take him. It'll be OK."

Excellent. That was exactly what I had been hoping for. She untied my feet and hands but kept the rope tied around my waist pinning my arms to my side. That way I could move unaided and at the same time have enough use of my arms to have a wee.

As we walked to the toilet, Jane whispered to me, "Don't you know who One is?"

"What?" I really didn't.

"One. Don't you know who he is?"

"He's a bloke Gary met at a rave, and I got to know him a bit. Then he turned out to be a complete bellend. Apart from that, I don't know a thing about him."

"So you don't recognise him from anywhere else then?"

Why was she going through this line of questioning? Why wouldn't she just tell me who he was?

"Question is, Jane, who the fuck are you?" I think that was a fair thing to ask, considering she'd taken the liberty of kicking me in the nuts earlier.

"Don't worry about that for now, Tom. Don't you know what One's real name is?"

"I don't have a clue."

Just as I felt she was about to tell me what she clearly so desperately wanted to, another voice came from just behind us.

"Are you fucking done yet?" It was one of Bob's bouncers.

"Nearly," I said. "Tell me, Jane," I whispered. "Tell me who he is."

"Right. Get out." He grabbed my shoulder and spun me around and, at the same time, sprayed my urine all over his foot. He bolted backwards. I saw my chance to get free.

I ran for the exit as fast as someone could while having their hands pinned to their side. I must have looked like a penguin trying to escape the attack of a polar bear. The bouncer gave chase, but he was well out of shape, and I was too quick for him. He shouted that I was getting away, which brought the rest of them out. Bob looked panicked and yelled at me to get back. I didn't listen and carried on. I had to get out of there. The door was only a few feet away, but just as I approached it, it opened and standing in front of me was the man they had obviously called on the phone.

Silence fell in the warehouse once more as the two of us stared at each other.

The figure stood in front of me was a weak one, and I'm sure that even someone of my size could have knocked him flying when running at speed. But the shock stopped me. And, therefore, my momentum and any advantage I might have had while travelling at speed was gone.

"Hello, Tom. And what are you doing here?"

"Hello, Mr Tovey."

"Let's go and sit down, shall we, Tom? Have a little chat."

OK, this was getting ridiculous. What next, Trevor? My mum? Morrissey, for fuck's sake. Was anyone that I knew or loved dearly not involved in this? And where the fuck was Big Chris?

Mr Tovey grabbed my arm and led me to the office. Gone was the pathetic figure of a man who ran an accounts office, replaced by this scarily calm individual who seemed to have complete control over the situation.

As I watched him, I started to think about the bloke who'd given me the job, the bloke who'd seemed so afraid of my own dad. I questioned why a bloke with the sort of influence he clearly had would be so keen to please my dad. I imagined him sitting at his desk, nervously bumbling around like an idiot. It was obviously all an act. But Jane must have known about it. Her reaction when he'd turned up certainly had suggested that. She didn't seem in the least bit surprised to see him here.

The image of him sitting there shuffling his papers and trying not to make eye contact with me became more and more vivid. And then it had hit me. On his desk there was a picture of him with his family – a buxom-looking woman and two sons. It was obviously taken a while ago, but the more I thought about it, the more it became clear. One was one of those sons. His surname was Tovey. That's what Jane had been trying to tell me.

"So, Tom," went Mr Tovey's opening gambit. "I suppose you're wondering what is going on here." He was right. I was.

"Not really," I said. He took a step back, looking almost shocked at my apparent disinterest.

"What do you mean, not really?" he enquired, leaning back in, just a few inches from my face.

"Well, I'm not interested. You don't need to tell me anything. Whatever it is, it doesn't have anything to do with me, does it? You might as well just let me go."

He stood back upright and developed a strange smirk on his face as he looked around the room for a similar reaction. They all looked at each other like they knew something that I didn't, even Jane. But then I presumed she was still playing along with it all. I still didn't know what her involvement was, but it clearly wasn't the same as I'd presumed earlier when her foot had met my groin at speed.

The only person who didn't seem to be either playing along with it or genuinely involved was Gary. He was still sitting silently staring at me and shaking his head. I was the one with his arms tied to his side with a trickle of blood coming down his face, but he was the one who looked scared.

"What makes you think you're not involved in this, Tom?" Bob piped up. I would have thought that was fairly obvious. Because I wasn't. Idiot.

"You've been involved in this right from the start," One added.

"And when your dad finally gets round to working any of this out, the trail will lead to one person, Tom. And that's you."

"My dad?" I said, "What's he got to do with this?"

Now the look between them all changed. It seemed that they were expecting me to know what they were talking about, but I genuinely didn't have a clue. It had been obvious to me that Tovey was in fear of my dad right from the first time I'd met him, but I'd just presumed that they went back a long way, and he knew something about him that he didn't want anyone else to know. Of course, that was probably the case given these developments, but it certainly wasn't what I thought. I imagined he might have had some pictures of him at a gay bar, snorting cocaine or something like that, but now there seemed to be a bit more to it.

"You know full well what your dad has to do with this," Tovey insisted.

"No, I don't," I also insisted.

"So you don't know what your dad does for a living?"

"He's an accountant." I was pretty sure I knew what my own dad did for a living, although the chuckle now coming from the rest of the room suggested to me that I might have had it wrong.

"Your dad, Tom, is not an accountant. Well, that's what he would have everyone believe. Your dad is an undercover policeman. But then why am I telling you that? You already know, Tom, don't you?"

"No, he's not. He's a fucking accountant."

It was laughable to even suggest that my dad, the piss-taking git that he was, could be anything like that.

"OK, well, let's see, shall we? Hand me the phone, Bob."

Bob did so, placing it right in front of me so I could clearly see what number he was dialling. It was the number of my house alright. Tovey put the receiver to his ear and placed a hanky over it.

"If you want to know who is bringing all the drugs in, I would go and have a look in your son's bedroom, in particular, his record collection. Look for *Dark Side of the Moon* and 'Blue Monday'." Then there was silence.

What the fuck was going on? Neither of those records had the name on the front, so he wouldn't be able to recognise them anyway.

"Oh right. Can I speak to Mr Reeves, please?" Idiot. He had just said that to my mum.

"You really are a fucking amateur, ain't you, Tovey? You total prick."

I decided that once again my best defence was attack. It had worked for me in the past, even with some of the people in this room, so why not try it again?

"Shut him up, would you?" OK, so it hadn't worked. On reflection I was not sure why I thought it would, now that things had escalated this far.

One then covered my mouth again with gaffer tape. Then his dad, Mr Tovey, repeated word for word what he'd just said to my mum and slammed the phone down. Now his attention came back to me.

For the next five minutes or so, Mr Tovey shouted at and walked around me. I wasn't really listening. I was imagining what must be now going on between my parents back at home and how I never really wanted to be there even when they were getting on well, but now that I knew that they were bound to be at each other's throats, all I could think about was getting back there.

The imagined sounds of my mum being unreasonable and my dad trying to calm her down were like the sounds of Joy Division or The Smiths compared to the sound of these knobheads yelling at me. Normally that sort of noise made me think of the worst type of commercial shit music, but now I longed for them like never before.

After a while, I came 'round and once again saw the situation before me. I was not sure if I would ever get out of this, but what was more concerning was that I had obviously inadvertently become a pawn in this. The two records he mentioned were the two that I had sold via the window of Gary's shop.

I had no idea what the connection was. I just hoped and prayed that my dad saw through it. He knew me better than anyone. If he was what Tovey said he was, an undercover cop, then he must by now be filled with a mixture of suspicions. Towards me, yes, I supposed. But I just hoped that his suspicions towards the rest of the people in this room were greater. I was in a tight spot.

"I suppose you're wondering why I told your dad to go and look at your records," Tovey said.

He was right; I was wondering that, but I couldn't confirm it to him, as I had bloody gaffer tape over my mouth. I muffled a response.

"Take that off, will you, Bob?" he instructed.

Bob ripped the tape off my mouth in one go, thus taking the top layer of skin off my lips. By now the blood had stopped trickling down my face, and I could feel the cut on my forehead beginning to dry up. But now I had a new fresh layer of blood coming from my lips and covering my chin.

"Go on then, you dick. Why?"

I now completely threw caution to the wind. I was already bleeding and three signed Jam singles down. What else could they do?

"Your fucking dad has been on my case for years, but he's never had any proof, so I decided that I would throw the blame in another direction, a direction that he wouldn't be able to fight – his own family. You, Tom."

This still wasn't making any sense. I could understand that if he managed to blame me in some way that my dad wouldn't be able to turn me in. Or at least I hoped not. But why the records?

"Bob told me that you would go to any lengths to get those records back, so I bought them. That was when your fucking idiot mate, Gary, became involved. Those aren't records. I take it you haven't played them. If you did then you would know that they don't work. Why? Because they're made of compressed heroin, and the sleeves are dipped in LSD. Didn't you ever wonder how the sleeves and the records became separated? You see Tom, you're the dick, and your dad is too. He will now be in your bedroom finding those records and testing them. And what will he find? He'll find one hundred per cent proof heroin and acid. Then he will add two and two together, unless he really is as stupid as he looks, and you will be in the frame. Brilliant, eh?"

It was quite clever, actually. But there was one thing that this bellend wasn't counting on, that although I might be, my dad was most certainly not a dick. He had managed to hide from me that he was a cop to the point where I still couldn't believe it now. And those were not the actions of a dick.

A few minutes ago, the revelation about my dad had been the worst possible thing to imagine, but now I was relying on it being true. If it wasn't, well, this whole thing was a complete waste of time.

"Yes, you are indeed very clever. You better hope that you're as clever as you think you are I suppose," I said.

"Meaning?" he replied.

"Well, given what my dad knows about you, why would he think for one minute that you're not involved? Even if he does suspect me, he's still going to think you're behind it."

Tovey stood up and laughed to himself. It was clear that even though he thought he was as clever as he did, it hadn't crossed his mind for one moment that someone might see through his plan.

He walked to the back of the room and stood staring out of the window with his hands behind his back.

"I mean, for a start, if you're that clever, you wouldn't be standing in a lit office looking out of a window when it's fucking dark outside, would you?" I said.

"He's right, you know. You should probably come away from there," Bob said. Tovey turned, and his eyes widened.

"You don't fucking tell me what to do at any time, you mongrel. I run this operation, and what I say goes. This is air tight. Don't worry about it."

Tovey turned and stood with his back to the window as he admonished Bob. The rest of room hadn't said a word for quite a while now. I looked around at them. They all had a look of panic on their faces as they realised for the first time that maybe Tovey wasn't as smart as they were all banking on him being. They had all put their eggs in one basket, and now it seemed that they thought the weave might come undone.

"Even if he does see through it, which he won't, how is he going to know where we are?" Tovey said with the most arrogant look I had ever seen on his stupid little face.

Just as he finished the last word, the window behind him smashed violently scattering glass all over him and the room. A pair of arms reached in and grabbed him. The arms in question belonged to my Dad.

"Are you OK, Tom?" he shouted.

"Do I fucking look ok? Get me out of here."

At the same time, Jane and Justin both stood up, producing guns from their coats, and trained them on the room. As I suspected, Jane was not who I thought she was. Justin's reaction, however, was a complete surprise and on some levels a bit disappointing.

Bob then grabbed me 'round the neck and began to drag me out of the room. He held a knife held firmly to my throat, so firmly that I felt it dig in slightly as he struggled to get a good grip on me.

Mick, One, and the bouncers all stood around the table with their hands in the air.

Dad was not alone. He'd brought several policemen with him who all pulled Tovey out of the window and into the open air. My dad and two of the cops climbed through the window and into the room.

"Let go of him and put the knife down," Dad yelled like he was in a Hollywood movie.

My god, this was impressive. Bob, not surprisingly, did not oblige.

He dragged me off my feet and to the back of the warehouse, the front of which was now teeming with police, all of them with their weapons trained on him and just missing me. I hoped.

"Drop the knife," came the instruction again.

"We're off, Tom. You still want that *Magical Mystery Tour* EP?"

I did want it but having the knife to my throat was a far more pressing issue.

"Of course, I fucking do Bob."

"Well why don't we go and get it then eh?"

Bob dragged me towards the back door of the warehouse. I prayed that the cops would know about it and be waiting on the other side.

To be honest, though, I was thinking more about the record. It wasn't the rarest in the world, but I suspected this might be my best opportunity to get it back. It would complete the collection, minus the Jam singles, and get me back to where I was before I had met any of these idiots, apart from Bob, of course, but now he was idiot number one and held my life in his hands.

He backed into the door, and it opened. There was a huge amount of shouting from the front of the warehouse. They obviously hadn't thought about the back door.

My only hope of this ending right now was for Bob's car to be parked 'round the front. On foot I was fairly sure that the cops would be able to catch up with us. But nothing else had gone right tonight, so why would that be the case.

Bob's car wasn't even there. However, there was a car, and that was all he needed. As he reversed, the path out soon became blocked by police. They fired several shots, but he still managed to pick up enough speed to ensure they dispersed rather than getting run over. He slammed the car into first gear and headed out with me in the back, sliding up and down the leather seating, banging my head on the door as we went.

"Fuck!" Bob yelled. One of the shots had caught him in the shoulder. He held it tight in an attempt to stop the flow of blood.

For the first time in a while, Bob's attention was not fully on me, and so I took the opportunity to try and release my arms. If I could, there was a chance I could do something about my predicament. The option was also there to go for him with my head, but that was fraught with danger. I'd never headbutted anyone in my life, and I certainly didn't want my first effort to be done from the back of a speeding car with both my arms tied to my side.

"Stay still, Tom," he said.

"How the fuck am I supposed to do that, Bob. Just stop the car, mate. This can only end badly."

"You should hope it doesn't, Tom. It'll go worse for you. At least I've got an airbag." He laughed. "You haven't even got your balance. You look like a dog trying to stand up in there." He was right. Should we crash suddenly, my body would surely be crushed.

Now we were on the open road. The cops gave chase, sirens blazing. I knew my dad was in one of those cop cars, so I had high hopes that they would think twice before doing anything rash.

One of the police cars pulled up alongside, matching Bob's speed easily. He opened his window and pointed his gun at Bob.

"Pull over!" he shouted.

Bob slammed the breaks on, and I hit the footwell at speed. Didn't hurt, though. The copper did the same, but he wasn't quick enough, and Bob managed to turn 'round and head in the opposite direction. Now we were going the wrong way down a dual carriageway. The cops gave chase but held back.

As soon as the opportunity arose, Bob crossed a gap in the barriers and ended up going the right way. The cops missed the target and remained on the opposite side. Up ahead, I saw a slip road. The cops would have to get on the right side before that, or we would be away. But it didn't happen, and we exited the carriageway.

Now we were on a country road, still at speed. The cops were out of sight. I could still hear them, but their error on the dual carriageway had left them well behind.

"You should pull over, Bob. We can hide up one of these side roads," I said as I managed to get a modicum of balance back.

"Keep your fucking head down. I know where we're going."

"Where?" I asked.

"To get your record, of course, Tom. It'll be the last fucking record you ever see, mate." With that he buried his foot to the floor and propelled me back into the footwell. This was hopeless.

For the first time since this whole sorry saga began, I genuinely thought it was unlikely that I would get out of this alive. Many threats had been made to my life tonight, but for some reason, only now was I taking any of them seriously.

The police sirens were getting fainter. We were getting away.

Then suddenly, as if from nowhere, another car rammed us full on from the side. My body, completely limp, smashed against the door, breaking the window. Bob's airbag went off, and as the car came to a standstill, he struggled comically to break free from it. Now was my chance.

The force of the crash slid the rope tying my arms to my body up to my chest. I had slight control back. The door was mangled, so my only hope was to get through the window. I managed to get just enough purchase to stand up on the seat and leap through it.

In the pitch dark, I ran as fast as I could. There were no houses in sight, but I could see a small light in the distance. I headed for it. But it wasn't long before Bob was on my tail.

"Tom," he shouted elongating the vowel. "Come here, you little bastard."

I could feel the anger and desperation in his voice. Despite everything that had happened tonight, I had managed to stay alive, but if Bob caught me, in his current mood, I doubted that would last.

The light in the distance was getting closer, and even more reassuringly, the police sirens had returned. Still distant but at least I knew they were going in the right direction. Soon enough, the sirens went past me. *No matter*, I thought. They would soon see Bob's car and realise where we were.

I could feel the thud of Bob's feet as I ran. He was getting closer. Then they stopped. I looked over my shoulder, still running, but I couldn't see him anywhere. I stopped and turned 'round. *Where was he?* I walked back towards where I had come from a few moments earlier. I could see in the distance a group of police cars parked up with sirens blazing.

"I'm over here," I shouted as loud as I could, sounding a bit like C-3PO attempting to gain the attention of a passing Jawa transport. They heard me. Their flashlights turned in my direction.

Just as I began to allow myself to think I was saved, a hand grabbed my ankle. Bob had fallen down a ditch. I tried to shake him loose, but he soon got out and grabbed hold of me again. He slid the rope back 'round my waist, grabbed my arm, and off we went again.

The cops weren't far behind now, and they had dogs. How would the dogs know that I was not the bad man and go for Bob? I hoped my dad was with them.

The closer we got to the light, the more I could see what it was coming from. A lone house stood in front of us. Bob pulled me towards it. He banged frantically on the door.

It didn't take long for it to be opened by an elderly gentleman. Bob barged past him, flinging the poor man to the floor. Bob then pushed me against a wall and leant down to pick the old man up.

"Who else is in the house?" Bob screamed.

"Just me and my wife. She's in there."

He pointed to a door, and in we went. Bob pulled the curtains shut as the old man, his wife, and I sat on the sofa.

"We haven't got any money," the old man pleaded. Bob laughed menacingly.

"I don't want your money, old man. I'm afraid this is the end of the road for all of us."

The old man and his wife were petrified. They looked at me for some sort of hope, but I had none to give. I had accepted that this was the end of the road. If Bob had had a gun, then I'm sure we would have all been dead already.

Now shouting came from outside. The cops had arrived.

"Just give it up, Bob. They've surrounded us. There's no way out," I said, pleading with him.

"What makes you think we're getting out of this?"

"What about the record?" I said.

It was my last hope. I appealed to his love of music. There was nothing left that I thought I previously knew about Bob that I could still rely on. But one thing I suspected he had never faked was his love for his music.

"Shut up, you idiot." Oh well, it had been worth a try.

So we were in a strange house in the middle of nowhere, a fucking desperate lunatic wandering around the living room with a knife, two elderly people and me tied up on the sofa, and a squad of police surrounding the house shouting at the tops of their voices. This was not a pleasant situation, but at least we were warm. Bob was still bleeding badly from his shoulder. His left arm was covered in blood, and it didn't look like stopping any time soon.

"You need to get that looked at, Bob." He really did. "You're going pale, mate."

"Just shut it, Tom. I know what I'm doing."

If there was one thing that I knew at this point, it was that Bob did not know what he was doing or what was likely to happen.

"Come and sit down. You need to keep pressure on it."

As much as Bob clearly believed he knew what he was doing, he also must have known I was right. There was nothing in this house, or anywhere else other than a hospital ward for that matter, that would be able to stop the flow of blood coming from his shoulder. He sat down opposite us.

I could tell by the look in his eyes that he knew this was the end of the road. If he gave himself up now, there was a chance that he might get out of this alive. If he didn't, then his choices were either to get taken down by the police or to bleed to death in front of us. But he wasn't thinking straight. I mean, how could he be? He and his band of merry morons had orchestrated this whole situation, and now he just had to take what was coming to him.

I was not concerned about him at all. My only concern was for myself and the old couple who were having a nice quiet night in until the knock at the door just a few minutes earlier.

Bob was becoming paler by the second. The end was in sight for him, and maybe for us. I looked into his eyes, and I knew full well that he was aware of what was coming. He was struggling to keep them open. They shut slowly, and then opened suddenly, as he realised he was drifting away.

I know I shouldn't have, but I started to think about the *Magical Mystery Tour* EP. He was the only one who knew where it was. Or at least that was what he would have had me believe. He might not have had a clue.

The old couple looked at me, the panic in their eyes beginning to dissipate as they realised that the reason we were in this situation was drifting away in front of us. Bob sat slouched on the chair, mouth wide open. His left-hand side was drenched in blood. It was not going to be long now.

He shut his eyes for the last time, and in the silence of the situation, we heard his last breath leave his lips. It was over. I sat motionless for a few minutes, waiting to see if he would come 'round, but he didn't. He was gone, and now it was time for us to go.

I walked over to him, my arms still tied to my sides as they had been for most of the night. I leant in to check that he had stopped breathing. Even if he had suddenly and briefly come back to life, he wouldn't have had the strength to do anything.

I made my way to the front door. The beams of light from the police torches broke through the small window in the middle of it. I opened the door to find about thirty policemen, all with their guns trained on me.

"It's over," I shouted. "He's dead."

They lowered their weapons and made their way towards me. Then through the crowd my dad emerged. He flung him arms round me.

"Thank god, you're OK, Tom," he said, clasping his hands to either side of my face. "Have you not got a hug for your dad, Tom?"

"Of course I have, Dad, but how the fuck am I supposed to do that with my arms tied to my side. You really need to pay more attention, you know."

He smiled, and with tears in his eyes, he removed the rope. I flung my arms around him and started to weep myself.

"So how did you explain what that phone call was about to mum? Must have freaked her out."

"I didn't. I just took her back in the front room and told her it was a crank call."

"Oh yeah," I said.

"Yeah. And then I put a sedative in her coffee. She was out like a light in seconds. She's probably still there now."

"How come you haven't used them on her before? You've had plenty of opportunities to. And reasons."

"Who says I haven't? She's not always shouting, is she?"

"Suppose not, no. We going then?"

"Yep."

We walked to the nearest police car, arms around each other, and got in.

It was over. The whole ordeal was over. I looked out of the back window and could see the old couple being looked after by the police, and Bob's body, covered in a sheet, being put on a stretcher. The only question that now needed to be answered was where the fuck was my *Magical Mystery Tour* EP?

25. Aftermath

Over the next few weeks, several arrests were made, including Gary. Mick, One, and the bouncers all got prison sentences of a couple of years for their parts. Mr Tovey's office was raided, and several items of evidence removed. He was tried and sentenced to eight years in jail. Turns out that, although he had started quite small, using my bloody records to hide his crimes and simultaneously attempt to pin the blame on me, by the time that night in the warehouse had occurred, he was shifting huge amounts of heroin, cocaine, Ecstasy, and LSD.

Jane and Justin, it turned out, had never been a couple. They had been hired by my dad to infiltrate the gang, and a good job they'd done of it too. I still hadn't really forgiven her for kicking me in the nuts, but I did understand why she'd done it.

I still didn't know why she'd been so distraught the night I'd gone 'round and saved her from supposedly being punched by the bloke that I now knew wasn't even her boyfriend, Justin.

She rang me after a few weeks, and I agreed to meet up with her in the hope of finding out.

I didn't really have those feelings for her anymore. Too much had happened. And apart from my dad, I was not really keen to see anyone that I'd spent that night with in the warehouse ever again.

I did want to see Gary, I must admit. He was my mate, and although he was involved and convicted of being so, I was not convinced that he'd had much choice. Mick, One, and the bouncers could go to hell as far as I was concerned, and I imagined they probably would if such a place existed.

The doorbell went the following Friday night. I had arranged to go out with Jane for the evening. She stood on the doorstep, and we held each other's gaze in silence for a moment. Then we both burst into laughter and hugged it out.

"How are your balls?" she said.

"That's not funny, Jane. That really fucking hurt. I understand why you did it, but you could have aimed a bit to the left."

"They would have known if I had done that on purpose."

"How would they have known?"

"Well, for a start, it wouldn't have hurt you as much. Plus, One and that bouncer from the club are used to looking at people's balls."

"Thought so. There was a thing at an illegal rave once where the bouncer slapped him for coming on to him. I always suspected that the feeling between them was mutual."

We went into the front room where my parents were sitting. Mum still had no idea about Dad's extracurricular activities, bless her. As far as she was concerned, that phone call from the warehouse that night and subsequent loss of consciousness had been just what my dad had said it was, a combination of a crank caller and tiredness.

My dad and Jane still maintained their position of not knowing each other for the sake of my mum. It was amusing, watching them pretending to get to know each other now that I was aware of the connection between them.

As far as Mum was concerned, this was only the second time they had met. In fact, I'm pretty sure she thought it was the first as she'd said she couldn't really remember the night she stayed 'round ours. Maybe she can but just didn't remember who it had been.

We retired from the front room to my bedroom so we could chat about the events we'd both become involved in. I put on The Smiths second album, *Meat Is Murder*. It was just a few moments into the first track, "The Headmaster Ritual", when Jane leant over and kissed me on the cheek. She stayed in close proximity, and then I knew that she wanted more than just a kiss.

Like I'd said, I didn't really feel that way about her anymore, but now that she was here, rather pathetically, I had a different opinion.

"So what happened that night you stopped 'round here?" I asked her.

"Exactly what I said happened. Justin punched me."

"But why did he punch you? I didn't think you were a couple. Not that you should only punch people you're in a relationship with. In fact, er, that's the last person you should punch, isn't it?"

She put her finger over my lips to stop me digging my hole and let off a small chuckle. I still wanted to know the answer, though.

"Well," she said, "he did punch me, but only after I punched him several times first."

"But you were crying. In fact, sobbing."

"Well, it really hurt. He's a big fella."

"Suppose so."

We laughed about it, but as it seemed that we were about to get into a relationship together, I had to be honest: it scared me too. What if she punched me? I was only half his size. Not that I would punch her back, even if she'd stabbed me, but it was enough to be worried about. She knew. I could tell she knew what I was thinking.

"I'm not going to punch you, Tom."

"I should bloody hope not. I'm a very nice person. Why would anyone want to punch me?"

We held each other in silence for a few minutes, silence, that was, apart from the beautiful sounds of *Meat Is Murder* by The Smiths, now at the midpoint of the album, halfway through the song "That Joke Isn't Funny Anymore". Seemed quite apt.

"Oh, I've got something in the car for you," she said.

A minute or so later, she returned with her hands behind her back. Whatever she had for me was being hidden behind her. Then she showed me.

"Oh my god. Where did you get it?" It was the *Magical Mystery Tour* original gatefold double EP film soundtrack.

"Bob's house. We removed everything from it last week, and I found this in a cupboard."

"It's still mint," I said excited.

A strange feeling came over me, one of a newfound respect for Bob. He'd looked after it so well, bless him. And then I remembered all the other stuff about him. What a dick. And talking of dicks, what had happened to Big Chris?

THE END

About the Author

Jon Reeves is now in his mid-forties and has an unconditional love for music. His desire to discover new sounds and learn about how musical history has allowed that music to grow has been with him for as long as he can remember.

His life has often not been a bed of roses, relatively speaking. It's not like he wonders each day if he will survive to the next. It's more to do with his desire to be a good person, which more often than not, has left him alienated from his peers. But not all of them. He has met some amazing people along the way who have inspired him to use his experiences to write stories.

The only thing as important to him as music is to grow emotionally each day and attempt to take positives from everything that happens to him but, at the same time, keep a realistic head on his shoulders.

About the Book

Some describe Tom's obsession with music as "unhealthy".

Growing up in the 1970s and early '80s middle England, developing his love for music, and building a record collection to rival that of people twice his age, Tom becomes fascinated by the musical cultures of the day.

In 1989 he turns eighteen and becomes part of his own culture, the rave scene, selling all of his beloved record collection along the way to fund his new lifestyle.

After a while, he decides it is time to regain his lost collection. He makes a list. And at the top, is a small list of rarities he regrets selling the most.

As he follows the trails of the records he sold, each one reveals alarming information involving a close friend and a group of people he thought he had left behind. But to what extent is Tom involved?